SHADOWS OF TOMORROW

SABER

BOOK TWO

MONICA RED

To my whole world, Josephine

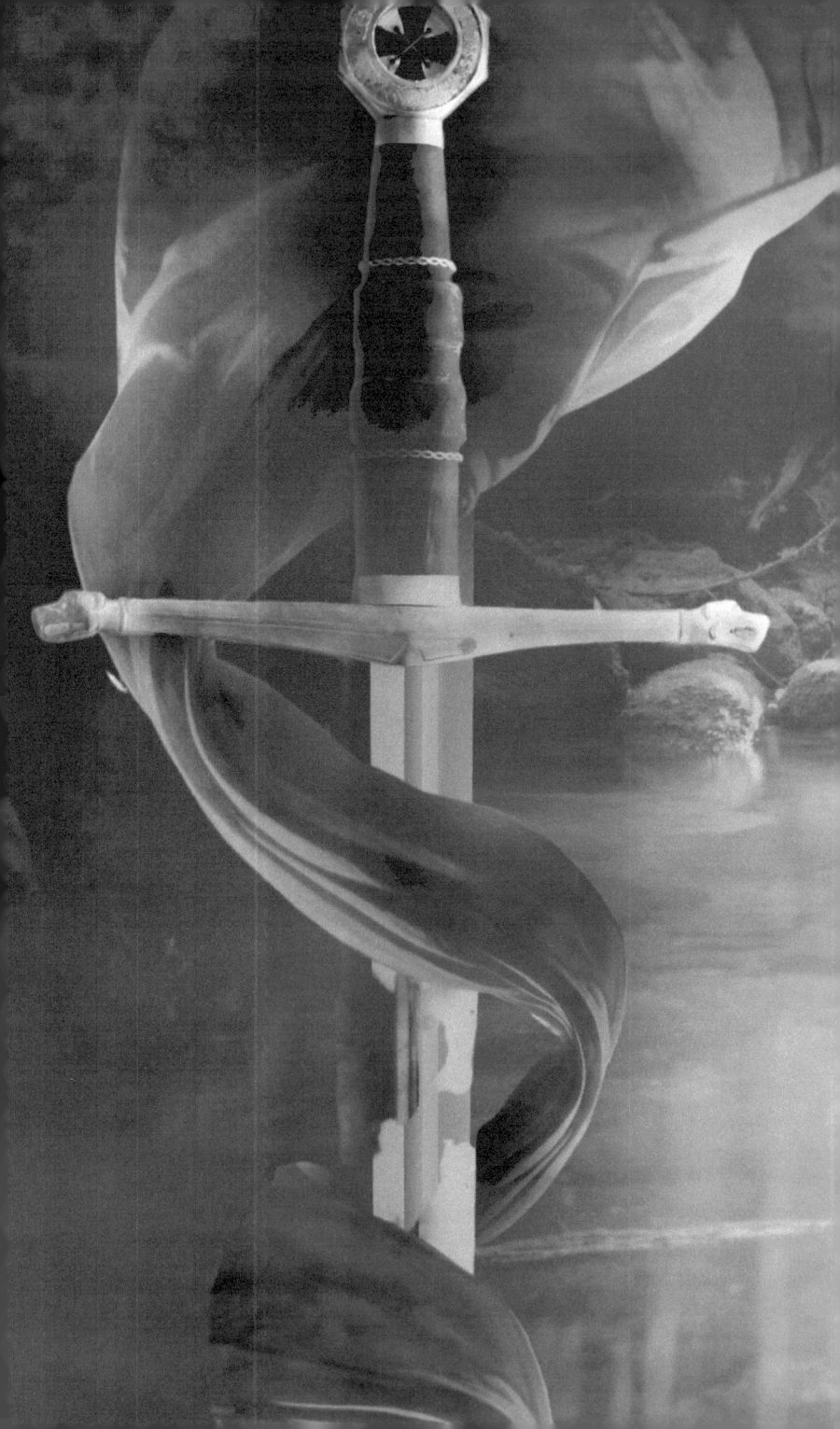

CHAPTER ONE
DURING THE WAR

The dirt walls disappeared as the soldiers above sealed the metal cover. Chris closed his eyes, trying to adjust to the lack of light, but when he opened them again, the faint holes on the lid weren't enough to illuminate anything. Time slowed as his new reality sank in—and with it came despair and a suffocating sense of pain.

Worse were the memories of the past few days. The vivid image of the valsings' settlement mocked him: a forest lit up with glowing streets and large tents filled with furniture, warmth, and the aroma of baked bread and smoked meats. Luxuries no soldier's camp could afford.

He could still hear the laughter of those fools—especially the smug voice of their ridiculous king. Orson, who had not only rejected humanity's request for an alliance but had humiliated Commander Daniel in front of them all.

Inside the vault, rage built in Chris's chest. That

king had crushed the army's morale. The soldiers *knew* what the valsings' help could have meant. The reisers were growing in number and strength. Without support, their chances of survival were thinning fast.

Chris slammed his fist against the metal above him. "Gods be damned!"

His fingers cracked. He could feel warm blood dripping down his hand.

He pulled it close and tried to convince himself it had all been worth it. He *knew* alcohol clouded judgment, but he couldn't stand seeing his friends crushed by the arrogance of a fool. Orson needed to pay.

Maybe if he'd found the king instead of the princess, it would've been simpler. Both of them dead. Or just him. But it was *Cassandra* in that tent, and her warning had made sense: if a human killed the valsings' king, the entire race would join the war—and not in favor of the humans.

Spending the night with the princess had worked. Remembering her still made him smile. It humiliated Orson in a way no blade ever could. Even now, in the dark, he could see the king's face—flushed with fear and rage.

He could still hear the chaos of that morning.

"You repulsive human!" Orson had screamed as Chris was thrown from Cassandra's tent.

"We'll show you how to treat a lady!" one valsing said, stepping forward with another behind him.

Cassandra, still in her nightgown, turned to her father. Her tears looked real. Her concern, too. She came close to convincing Chris, in spite of his awareness that their arrangement was strictly professional.

One valsing tried to kick him. Chris grabbed another by the arm and pulled him forward as a shield. Both of them landed face-first in the mud. Chris sprang up, disarmed one of the guards, and pulled out his own dagger.

"How did you—?" Cassandra began, and only then did Chris notice she had stepped closer, holding a small blade—one she must have been trying to offer him.

Orson seized his daughter's arm and raised his hand to slap her. Chris reacted instantly—one hand pressing a dagger to the king's throat, the other pinning him to a tree.

"You *never* hit a lady," Chris growled.

It was the first time in his life he realized how much fear he could cause. It shook him, and he let go.

The king made the mistake of smiling.

Chris's eyes sharpened. A shadow moved. A tall valsing lunged, but Chris stepped back and punched him clean across the nose. The valsing screamed and covered his face while blood dripped everywhere.

Around him, the other valsings gasped and a few screamed. Cassandra touched Chris's arm, but it was the voice of Commander Daniel that cut through it all:

"*Captain, that's enough.* Arrest him."

After that, everything unraveled.

Chris was sent back to the barracks—to face his father.

He lied in his defense, claiming the princess had been watching him during their first visit and had sent for him that night. It hurt to say it, but the worst part was how *easily* his father believed him.

Colonel Alexander Riddley made his disappointment painfully clear.

"I wish you'd just leave the army, Christopher," he'd said, loud enough for the other superiors to hear. "You're killing your mother. If it were up to me, you'd be walking into Soto Forest, begging the Zhortas to take you in."

His sentence: an *undefined time* in the vault. Ordered by the full council.

The worst part was not knowing what had happened to Cassandra. Orson's retaliation would be brutal. Chris had asked Charlie to find out—but never heard back before the vault swallowed him whole.

Now, time no longer made sense. Hours. Days. Maybe longer.

His father's words echoed endlessly, digging into his soul. The pain in his body sharpened. He could no longer sit, lie, or stand without agony. His spine throbbed. His breath came in with the sharp sting of dust and blood. His mind frayed.

When he finally blacked out, it felt like mercy.

In that darkness, a sound—waves crashing. Not real. The ocean of Tundra had long since turned to sand.

But still, he could see it. Stars overhead. The stone path beside his childhood home.

Footsteps. A girl walked along the shore. Wind played in her dark, wavy hair. City lights scattered gold over her features.

"You're so beautiful," he whispered.

She startled, then stepped closer. "Are you hurt?"

As she neared, he cursed silently. Perfect skin. Bright blue eyes. No doubt—she was valsing.

"Are you a valsing?" he asked anyway.

She laughed—and the dream crumbled.

The prison closed around him again.

It could have been hours or days, and she kept returning. Bringing a sense of peace and relief, he couldn't resist.

He told himself she wasn't real—just the voice of desperation. But he couldn't resist her presence. She taught him Hune's legends, old stories, and how healing didn't always come from power. She softened something inside him.

And he fell in love with her.

Until the world came back.

CHRIS DIDN'T KNOW HOW LONG HAD PASSED when he heard the lock above. The sun blinded him. Arms pulled him out. Pain wracked his body until the world went dark again.

In the infirmary, nausea was his only constant. Faces came and went. Friends. Medics. Yet none of them felt *real*—not like her.

One morning, he finally saw the trees outside the window, and reality sank in.

"Slow now, son. "We weren't expecting you to be so aware for at least another week."

Chris's throat was dry. The air going through it felt like a knife scratching and peeling his insides.

But when the nurse gave him water, it made him sicker.

"Easy, son," she soothed. "You were in there *three and a half weeks*. I've never seen that before. What a waste of good soldiers."

She took his vitals, fluffed his pillows, then hesitated at the door.

"Was she worth it?" she asked.

For a heartbeat, Chris thought she meant *her*—the dream girl.

Then he realized she meant Cassandra.

Daniel's voice saved him from answering.

"Captain," the commander said.

Daniel sat by Chris's bed and looked at him for a moment. It gave Chris time to notice the missing medals on his jacket.

"Did they punish you, too?" His voice sounded raspy and weak.

"No, Chris," Daniel said, and after a deep breath, he added, "I'm leaving the army, though."

Chris stared. "Because of me?"

Daniel gave a small smile. "Yes. But not for the reasons you think."

He sat beside the bed. "I *know* why you did it, Chris. And it worked. Orson crushed our hope that day. And you? You made sure he paid for it. You humiliated him—without drawing blood. Although, that wasn't your original plan, right?"

Chris looked away.

"When a valsing came running to camp, I never imagined it'd be you she was warning us about. But when

I saw your sword in the mud... I was so relieved when I saw the freaking king alive!"

Daniel patted his leg. "You got our hope back. By the way, Princess Cassandra is fine. Orson sent her away that day. She has been with her mother ever since."

Chris sighed as a weight left his shoulders. "Why, then?"

"Well, I defended you, and it was too much when even your father denied your actions did more good than bad for the soldiers." Daniel shook his head. "I never thought Xander's parenting would intervene in his decision as a leader."

A weight pressed down on Chris's heart. His father's words were still too clear and too loud in his mind.

"Damn idiots!" Daniel shouted. "This war will not be won by an orthodox protocol, Christopher. Remember that." Daniel stood and put his hand on Chris's shoulder. "For what it's worth, I'm proud of you."

After he left, Chris sat in silence.

He appreciated Daniel's words, but he wasn't sure he deserved them. Maybe the soldiers had regained their hopes, but he hadn't. He knew how lost they were and how bad things were going to get. He could only give the best of himself and pray it was enough. Being a soldier should be his priority.

A pair of blue eyes crossed his mind and this time, he pushed them away. He needed to stop dreaming.

CHAPTER TWO
PRESENT TIME...

The weight of secrets didn't lie in what was hidden—but in what would happen if the truth ever came out.

Saint Peter's Abbey was built on secrets. So were the zhortas who had lived in it for generations. And so, Sara's life had been shaped by silence.

She had grown up learning that the best-kept secret was the one never spoken aloud. Zhortas wrote them down, filed them away in thick, coded tomes, but rarely dared to speak them. If someone did share one, the listener bore the responsibility—either protect the truth or expose it.

The last prophecy of Hune was the most dangerous example of all. The zhortas' decision to deliver it to King Leonard had ignited a war. And now, Sara held a secret of her own. One that didn't belong to her. One that might cost her more than she was ready to lose.

"Sara!"

She blinked, startled.

Zhorta Wilson stood above her on the scaffold. "The scissors. Now!"

"Right—sorry!" She passed them up, flustered.

It was a crisp, golden day in Soto Forest, perfect for harvesting. The mushrooms and root vegetables grown in the abbey's greenhouses would be delivered to Andromeda before sunset. A quiet effort, hidden from most humans—just another way the zhortas tried to help, without stirring fear or resentment.

Wilson climbed down beside her with a grunt. "You've been off all morning. Talk to me."

"I'm worried about Lily," Sara admitted. "And... maybe more than that."

Wilson raised an eyebrow. "Not the soldier?"

"What? No!" She dropped a basket into the cradle a little too hard. "Why does everyone assume that just because there's a man in the abbey, I must be falling for him? I don't even *know* him. And the times I *have* seen him, I've been trying not to have a panic attack while having a civilized conversation."

Wilson smirked but said nothing. At least not yet.

Sara kept her gaze on her work. "It's Lily. We fought. She's gone, and I don't know if I want her back. She said some horrible things. About the zhortas. About... me."

"Lily's hurting. She doesn't mean it."

"She meant it." Sara's voice cracked. "She said I'm not a real zhorta. That you all taught me out of pity. That I'm just... in the way."

Wilson set down his baskets and took her hand. "You know that's not true."

"She said I'm nothing. That no one would ever look at me that way."

Her voice broke.

Wilson didn't flinch. "You are *not* nothing, Sara White. And one day, someone is going to see you exactly for who you are and be absolutely wrecked by it."

Sara gave a soft, trembling laugh. "You always say the right things."

"I don't. But I've lived enough to know cruelty when I see it. And love, too."

Sara blinked hard, pushing back tears. "I think I've felt both."

"Is this about the soldier, then?"

"I don't *know*," she whispered. "There's something familiar about him. And when Lily said what she did, it... it hurt worse than it should have."

Wilson looked at her closely. "You think you've met him before?"

"I don't remember it. But my heart does."

He gave a long sigh. "You know you don't have zhorta foresight. But sometimes, we sense things not with the mind, but with the soul. You may be remembering something from *his* side. A connection. Something unresolved."

"That's what scares me," Sara said. "Because if it's real... then what am I forgetting?"

Wilson turned away and adjusted the packages. "Even if it's real, Sara, you deserve answers. Just be careful where you look for them."

They worked in silence for a moment, the tension softened by the rustle of wind through forest leaves.

11

Then, Wilson said, "So—Lily's in love with the valsing. But she left him anyway."

Sara nodded. "She thinks he's going to die. That she's the reason he will. So she's trying to protect him."

"By vanishing. How noble." Wilson rolled his eyes, then softened. "She's wrong, of course."

"I tried to tell her. But then she said I only cared because I liked Donald. And that I'd never be important enough to matter to anyone—not even to my own kind."

Wilson's expression darkened. "The valsing, not the soldier? She is way off. Obviously, she wanted to hurt you. But she's wrong."

"She said the zhortas support the reisers. That we ran away and left the world to burn."

"That's what pain does, Sara. It distorts what you know into what you *fear*."

Sara exhaled. "Maybe. But I told her she was stupid. And that she didn't belong with Donald either."

"You were angry," Wilson said. "You had every right to be."

"I still should apologize."

"You should do whatever feels right. But don't take the blame for someone else's brokenness."

Sara bit her lip, remembering how she'd implied Lily wasn't even brave enough to show her face to the man she claimed to love. It was cruel. She hadn't meant it. But the words had come out anyway.

Just then, Daniel burst into the kitchen. "Only you can help us now," he said with theatrical flair.

"Daniel..." Wilson groaned. "This better not be about the prophecy or our *guests*."

"What? No!" Daniel popped a berry in his mouth. "It's Rafael. He's decided to cancel all deliveries to Andromeda."

Wilson swore. "He's lost it."

Sara stood, brushing flour off her skirt. "What? Why?"

"Something about outsiders. Security. Distrust. You know how he gets."

Wilson crossed his arms. "You'd think after centuries of secrecy, we could trust a few townspeople with turnips."

"Honestly," Daniel said, "it's just Rafael being Rafael. But Stuart wants you to talk to him. So…"

Sara nodded and peeled off her apron. "I'm on it."

Daniel grinned. "You're the only one who can talk sense into him. Go work your magic, prophetess."

"Don't call me that."

But she smiled anyway.

As she left the kitchen, she felt Wilson and Daniel's eyes on her. Behind the fear, the anger, the confusion, something else was building.

Like the slow rising of a tide.

Like a memory just out of reach.

CHAPTER THREE

I t felt to Chris as if the library of the abbey had become his second prison—though admittedly a more comfortable one. For days now, he and Donald had dined on things he couldn't identify but tasted divine. They'd spend the daylight hours buried in scrolls and texts, searching for anything about the prophecy, the saber, and whoever was destined to wield it. They read until the bells rang for supper, when the zhortas would silently file out, signaling the library's closure.

Chris had learned two things in that time.

First, the prophecy wasn't kept in the library—it was in Rafael's personal keeping, which Chris found deeply suspicious.

Second, finding anything meaningful in the library was next to impossible.

The abbey's archives were overwhelming—endless centuries of history, legends, and lore from Hune and beyond. Parchments, tomes, and journals layered in languages old and forgotten. Every aisle bled into the next, and nothing was categorized in a way that made sense. Chris had once thought the military training grounds were disorganized. Now he knew better.

In short: nothing they'd found advanced their cause. The prophecy Rafael spoke of? Still unseen. The saber? A shadow. And the person who could wield it? A mystery buried under too many myths.

Donald didn't seem bothered. The valsing had thrown himself into the task like a child loose in a candy shop. He wandered from scroll to scroll, muttering excitedly about unrelated details and charming linguistic puzzles.

Chris envied his enthusiasm. For the first time in years, he wasn't in immediate danger. He had warm food, a soft bed, and still, he couldn't enjoy any of it. The writings painted a dark, hopeless future—where the reisers would win, the races would fall, and Hune would never recover.

And then there was Sara.

He hadn't seen her since she'd healed his hands. It was easy to tell himself she simply avoided the library... but harder to ignore the thought that maybe she was avoiding *him*.

Even harder were the memories—of what he had once thought were hallucinations. The dreams where she cried, held his face, begged him to believe she was real. That they had touched the sand, felt the water, breathed the same air. And he, too broken then to trust in anything soft, had rejected her.

She had kept her promise never to return. Until fate brought them here.

And now, he didn't know what to say to her—how to apologize for something that didn't make sense even to him.

"Donald," Chris said, snapping his friend out of his scroll-induced trance. "This is pointless. I'm done."

Donald blinked at him. "Done? It's not even midafternoon. We still have so much—"

"That's the problem! There's too much, and none of it's helping."

Donald set down the scroll, grinning. "And what do you suggest, Commander?"

Chris stood, pushing his chair back with such force it nearly toppled. "I'm getting help."

Donald lifted an eyebrow. "Let me guess. This help has bright eyes and an enchanting laugh?"

Chris rolled his eyes. "More like a beard and glasses."

He left the library before Donald could tease him further. If they wanted answers, they needed the prophecy—and Rafael was the only one who could provide it.

Outside, he caught a zhorta in the hallway. "Excuse me—do you know where I can find Zhorta Daniel?"

"He's with our prime zhorta in his office."

"Thanks."

The abbey had its quirks, but it wasn't hard to navigate—half its rooms were abandoned, and the ones still in use were mostly on the ground level. The structure was crumbling, and his residents weren't many. Chris assumed the population used to be much larger, but the war had altered that.

Just as he reached the main foyer, he heard Sara's voice coming down the stairs.

His heart stuttered at the sound.

"Do not worry," she was saying, "we leave as soon as we get there."

Chris turned and saw her. Her steps were light, her face glowing despite the dim corridor. She didn't belong in this ruined place. She looked... radiant.

"For all of them," she continued, "nothing has changed... that we know."

"Hi, Sara," he said, unable to stop the smile tugging at his lips.

She turned at the last step. Her gaze went to the emblem on his uniform, and her posture shifted. She placed her hand over her chest—whether out of habit or fear, he couldn't tell.

"Oh, boy," she muttered. "Still not used to seeing that uniform here."

He hated what that meant. Hated that his presence —*he*—could cause her fear.

"I didn't mean to startle you. I can ask Stuart for other clothes."

"No," she said quickly. "Please. I have to get over this."

He nodded, trying not to show how much it bothered him.

"Were you looking for Rafael?" she asked.

"Yes, and Daniel. But I'm glad I ran into you... unless you were avoiding me?"

Sara bit her lower lip. "I wasn't—"

Their eyes met, and her words fell away.

"I've just been working outside," she finally offered.

He smiled faintly. "I hope the weather's been kind."

The last thing he wanted was to bother her, so he headed upstairs.

"Chris?" she said, and immediately he turned back.

"What do you think about secrets?"

Chris raised a brow and crossed his arms. "Not a fan of them."

Sara's face fell.

He softened. "But it depends. Secrets can protect or destroy. I've kept many myself—some to spare others, some out of duty. It all comes down to why you keep them."

She leaned against the wall, clearly weighing her thoughts.

"I want you to trust me," he said gently, moving closer.

She met his gaze, something soft and luminous in her eyes. "I want to."

"Then let me ask you this—if you told me your secret right now, would it change anything? Would it solve something important?"

Sara hesitated, then shook her head. "No. Not anymore."

"Then maybe it's not time to share it. What matters is that I trust you will, when it is."

"You're... kind," she said quietly. "A good person."

That shook him more than he expected. It had been years since anyone called him that.

He stepped closer. He feared that after he finished talking, Sara would avoid him because he'd lost his mind, and not just for being a soldier. "Do you know why I'm here? You brought me."

Sara frowned. "I told you—I don't know what Rafael said. I don't know how to—"

"I don't mean Rafael. I mean you. I had visions of you—with you." He paused, not daring to face her. "Not terrible visions—or weird visions. And not only visions. Things were—felt real like the smell of flowers around here." He exhaled and shook his head. "Just the idea of visions must be weird enough to you."

Sara smiled and tilted her head. "You realize where I live and who live here, right? Visions are kind of important around here."

"Yes! They are, but to me..." He took a deep breath and wondered how much he should tell her in that moment. "On our way here, the flowers—you smell like those, by the way—when that essence surrounded us—me. When I perceived it, I knew we were on the right path."

Sara nodded, lifting the corner of her mouth. "That's not weird. It is the way of Hune to reach you. Although it isn't flowers, it's more ferns and mushrooms than flowers. I loved it and I'm sure I would have followed it, too. Do you think you would have believed the scents of books and Rafael were the right path?"

The reference amused Chris.

"It is probably just the glacier orchid, anyway," she said. "Not weird at all."

Chris chuckled, shaking his head. "You know how strange this is for me, right?"

"I do," she said. "But there's a lot more to Hune than what you've learned."

Chris leaned back against the wall. There was no doubt she was beautiful, but it was the kindness in her eyes that made him like her.

"Chris?" she said.

"My lady?"

Sara's cheeks turned red, and her smile became one of the ones he liked so much. "My lady? You are the only one who has called me that."

Chris put a hand on his chest and opened his eyes wide.

"Well, that is ridiculous! Doesn't anyone around here have manners?"

Beside her smile, Chris never heard what she had to say.

THE ABBEY DOORS BURST OPEN, SLAMMING against the stone wall with a resounding bang. A rush of cold air swept in, scattering loose parchment and chilling the already drafty hall. Stumbling inside was an elderly zhorta, breathless, his heavy robe tangled around his legs.

"Rafael! Rafael!" the old man cried, nearly doubling over at the base of the stairs.

"Stuart?" Sara called, startled. She steeped toward him instinctively.

"What's going on?" Rafael's voice echoed from the

top of the stairs. His tone was sharp but carried the weariness of age. "Stuart, speak!"

But Stuart wasn't looking at Rafael. His eyes locked on Chris.

"You!" he rasped. "Come. Now!"

Without another word, he turned and hobbled back out the open doors.

Chris didn't hesitate. He rushed forward, overtaking Sara, who looked to Rafael in alarm. But Rafael had already started down the stairs, muttering under his breath.

Outside, the Soto Forest churned with unease. Zhortas were hurrying down the slope toward the castle, while others clustered together in a tight circle not far from the gate. The wind howled between the towering roots, and the scaffolding groaned overhead like an ancient warning.

Chris broke into a run. As he approached the crowd, one zhorta stepped aside, and in the gap, Chris spotted a man collapsed on the muddy ground.

His heart dropped.

The uniform—torn, soaked, and caked in dirt—was unmistakable beneath the grime. And the face, though pale and drawn, was one he could never forget.

"John?" Chris knelt beside the man, gripping his shoulder. "John Monder?"

The lieutenant's head turned slightly. Mud streaked his forehead, and leaves clung to his dark hair. "Commander," he croaked. "Thank the gods I found you."

Chris's grip tightened. "What happened?"

John shook his head slowly. His voice cracked as he

forced out the words. "They got them, sir. All of them. The soldiers, the civilians... everyone. The damn reisers."

A sick chill slid down Chris's spine.

Behind him, Rafael appeared. "We should speak inside," he said quietly, though his eyes were already scanning the growing crowd of shaken zhortas.

Chris nodded. He helped John to his feet, slinging the soldier's arm over his shoulder. The man's legs barely held him upright, and every step seemed to cost him more.

Donald met them at the base of the stairs, his face pale. "Chris, what—?"

"Later," Chris said sharply.

Rafael led the way, clearing the path. No one dared speak as they climbed the stairs to his office. John's ragged breaths echoed off the walls.

Inside the office, Chris guided him to a chair near the fireplace, then crouched in front of him. The heat of the flames barely seemed to register on the soldier's skin.

"I need you to breathe, John. Then tell me everything."

John's hands trembled. "They... they took everything. Even the armament. Commander, we didn't stand a chance. We thought we'd make it through the canyons. But they were waiting."

Donald had entered silently and stood frozen near the door, disbelief etched across his face.

"Who did this?" he asked.

John snapped his head up, eyes burning with exhaustion and anger. "Who do you think? The reisers, of course! Do you need a personal reminder of the war?"

"Enough," Chris said firmly. "John, sit back down."

But the soldier surged forward. "No! We need to go now. We have to rescue them. If we wait—"

"You can't leave," Rafael interrupted, stepping forward. "The only way to stop this is—"

"Of course, you think you know!" John spat. "You've probably known all along! Sitting on your answers like a bunch of cowards while good people die."

Chris stood quickly and pushed John back into the chair. "That's enough."

"What, are you defending them now?" John snapped. "We've been out there dying, while you—what? Rested in a library? Ate hot meals?"

Donald's hands clenched at his sides. "You do not understand what's happening here."

"Please," John scoffed. "A valsing? What are you even doing here?"

"Leaving is a fatal mistake," Rafael shouted. "Sara needs—"

"Who the hell is Sara?" John said. "And what do you know about fatal mistakes? You are just a traitor zhorta!"

"John!" Chris barked. "Control yourself."

But John's temper wasn't cooling. "You've lost it, Commander. What, chasing a girl now instead of a mission? Is that why you've gone soft? Please tell you didn't get her pregnant!"

Chris slammed a hand on the desk. "Shut up."

He turned, catching a glimpse through the open door—Sara's silhouette disappearing down the hallway. She had heard. All of it.

"Rafael, close the door. Now."

The prime zhorta obeyed, but the tension in the room was unbearable.

Chris turned back to John. "I haven't heard a proper report yet to your superior, Lieutenant."

John stood quickly and saluted. "Commander."

"Sit. And tell me, soldier. From the beginning."

John's tone was more controlled this time, but the pain was still there. He recounted Charlie's evacuation plan, the escape through the canyons, and the eerie emptiness of Andromeda. And then—Leonard.

"He brought the armament," John said. "But it was a trap. One of his own men warned us just before the reisers struck."

Chris stilled. "Leonard? King Leonard?"

"With all due respect, sir—I won't call him that. Not anymore. He's a traitor. He's been working with the reisers all along."

A gasp escaped Rafael. Chris turned to him.

"Do you have something to add?"

Rafael hesitated, then reached beneath the desk. He pulled out a letter, folded but worn at the edges, and handed it to Chris.

Chris opened it, reading slowly, each word carving deeper into his thoughts.

Prime Zhorta Rafael,

This is the time to choose where we will
lead our future, and I decided to
change our destiny. I am sending you
my first guard. It is my royal

command that you step down from
your role as original protector and
give our dearest treasure, Sara, to the
commander of my guard. He is to
move to Laconia, where he will
receive his next orders.

Your Magnificent Grace and Ruler,
King Leonard the III and the High
Council of Hune

Chris read the letter more than once, knowing the message had a deeper meaning. He couldn't tell how much more Rafael could read between those lines.

"Chris, I told you before," Rafael said. "What the king said didn't seem right. The high—"

"Why you didn't tell me about Laconia?" Chris said.

Rafael grabbed the edge of his desk. "Chris, no! The last place you should go is Lac—"

"I'm not dumb, Rafael. But if you really want to protect Sara, I need the truth. All of it."

Rafael looked down, and his shoulders dropped.

Chris shook his head and he slammed his fists on top of the wooden desk, making Rafael jumped back.

"You and your stupid secrets are condemning everyone, and you freaking know it."

He helped John up and flung the door open. From behind it, a few zhorta screamed and jumped out of his way.

Once downstairs, he made sure Donald was behind them.

"Donald, we need to find out everything about Laconia."

"Laconia?" Donald said. "I thought we weren't going there."

"I thought we were saving our people," John said.

Chris stopped and made sure both were looking at him.

"We are saving our people, and we are not going to Laconia, but..." He raised his hand at both, and his tone became deeper and lower. "I need to know why the freaking kin— Leonard wanted us there. And John, you need to eat and rest, or you won't be any help."

CHAPTER FOUR

Sara pushed the forest roots aside with more force than necessary. She knew the soldier's assumption was ridiculous—but understandable. And yet, every time the words replayed in her mind, the need to hit something surged again.

What gnawed at her even more was Chris's silence. He hadn't defended her. He had just stood there, letting that muddy, broken soldier imply things about her as if they were true.

Unlike Chris, she didn't need to hear any more. One look at the man's battered condition told her everything. The reisers were coming. The only question now was: how close?

She went looking for help.

"Daniel," Wilson asked, brow furrowed, "do you really think there could be—"

"Reisers?" Daniel cut in, already striding for the door. "Yes."

Before Sara could even finish recounting what she'd

witnessed, Daniel had grabbed an axe from the scaffolding and tossed another toward Wilson, handing a third to her. Without another word, he marched into the forest.

"Maybe he's overreacting?" Wilson offered weakly.

"Few things make a soldier run," Daniel muttered, not looking back. "Reisers top the list."

Sara kept close, maneuvering between the curling roots as Wilson pushed a thick one aside to let her pass.

"I get that," Wilson said, "but he might've come from somewhere else—just looking for his commander."

Sara hoped he was right. She wanted to believe this was just a misread—a trauma-fueled overreaction. But the sweat on her palms and the pounding in her chest said otherwise.

"It's possible," she said softly. "But better to check than be sorry."

"Daniel," she called, "how do you kn—"

A thick root tore upward from the ground in front of her and slammed beside them with an echoing crack. In Soto Forest, roots always shifted... but never this fast. Never this violently.

She froze.

The crunch of leaves and snapping wood came next —rhythmic, deliberate, close.

"For the gods," Wilson whispered, raising his axe with trembling hands. "I never thought I'd see them again."

Daniel reached out and gently pushed the axe up.

"These won't help against the reisers," he said grimly. "They're for the roots. To buy us time."

Wilson met his eyes, and something passed between them. Shared understanding. Old fear. Maybe even old orders. After a breathless pause, Wilson nodded.

Daniel turned to Sara and took her by the shoulders.

"You need to go back," he said. "Warn the others."

"No." Her voice shook. "I'm not leaving you. If they see you—"

Another root pulled violently from the earth—and behind it, she saw them.

Dark silhouettes emerged through the undergrowth. Hundreds. Twice her height. Clad in dripping armor so thick it looked alive, like it had grown over their bodies instead of being forged. It reeked of rot. Of death. A thick ooze clung to them—flesh? Decay? She didn't know.

The dissected arm Lily had shown her rose in her mind like a scream.

Daniel saw them too—but his gaze returned to her instantly.

"We don't have much time. You know this forest better than anyone. Wilson and I will draw them off, take a different route—buy you minutes, maybe more."

"No, you can't stay here! They'll—"

"Go, Sara," Wilson said. He leaned in and kissed the side of her head. "You need to reach them. That's the only thing that matters now."

Tears stung her eyes, and her body started to tremble.

"Sara," Daniel said, firmer this time. "Only you can get there in time."

She nodded, once, even though every part of her

wanted to scream and stay and fight. But she trusted them. And they trusted her.

The roots beneath her feet lurched. She barely had time to grab a low branch before everything twisted. The forest shifted around her, bending its paths to obey her need.

In a blur of motion, she was gone.

Sara darted across the rising terrain, the roots flinging her forward like a stone skipping across water. Though she'd already been in the woods nearly an hour, the forest was helping now, hurling her back toward the abbey at unnatural speed.

Within minutes, the towering scaffoldings came into view. The familiar outline of home—crumbling, rusted, but still standing—rose like a beacon against the gray sky.

Her legs faltered.

The weight of it all—the soldiers, the friends she'd just left behind, the threat approaching from the forest—slammed into her at once.

This was her home. These zhortas were her family. And she was about to lose everything.

Her eyes flicked upward.

In the highest tower, the ancient bell sat untouched. It hadn't rung in decades. Not since the first fall. No one even knew if it still worked.

She didn't care.

Sara ran for it.

CHRIS LEANED AGAINST THE KITCHEN'S STONE wall, watching John devour his second bowl of soup. It had taken two full plates and at least four hunks of bread before the man slowed enough to chew.

Across the room, Donald paced like a trapped animal. He shuffled through books and old scrolls he'd brought from the library, reading one, tossing it aside, then grabbing another.

"Donald," Chris started, "you have to stop or—"

A deep, resonant clang shattered the air. The ancient bell roared through the abbey like a thunderclap. The walls groaned. Dust and chips of plaster rained from the ceiling.

"What the hell...?" John muttered, already halfway to his feet.

Chris stormed toward the door, but a crowd of zhortas rushed in from outside, blocking his way. Chaos reigned. Between the tangle of hoods and limbs, he glimpsed the roots lifting outside, their massive coils pulling free from the earth like awakened beasts. Several scaffolds creaked dangerously under the shifting weight.

"They're coming," Stuart said.

He didn't need to ask who was coming. None of them did.

Then he added, breathless at the far side of the kitchen. "You need to leave, Chris. Now. Save her. Take her with you!"

"John," Chris barked, "get to the stables—see what horses we've got left. Meet me at the main entrance. Donald, grab our gear."

He turned to Stuart. "Where's Sara?"

"Rafael's trying to stop her. Come!"

Hallways overflowed with zhortas, all carrying bundles of papers and tomes. When they passed the library, Chris froze. Scrolls and parchment were being tossed by the armful into the fireplace. The flames licked ancient knowledge into ash.

"We need to protect our world," Stuart said, glancing back. "There's information here too dangerous to fall into enemy hands."

Chris felt a knot tighten in his gut. These people knew what was coming. And still, they didn't run. There were no screams—only grim, purposeful action. Dignity. Resolve.

They couldn't fight the reisers. Not really. But they wouldn't let them win either.

He followed Stuart into the vestibule. Sara stood just beyond it, near the threshold of the open door. Rafael gripped her arm, speaking quickly, urgently. Chris couldn't hear the words—only saw the anguish on both their faces. Then Sara tore free and stepped outside.

"There's no point in trying, Sara," Rafael called after her.

Chris quickened his pace.

"Rafael," Stuart said, guiding Chris forward. "I found him."

Rafael's whole posture sagged in relief. "Thank the gods." His voice was hoarse. "Chris, you have to leave. I just need to speak with Sara—"

Chris followed them both into the open.

The rumble of the forest had grown into a monstrous hum. The air shook with power. Roots towered, groaning and splitting rock. It felt like the desert storms of Tundra—but this time, the earth itself moved.

John was already waiting, two horses in tow. It wasn't much, but Chris had expected that.

Rafael stepped up beside Sara.

"Sara," he said softly, "there's no time. There's nothing left for us here."

Her jaw clenched. Her eyes burned with anger—and grief.

"If you want to give up, that's on you," she said. "But we *can* escape. Why else would Daniel and Wilson have sent me back? Why would they—"

Her voice cracked. She looked down, fighting back tears.

"They sent me back to *warn* everyone."

Rafael touched her cheek. "My child, you must help them—"

"No!" she snapped. "I'm not your— We can fight! We can free the trees, block the reisers. We can—"

Chris noticed the axe in her hands. Her plan was clear. And honestly? It could work... if they had more time.

But Rafael's voice dropped low. "It won't stop them. They're marching with *one of us*. Someone who knows these woods better than even you."

"What?" Sara whispered. "Who—?"

Stuart stepped forward. "He's right. It won't stop *him*."

Sara's breath caught. The axe trembled in her hands.

"I need you to do something," Rafael said, taking her hands in his. "Only *you* can do it. Only you can get them out of here." He looked back at Chris and when Sara turned, tears were rolling down her cheeks.

Rafael leaned closer and handed her a sack.

"Sara, whatever you learn about me, none of it matters. Just remember—I love you. And you'll always be my daughter."

She hugged him tightly, and Stuart joined them. He kissed her forehead, voice trembling.

"We'll see you later, my beautiful child."

Rafael turned and walked back toward the abbey. Stuart followed, vanishing behind the heavy wooden doors.

"Commander," John called, "only got two decent horses. The others are old—might not make it."

"That's all right," Chris said. "Take Donald with you."

Sara stood with the sack clutched to her chest, her eyes locked on the retreating zhortas.

Chris placed a hand on her shoulder. She nodded, didn't speak, and climbed onto the horse.

He looked back one last time. He imagined what the abbey would look like once the reisers arrived. The place that had held harmony, knowledge, peace... would be dust.

He pulled himself into the saddle.

"Up the hill, Lieutenant."

They had barely crested it when the stench hit him— thick, acrid, unmistakable.

Then came the screams.

Chris swore and veered into the trees.

"They're too close!" he shouted. "We can't risk the horses in the roots!"

He dismounted, helping Sara down as well. Donald leaped from his horse like a dancer landing a practiced step.

Chris dragged a hand over his face, trying to think.

Then he noticed Sara, already climbing one of the roots. She held something small in her hand—shimmering faintly.

"Listen," she called. "Only step where I step. Don't touch anything you don't need to. If you get lost, *stay put* —I'll come back for you. Move fast."

She tossed a pebble to the forest floor.

Instantly, a root by Chris's feet groaned and lifted. Mushrooms and moss sloughed off like dust. The bark darkened and twisted upward.

Chris leapt beside her. She didn't wait. She jumped to another root, and it too responded—rising and bending to her will.

He grabbed a branch to steady himself as the root lurched upward beneath him.

Behind him, Donald clung to the side of the shifting root. John had to leap from his saddle just in time before the forest moved under him.

"Hurry!" Sara shouted, already ahead. "Keep up!"

Chris pressed forward, heart hammering. He glanced back—but the roots twisted so fast, he could barely track the others.

"Just keep moving!" she called again. "I won't leave them—but you *have* to hurry!"

CHAPTER FIVE

C hris realized only a few minutes had passed, though it felt like hours. Sweat slicked his palms, his fingertips stung from brushing rough bark, and his lungs ached from chasing Sara through the forest's dizzying maze. High in the roots, where the air thinned and the ground vanished beneath them, she moved too fast to follow—an arrow cutting through chaos.

He lunged to the next root and grabbed a brittle branch. It cracked. His heels slipped, and his weight tilted dangerously toward the chasm below. He flailed—

And Sara caught him.

"There's moss up here," she said, not winded, not surprised. John and Donald landed beside them, breathless.

"I see that now," Chris muttered, steadying himself. "Thanks—"

"How far do you want to go?" she interrupted, sharp.

"Ten thousand miles," John gasped, bent double.

Sara shot him a look. "As if you could walk that far."

Chris offered a weary smile. "As far as we can... but maybe we should—"

"We can't slow down," she snapped, already stepping away. "The trees are listening. I won't anger them again."

Her voice brooked no argument. She leaped, and the roots shifted in her wake.

Chris helped John up. "You okay?"

"Not sure," John said breathless. "I can't feel anything anymore."

Chris helped him up before following Sara.

They pressed on, root after root. Higher into the canopy, surrounded by gnarled wood and the hush of ancient magic, there was no sun, no direction—only Sara's fluid path ahead and their own bruised resolve.

Occasionally, Chris glimpsed the outline of desert sky far off, only for it to vanish into the tangled dark. He stopped looking back; Donald and John were still following—though just barely.

Then the forest changed. The roots thinned, lowering toward the ground, and a shimmer of blue peeked through the canopy.

Relief pulsed through him when he watched Sara descend, and he followed without hesitation.

"What was that?" he asked, crouching beside her.

Donald collapsed behind him, chest heaving. His hair stuck out in every direction, but Chris didn't have the breath to tease him.

"He better have waited," Sara said and moved to another branch before vanished from Chris's sight.

He stood up, watching the trees and unsure of what to do—not a welcoming feeling.

"She knows what she's doing," Donald said, sitting up. "At least one of us does."

Chris glanced around, uneasy. "But what if—"

The roots shifted. He turned, hand on his sword.

John emerged from the forest, half-carried by Sara. Chris rushed over and supported his other side, guiding him down.

John's skin was clammy, his face drawn. "That... was a nightmare."

"Agreed," Donald muttered.

Sara stood again, gripping the side of a tree. "The Northern Forest should be about twenty or thirty miles northeast. Follow the cold. When the air bites, you'll be close."

She turned to leave.

Chris grabbed her arm. "Where are you going?"

She tugged free. "Back. Where else?"

"What?" Donald said. "You're not serious."

John's eyes widened as he stood up.

"I brought you here," she said, voice firm. "Now I'm going to help my people."

Chris blocked her path. "You can't go back. You saw the reisers. Heard them. They're already there."

"So what?" she said. "That doesn't mean I won't try. You go. Save your world."

John stepped forward. His voice dropped low. "You can't go back. Whatever was left of your home... it's not there anymore. You don't want to see what they leave behind."

41

Sara squared her shoulders. "Did you stop fighting to save yours?"

John faltered.

Chris took her hands, held her gaze. "Sara, if there had been even the smallest hope of saving the zhortas, do you think I would've left them?"

Her jaw tightened. She didn't answer.

He stepped back, trying to contain the pain rising in his chest. "You think I abandoned them."

"You didn't come to the abbey for us," she said. "You were looking for something to save your world. We were just in the way."

Chris's mouth opened, then closed.

"You can't blame him," John said. "The zhortas kept the prophecy from us. They could have shared it."

"Kept them from you?" Sara's tone darkened. "What do you think we kept hidden?"

"Everything," John said and took a step forward. "For starters, how about predicting a war we had no idea how to finish? And how about making sure the freaking reisers don't have a shield that makes them invincible?"

"Invincible?" Sara raised her voice, not caring to hide her anger. "Do you know how stupid you sound? Are you expecting a bunch of scholars to tell you how to fight? What about you start doing your job?"

"Doing my job? What do you think I have been doing all my life? Actually, what have you done for our world?"

"John, that's enough," Chris said. "This is not the time to—"

"Why, Chris? You heard her!" John pointed at Sara.

"She wants to go and save the zhortas by herself. Let her. That will teach her—"

"You better watch it." Chris jumped down from the root and stood in front of his friend. "In case you forgot, she just saved your life."

"So what?" John said. "She also brought us a million miles away from the desert. Now, how are we going to save everyone? With every minute that passes, we may lose one of our soldiers, or one of our people is getting killed. Have you forgotten about them? I can see she is pretty, but how could you—"

Chris pushed him back, and John had to catch himself to avoid falling.

"No, Chris," Donald said. "We all need to stop and—"

Chris pointed at Donald. "Stay away from this one." He turned to John again. "Do you think I can forget them? Do you think you can come and yell at me, pretending to know what has happened or what I have been doing?"

John crowded into Chris's face. "Oh, no! I can see exactly who you have been doing."

Chris landed his fist in the middle of John's face.

John fell and groaned, but he didn't stand up. Instead, he grabbed something from his pocket and threw it at Chris.

A heaviness grew in Chris's heart when he recognized Terry's locket.

"He is gone, Christopher," John said. "So is Fred, and whenever you care to ask, I can tell you the names of the others." John wiped the blood from his mouth. "His last words were for you. He said he never forgot." John's voice trembled then. "Please tell me you haven't either."

Chris's throat closed around a thousand unsaid things. He gripped the locket until the metal bit into his skin.

"We still have scrolls," Donald said softly. "We can still stop the prophecy."

"The prophecy?" Sara repeated.

"Yes," John spat. "The prophecy! And unless you know how to stop it, you should shut up."

Chris took a step towards John, but Sara's words froze him.

"You can't stop it. It's already been fulfilled."

Everything fell still.

"What...?" Chris said.

Sara's voice was distant. "Unless you can go back in time and save the zhortas, it's done."

Chris crossed his arms. "Rafael never even showed it to me."

"No. He wouldn't." She stared at the root, her voice turning hollow.

And then, she recited it:

Hune has been condemned by the actions of its races. The indifference among them, along with their arrogance, will deliver certain devastation to our world. Empowered, the hated race will conquer Hune, leading to the death of everything as we know it.

"That can't be possible," John said. "It doesn't even mention the reisers."

Sara nodded. "Everything else you've heard? Interpretations. Guesses."

"It doesn't mean it's done, though," John said. "It means just...nothing."

Chris turned and rubbed his face. "Gods be damned!"

Sara was right. Like the stupid prophecy said, the hated race had taken power and conquered Hune.

"How can that be?" Donald said. "It doesn't specify any of the races!"

"It was never about the races," Sara eyes flooded. "The death of everything as we knew it." She stopped as her voice broke. "As the zhortas knew it. Zhortas wrote the prophecy, not humans. It always meant the zhortas' world, our world. Not yours."

"And you all were aware of this and said nothing about it?" Donald said.

"Oh, they did," Sara sighed. "Why do you think humans learn about it? The zhortas reached out to the council for help. And when everything turned into a war, Rafael asked us to forget about the prophecy. He said it wouldn't matter who was condemned. The fighting and destruction of Hune needed to be stopped."

Donald put his hands on his forehead and sat down, while John let his head fall. Both of them looked defeated, and if Chris were being sincere with himself, he felt the same way.

After a brief moment, Sara grabbed a pebble from her sack and moved towards the trees

"So, it is done," Chris said. "That doesn't mean your work is done, Sara."

She turned and crossed her arms. "This isn't my fight."

"You are wrong." Chris stood in front of her. "Rafael, Stuart, and even Daniel believed you were more than a zhorta. I understand how you feel about that, but you won't let them down now, will you?"

She stared at him fighting the tears in her eyes, which Chris hoped were sadness and not hate.

"It is what you do when things get bad that makes a difference."

Chris dared to take a step closer. "You met my father. You know this is when you don't give up. If you go back, Sara, you'll waste their sacrifice."

She stared at him for a brief moment before pulling her hood up and walked into the woods.

His nerves frayed with every passing second, waiting —dreading—but the surrounding roots never stirred. And when the stillness stretched too long, a hollow fear settled in his chest. Maybe she just needed space... or maybe she was gone for good.

Terry's locket was still in his hand. Inside, it held the painting of a smiling woman hugging a happy little boy.

"He saved us all," John said, approaching Chris.

"That doesn't surprise me," Chris said, and he put the locket in his pocket, "but it does that you didn't mention it before."

"Chris, I just...I don't know. I guess I thought no one there would care about it. I mean, I know you do, but those others... A lot has happened, Chris, and you need to hear it, but—"

John looked up and cleared his throat. He used the

back of his sleeve to wipe his eyes, and then he looked at Chris.

"I have to tell you everything, but I don't want to talk to my commander... I need my friend."

Chris sat on the ground and rested his arms on his knees, waiting for John to talk.

CHAPTER SIX

Charlie woke with his hands and feet bound.

There was no blindfold, but only darkness surrounded him. Panic rose in his throat like fire. His breaths came fast and shallow until he realized: he couldn't see. Not because they'd blindfolded him —but because his world had gone dark.

His body broke into a cold sweat. A blind commander. That's what he was now. And in this state, he couldn't save his people. He couldn't save Jean.

He forced himself to breathe slower, steadier. Focus on what you can feel, he reminded himself.

His head throbbed. His eyes burned and felt sticky. He bent forward until the ropes stopped him, then rubbed his face against the coarse fabric of his sleeve. Dried blood cracked and flaked. Something tore—a sharp, searing pain sliced through his eyelid. He gritted his teeth.

Light filtered into his right eye. The left burned too

fiercely. The pain, the swelling... he might lose the eye. If it was even still there.

Groaning, he stopped trying to assess the damage. He needed to stay alert.

He lifted his head. Shapes swam into view—shadows kneeling, barely lit. The reisers had lined up his soldiers and forced them to kneel. Civilians sat in front of them, trapped in silent witness.

To the side: a pile of bodies. Smaller than in other battles. But not just uniforms.

Charlie turned his head, bile thick in his throat. He'd failed them. Failed everyone.

He hadn't prepared well enough. He hadn't accounted for panic. Amanda had warned him the reisers would take prisoners—and he hadn't seen it coming.

He remembered lifting a woman from the sand, Jean screaming his name, a sharp blow to the side of the head —then nothing.

Now he was alive, and he almost hated that fact.

Jean. She was his weakness. The one thing more important than duty. And if the reisers discovered that— if Leonard did...

Charlie forced his gaze to the ground. As much as he wanted to search for Jean, he couldn't risk it. His only prayer was that she was still alive, that she hadn't seen him, and that no one suspected the truth about them. If their connection was exposed, she'd become a target— and that was a risk he couldn't let himself take.

He remembered Amanda and John. Had John hidden Amanda for the same reason?

Footsteps crunched.

A reiser's voice rang out, smooth and cruel.

"Are you in charge of this sorry excuse for a guard?"

Charlie didn't move.

"I'm Colonel Hayden Green," the reiser said. "Your captor—and, for now, your owner."

Charlie raised his head slowly. "You're as foul and rotten as I expected."

"Interesting," Hayden replied, crouching beside him. "I was told I'd find a brilliant strategist here. A commander who'd slaughtered our kind. But all I found was you. So easy to defeat."

Charlie tried to move toward him, but the ropes tightened around his chest and wrists. His head pounded.

Hayden narrowed his eyes. "Just to double-check... you're not Colonel Alexander Riddley's son, right?"

Charlie shook his head once. He could handle the pain. But he would not give them Chris. He would die first.

"Excellent!" Hayden stood. "That means our real fun has yet to begin." He turned to a nearby reiser. "Major, give them water. Then we move out."

But before the major could obey, another figure approached. A reiser dragging someone behind him.

Charlie's heart sank.

Amanda.

Bruised, bloodied, shivering. Still in uniform. Her head hung low—he couldn't tell if she was conscious.

Then Leonard's voice sliced the air. "This is what happens when you betray your king."

He kicked her square in the back. She crumpled with a groan.

Charlie exploded forward. The ropes bit into his skin, but he didn't care.

"You freaking bastard!"

Silence fell. Everyone had heard it.

"You were born to protect your people! That's what a real leader does, you bastard."

Leonard stepped toward him, sneering. "I was born to—"

"To be a coward!" Charlie spat. "The reisers must be desperate if they're taking orders from filth like you."

Leonard raised a foot to kick him—but Hayden grabbed the so-called king and slammed him to the ground.

"These are my prisoners," the reiser said. "You don't give orders here. Murllen decides their fate."

Leonard stumbled to his feet, surrounded by reisers. His eyes darted wildly.

"I am the king!" he barked. "You must respect me. Murllen—he won't—"

"You're lucky he still wants you alive," Hayden said. His voice dropped to a snarl. "But don't test me, Leonard. We have a long trip ahead—and accidents happen."

He leaned close. "I don't like cowards. Or traitors."

IN THE MIDDLE OF A HEAVY SILENCE, THEY LEFT the canyons and stepped back into the heart of the desert.

The reisers had horses. Lots of them. And food. And water. It was the luxury of the winning side. Charlie noticed the difference in how they traveled now—the polished gear, the carefully organized guards. It all pointed to one thing: someone had paid a price for this efficiency.

Leonard.

He must've sold them out. Either that, or he'd taken the army's resources to buy his own safety. Charlie wasn't sure which was worse. The signs had always been there, but they hadn't wanted to see them. Leonard had never been bright, but somehow, they'd all been surprised when he turned traitor. That, Charlie thought bitterly, was the real stupidity.

Even more disturbing than Leonard's betrayal was how similar the reisers' organization was to their own. Charlie had no trouble following the way they moved, how they shifted formation, their rotations and sentry changes. It all mimicked human military patterns. Just... stripped of warmth. They didn't call anyone "sir," but they obeyed their leaders with the same dead seriousness.

He noticed something else, too: they kept him at the front of the caravan, hidden from his soldiers. It was tactical. Without their commander in sight, morale would erode. Escape plans would fail before they started. It was exactly what *he* would've done.

The worst question lingered at the back of his mind: why had the reisers started taking prisoners now? After years of slaughter, why change the strategy? He doubted it was mercy. And he was fairly certain he didn't want the answer.

Amanda came to mind.

They'd put her in a wagon ahead of him, too injured to walk. He wasn't sure she was still alive. Maybe he didn't want to know. His instinct was to blame her for everything. For not speaking up. For waiting too long. But deep down, he wasn't sure *he* would've acted any faster. And in the end, she *had* warned Chris. However little, it was all they had now.

THE DAYS BLED TOGETHER AS THE DESERT SAND stretched endlessly around them. The attack couldn't have been more than a few days ago, but it felt like a lifetime.

Charlie had never been this close to breaking.

Physically, he was reaching his limit. Mentally, he was already scraping the edge. The wounds from the battle still stung. But it was the faces of his soldiers—the civilians—that haunted him more than pain ever could.

During the day, they marched. Fast. Unrelenting. At night, they collapsed—hungry, filthy, aching. Sleep came in jagged slivers, never enough to rest. The food they were given was just enough to survive on. Barely.

"Gods, you look terrible," Amanda said one evening.

She didn't sit up, but her eyes were open. Awake. Alive.

"Hey, there," Charlie said. "I thought you were dead."

"I was hoping for it."

Charlie managed a grin as he scooted closer to her

wagon. His voice dropped low. "Well, you can't give up. That's an order."

"I didn't think you liked me, Commander."

"Not at all," he said dryly. "But I'm not in the mood to tell John you gave up."

At the mention of John, something flickered in Amanda's eyes—a brief shimmer, a memory maybe. Charlie hoped it would be enough to keep her going. The way Jean's garden had once kept him tethered to hope. That tiny window of color and warmth in Tundra had been the best time of his life.

THAT NIGHT, THE REISERS SAT AMANDA BESIDE him. She could barely keep her eyes open, and every movement made her wince. But she ate. Slowly. Carefully. Enough.

"I need to ask something personal," Charlie said. "And gross."

Amanda raised an eyebrow, just barely.

"My left eye. I... haven't opened it since the battle. Think it's still there?"

She blinked a few times, then shifted slightly. "I'm not a doctor, but... yeah. I think it's in there. Doesn't look great, though."

Charlie nodded, chewing his chunk of stale bread. The constant burning made it hard to focus, and the worst part was the maddening *need* to scratch. He could live with the pain, but the not-knowing was driving him insane. At least now he had an answer.

"You know how long we've been marching?" Amanda asked.

"No idea. Lost count of the nights. A week? Maybe more."

"Anything... happened?"

Charlie laughed. A real, bitter laugh that made his throat hurt.

"Has anything *not* happened?" he said. "Let's see. We got defeated, captured, betrayed by our king, marched across half the desert, watched half our people die, and now we're property. That about sums it up."

"I meant *after* that," she said softly. "What happened... after."

Charlie's laughter faded.

She was asking about soldiers. About *everything* he didn't want to talk about.

He looked away.

"I don't know," he said. "They keep me near the front. Can't see what's behind. I don't want to."

Amanda nodded. Her appetite vanished.

"Hey," he said, shifting closer. "Remember your pal Green?"

"You mean the reiser colonel?"

"Yeah, that one. Well—he saved our lives."

Amanda's head tilted. "He did *what*?"

Charlie leaned in. "No joke. I passed out during the battle. Next thing I knew, I was tied to this damn wagon. They dumped you beside me."

"I remember," Amanda whispered.

"You passed out. Then Leonard showed up—real

brave of him. Came over and kicked you while you were unconscious."

Amanda flinched slightly, and Charlie clenched his jaw. "I couldn't move, but I yelled at him. Loud enough for everyone to hear."

"And then?"

"I'm sure Leonard was going to kill me and then you, but Colonel Green picked him up and *slammed* him into the dirt."

Amanda's eyes widened. A slow smile formed. Charlie grinned, too.

"One of these days, I'm telling that story in a tavern. Especially to Chris. He's gonna be *pissed* he missed it."

"Please tell me he killed Leonard."

"I wish," Charlie said, laughing. "But no. Leonard panicked. Green told him he was lucky someone wanted him alive but that accidents happen on long trips."

Amanda let out a breath. "Why would a reiser do that?"

Charlie's smile faded. "He said *we* were his prisoner."

Amanda looked away. Her expression darkened.

"They're taking us to Murllen," she said. "Their leader."

Charlie stilled. "What do you know about him?"

Amanda closed her eyes. "Too much. And not enough. I do *not* want to meet him."

CHAPTER SEVEN

The morning came too quickly, and with it, the Treisers' decision to have Amanda walking beside him. The first few hours passed in silence. Charlie suspected Amanda wasn't strong enough to keep pace, and soon, a growing limp crept into her steps.

"So, what's her name?" Amanda asked, breaking the silence.

"Excuse me?"

He turned to find her wearing a childish smile.

"Oh, please. The one you're so desperate not to find behind us."

Charlie shook his head.

"I've been there before," she said, "trying too hard not to look in the right direction."

Charlie didn't reply for a while. "I may start believing you were better off sleeping in the wagon."

Amanda laughed. "I agree. I *was* better in that car, sleeping!"

"And speaking of avoiding people," he said, "what's going on between you and John?"

Amanda looked toward the horizon, eyebrows lifted like the sky had surprised her.

"Well, as far as I know," she said, "he is—or used to be—my husband."

Charlie stumbled. It was a miracle he didn't end up face-first in the sand. Like when he heard about Chris's engagement, he felt both stunned and stupid. But this was harder to believe. Chris getting married made more sense than John settling down.

John was the one friend he'd never pictured in a serious relationship. A joker no one took seriously. Then again... it could explain a lot. Maybe the attitude, the recklessness—it was all armor. And yet, Charlie remembered too many times John had been in questionable situations for a married man.

He shook his head. In the end, he had been the proper gentleman among them.

"You had no clue," Amanda said.

"No, I didn't. But I'd love to hear about it."

Amanda told him how and where she'd met John, and why they'd gone their separate ways. For the first time, the walk didn't seem so bad. The story held a bitter-sweetness, but Charlie found himself enjoying it.

"Do you think the armament was your only option?" he asked when she finished.

"At the time, yeah. We didn't believe things would get this bad. Now, I'm sure I could've joined any guard."

The silence that followed was awkward.

"I'm not sure about *any* guard," Charlie teased. "How good could you possibly be?"

Amanda raised an eyebrow. "Let's see. I was a captain when I met John. In a regular guard, I would've moved up faster. So, since I'm a major now..." She turned to him. "I would've been Christopher's first choice to leave in charge."

"What? No way!" Charlie scoffed. "I *know* Chris would've never picked you over me." He snorted. "Our *big commander* would never do that!"

"Big commander?!" she echoed. "That's not even an actual rank."

"I know, but I kind of like it. Makes me keep my current rank."

Amanda smiled but didn't laugh this time. Charlie noticed the sweat glistening on her forehead and the worsening of her limp.

As commander, he was responsible for his soldiers. And since the king had betrayed them, the armament was technically under his command now. That meant every human prisoner was his responsibility. It weighed on him like armor made of stone.

"Her name is Jean," he said, clearing his throat. "I'm trying to protect her—from what the reisers would do if they found out about us."

"What's going on between you and Jean?" Amanda asked between breaths.

Charlie resisted the urge to look back—to make sure Jean was among the civilians.

"Well... I fell in love with our big commander's fiancée."

Amanda laughed—until she saw the seriousness on his face. Before he could explain, a reiser rode over to them.

"Do you think this is a party?" the creature sneered.

He shoved Charlie, who fell hard. His legs hit the sand, and the sudden jolt of the wagon yanked his arms. The ropes on his wrists cut deeper into already-bleeding skin, and the worst was the sand in his nose and mouth, choking him as he coughed and gasped.

"No!" Amanda cried. "Stop this! Help him!"

The reiser just laughed. "But this is funny!"

The mockery burned worse than the sand. Charlie used the wagon's momentum and sheer stubbornness to push himself up, ignoring his throbbing muscles and raw wrists.

The reiser rode off, but the moment lingered like a shadow. It was a reminder: they were prisoners. Their lives belonged to the reisers.

"Bastards!" Charlie muttered. "Why don't you untie me, and we'll see who laughs then?"

He turned to Amanda. Pain radiated from every step she took. She wouldn't get back up if they pushed her like that.

"I'll tell you the story later," he said.

THE REST OF THE DAY PASSED LIKE THE OTHERS: too much walking, no rest, and no distractions.

Charlie couldn't understand why he hadn't seen Tundra yet. He'd convinced himself that's where they were headed. He turned, meaning to ask Amanda, and saw his soldiers through the gaps between wagons. Not the civilians. Not Jean.

"Hey! Getting a little lazy there!" he called to Amanda—but her pale face alarmed him.

Sweat poured down her cheeks, her muscles trembled, and each step left a wet, dark footprint in the sand. Earlier, she'd told him about her accident. If they didn't stop soon, she might lose her leg.

Charlie dropped back beside her. "Let me carry you."

"No," she said. "We'll just fall together."

She was right. He wasn't strong enough to save her—or anyone—and it was killing him.

Still, Charlie walked beside her, letting her lean on him, step after agonizing step. With every faltering breath, his doubt deepened. Not just about Amanda, but everything. How many had died already? How many were dying now? And when they reached their destination—if they reached it—would they regret surviving?

His thoughts turned to Jean. She'd always seemed delicate—gentle, even. But she cared so deeply, carried the pain of others as if it were her own. Everything that had happened might have shattered her already. A part of him ached to see her. Another part was relieved not to. If she was suffering, he wasn't sure he could bear it.

As soon as the caravan halted, Amanda let herself drop into the sand. Charlie exhaled and knelt beside her, easing her against the wagon's side.

"Thanks," she whispered, eyes closed.

"It's just your leg, right?"

Amanda gave a half-shrug, but Charlie noticed tears

slipping down her cheeks. He looked down. Her uniform was soaked from the knee to her boot—dark, glistening with something more than sweat.

He had no idea what to do. He didn't even know where to start.

"Let me check them," came a voice from behind them—a female voice, calm and commanding.

Charlie turned. His heart stopped.

It was Jean.

Her voice had changed—no longer the soft murmur he remembered. It had taken on a steel edge. Firm. Unafraid. Just like Chris had once described it.

From the back of the caravan, Colonel Hayden Green stomped toward them. And behind him, almost running, Jean—her dress tangled in her hands, fighting the sand as she struggled to keep up.

"I told you before," she called. "They can't keep going like this. You're going to kill them all!"

Hayden stopped. Jean bumped into him, but she didn't stumble.

The reiser leaned down, eye to eye with her. "Good. Let them die."

To Charlie's amazement, Jean didn't flinch.

"They need rest and proper food," she said. "Or at the very least, water while they walk."

Hayden straightened and turned as if to walk away, but Jean stepped in front of him again.

"They need treatment. Their wounds are festering."

He shoved her aside. She staggered but didn't fall.

"You *need* them alive," she pressed.

Hayden whirled around. Charlie braced himself—

expecting blood, a scream, a body crumpling. But Jean didn't retreat.

"You really think a little human girl can tell me what I need?" Hayden sneered, his voice low and mocking. "No wonder your kind falls so easily."

Jean's hands went to her hips. Her voice didn't shake. "I may not be a soldier, but I'm not stupid. If you just wanted them dead, you'd kill them outright—like you've done before."

Charlie swallowed hard. He'd forgotten who raised her. He'd let his love for her blind him to what she'd truly survived.

She didn't look fearless. She looked *determined*.

Hayden's expression shifted—less mocking, more dangerous.

"You are stupid," he said. "Otherwise, you wouldn't be shouting orders at me. I may need some humans alive —but not *you*."

"Please," Jean said softly, "if they don't get help, they'll all die."

Hayden shook his head and turned. But Jean followed. She walked right past Charlie, close enough that he caught the scent of dust and lavender and something faintly burned.

Her hair was tied back in a rough knot, her dress ripped and crusted with sand, sleeves torn. Yet in that moment, to Charlie, she looked more beautiful than ever. Not delicate. Not fragile.

Unbreakable.

"You think you're helping them?" Hayden asked

without stopping. His tone had changed—quieter, almost curious.

"You told the king they belonged to Murllen," Jean said.

"That doesn't mean I can't kill them."

He started to walk faster. Jean didn't hesitate.

"You're just going to let them die?" she called.

That stopped him. He turned so fast she couldn't move in time. Hayden shoved her against the wagon, claws wrapping around her neck.

Charlie surged forward—but Amanda's hand clutched his arm.

He clenched his fists, forced himself to breathe. If he stepped in now, Jean might die. And if she died, he had a terrible feeling he wouldn't survive the night either.

"Do it," Jean said.

Charlie's breath caught. Her voice wasn't loud, but it was steady.

Hayden leaned closer. "You really think I won't hurt you?"

Without warning, he slashed the wagon beside her head. Wood splintered inches from her ear.

Charlie turned away, unable to look, waiting for a scream that didn't come.

Amanda squeezed his arm again.

"I'm begging you," Jean whispered. "Please... let me help them."

Charlie turned back, just in time to see Hayden release her.

For a moment, something flickered in the reiser's

eyes. Not mercy—but something close. Understanding, maybe. A strange sort of grief.

"Stupid girl," he muttered. "You think you're helping these soldiers. But where they're going... they'd be better off dead."

He stepped away, but just before Jean stood upright again, he added, "You can work with them during the night. At your own risk. If you get tired—if you fall behind—I won't hesitate to leave you to the desert's mercy."

CHAPTER EIGHT

Charlie was still staring at Hayden when a soft touch warmed his shoulder. He didn't need to turn to know it wasn't Amanda. But when he did, Jean's eyes made his heart jump.

She kneeled by Amanda, avoiding his gaze.

"Jean, I—" Charlie began.

"I know. I got it."

She still wouldn't look at him. Only then did he notice her trembling hands and the fast, uneven rise and fall of her chest.

"I'm not supposed to let them know I love you," she whispered. "Or that we're—"

Charlie moved closer, just enough to breathe the same air. "You love me?"

Jean's cheeks flushed, and tears slipped silently down her face. For one precious second, she looked into his eyes.

Then she turned away, focused on Amanda's leg, and

he let her. He ached to hold her, to draw her close, but he settled for watching her breathe.

When his gaze drifted down, the shock hit him. Amanda's leg was worse than he'd imagined. Her old scar had split open, bleeding freely. The skin around it had turned a sickly mix of purple and green, and her leg was nearly twice the size of the other.

"I don't think there's much you can do for me," Amanda said, her voice raspy. "But maybe check his eye? He's been whining about it all morning."

"He can wait," Jean said. "I need to stop the bleeding. And there's no way she should walk tomorrow."

"Of course," Charlie said. "Bedrest will do. How do you think—"

"After she eats, we'll help her into the wagon and leave her there for the night. None of the reisers will care enough to bring her back down in the morning. Can you get that box?"

Charlie set the box down, and Jean propped Amanda's leg on it. He hadn't believed Chris when he'd told him about Jean's bossy side. Now, he was grateful for it.

"I don't think I've seen you with the soldiers before," Jean said as she tore a strip from the bottom of her dress and began cleaning it. "I'd remember. There aren't many women in the guard."

"I used to be part of the armament," Amanda said. "Do you know what that is?"

Jean shook her head.

"Jean," Charlie said, "this is Major Amanda Belk. She and the armament were in charge of protecting the king.

Thanks to her, we might have a chance. The message we left got Chris—"

Jean froze and looked up sharply. "Chris is dead," she said. "You *know* that. He died before you reached Tundra. Chris never came back because he died in the desert... with his father."

She turned to Amanda, who glanced between them.

"He's dead, Charlie. You delivered the news to Alleta. That's what she told Colonel Green."

Charlie's stomach dropped. If Alleta had lied to Hayden... and the civilians and soldiers *had* seen Chris in Tundra, the truth wouldn't stay buried for long. And whoever tried to keep it hidden would pay for it.

"Jean," Charlie said quietly, "what did Alleta tell the reisers? What about you and Chris? Does he—?"

Jean's hands trembled harder as she focused on Amanda's wound.

"The king sent for Alleta and me because of Colonel Riddley," she said.

"Did he hurt her?" Amanda asked. "Or you?"

Amanda's voice sounded weak, breath ragged—but her face hardened. Rage replaced her exhaustion, at least for a moment.

"The king tried to hit Alleta," Jean said, "but the reisers stopped him." Her voice cracked. "Alleta's going to do something, Charlie."

Charlie reached to comfort her, but she pulled away. Her alarm was real.

"She's grieving and furious. I know her too well. She's planning something. But I can't—what can I do?"

Jean covered her face with her hands, tears sliding

down her cheeks. Amanda reached over and placed a hand on her arm.

Charlie understood the danger. If Alleta acted, it wouldn't just risk her life—it could doom them all.

"Jean," he said gently, "you need to make sure Hayden knows what Alleta is thinking—"

"I *can't*!" she said, panicked. "He'll kill her."

Before Charlie could answer, a reiser stepped close, glaring at them. Jean said nothing more, finishing her work in silence.

When Amanda was finally settled in the wagon, Jean turned to check Charlie's eye.

"Oh, Charlie..." she whispered. Her fingers brushed his cheek. "This is going to hurt."

Agony burst behind his eye. He jerked away, clutching his face, breath sharp.

Jean touched his hands. "I'll find a patch and fix it tomorrow."

He leaned close and whispered, "If Alleta is in danger, you have to make Hayden protect her. That's what you tell him."

The reiser grabbed Jean by the arm and led her back toward the caravan. She didn't look back.

And though her strength made Charlie proud—it left a mark on his heart.

LIKE JEAN HAD PROMISED, NO REISERS CHECKED on Amanda the next day. She lay in the wagon, paler than the night before, a slight fever warming her skin.

Charlie, despite his exhaustion, felt better. Whatever Jean had done had eased the pain in his eye. Whether or not he'd ever open it again didn't matter. He could think. He could walk.

"She's sweet," Amanda murmured. "And kind."

Charlie exhaled, then chuckled softly. "Couldn't agree more."

"But what are you going to do about it?"

Charlie frowned. "Well, I'd marry her today, but we're not exactly—oh, wait. You think I need to *duel* Chris over her?"

Amanda shook her head. "She wouldn't let you. She knows what she wants. I just don't know what you'll say to your superior."

She coughed, her chest rising too quickly.

Charlie moved closer. "How are you doing in there?"

"I'm still here, right?" She closed her eyes, but even then, she looked restless.

A memory surfaced—Chris's words about mercy and the battle where Colonel Xander died. Charlie shivered.

"Tell me your story?" Amanda said. "I don't want to die not knowing whether Chris is going to kill you."

He smiled, but the weight in his chest was real.

Charlie began from how he'd never known Chris was engaged. How impossible it had been to look at Jean without letting the truth show. Amanda laughed when he recounted John's warnings—and what Charlie had almost done to his friend.

He wasn't sure how much she heard. With each breath, it seemed Amanda was slipping further.

Then came the sound of hoofbeats.

Colonel Hayden Green dismounted and peered into the wagon.

"She's dying," Charlie said.

"So?" Hayden replied.

"What are you going to do about it?"

The colonel looked at him. "What do *you* think I'm going to do?"

The caravan slowed. Other reisers moved into position, waiting.

Charlie braced himself.

"Humans," Hayden muttered, "so arrogant. You think you're better than us. So tell me—if *you* were me, and this was a reiser dying in your care... would you let her die in peace? Or would you tie her to a wagon and drag her through the desert until she fell apart?"

Charlie shook his head. "I wouldn't enjoy watching anyone suffer. Not even a reiser."

Hayden tilted his head, amused. "So—should I kill her? End her pain?"

Charlie hesitated. He knew what Chris would say. But he couldn't.

Not again.

"I would tend her wounds," he said. "And make sure she lives to face a fair trial."

Hayden stepped closer.

"With no hesitation," Charlie added, "I'd cut down any reiser in battle. But this isn't a fight. These are prisoners. And here... I'd try to save them."

Hayden signaled. A reiser lifted Amanda and carried her away. She groaned, barely conscious.

"You should be proud," Hayden said, a glint in his eye. "You almost sounded like a reiser."

Moments later, the caravan rolled on, leaving Charlie with nothing but dust and silence.

Charlie saw Jean again that night. He hadn't expected her. But the sight of her was exactly what he needed.

"Did she die?" she asked.

He shook his head. Jean didn't press. Instead, she knelt in front of him and silently began cleaning his eye again. It still hurt—but not like before. He didn't flinch. He didn't pull away.

"I hope she's all right," Jean said as she finished, tying a soft scarf across his brow.

Charlie only nodded. He longed to touch her—to hold her. But instead, he let her fuss over a scrape on his hand that didn't need fixing.

When she finished, she sat quietly.

"You shouldn't come again," Charlie said.

Jean looked up. Her eyes were full of tears.

"I know," she whispered.

And then, like a shadow, she disappeared into the night.

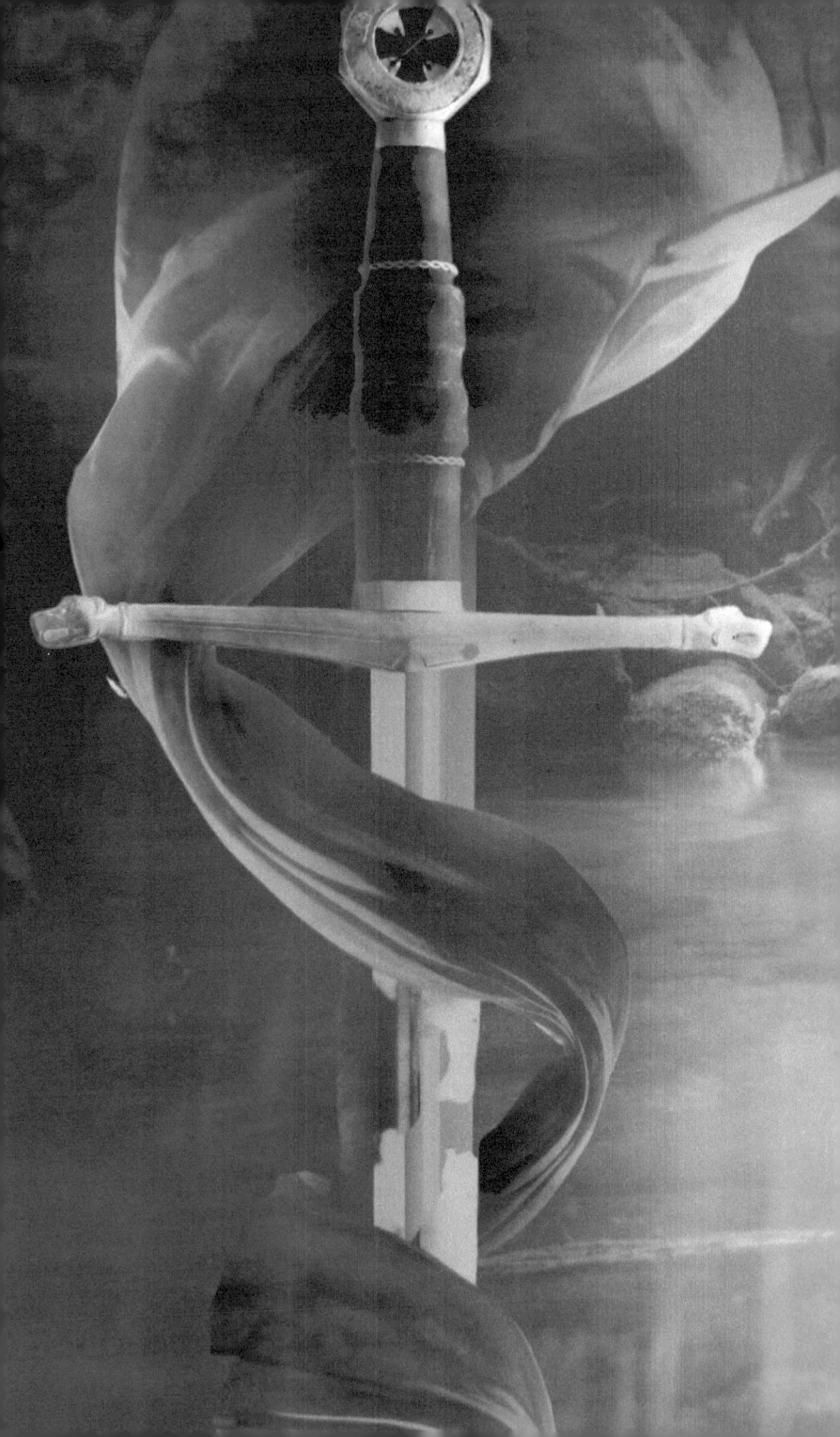

CHAPTER NINE

S ara spotted a tent nestled among the trees—
although smaller than the ones on Lily's settlement, it had a better structure. It flowed organi-
cally with the woods, its natural lines almost making it
disappear into the landscape. Lily had once explained
that Donald's people specialized in building living spaces
that harmonized with nature.

In a small clearing, Donald knelt beside a pile of
damp wood, trying—and failing—to start a fire.

Sara shook her head gently, her boots squishing in
the wet moss as she approached. She bent to gather
mushrooms and a bit of dry moss. Chris and John were
nowhere in sight, and for the first time in what felt like
hours, her chest loosened just enough for her to breathe.

"Here," she said, handing Donald the mushrooms.

"Thanks," he replied, though he eyed them with deep
suspicion before giving them a cautious sniff.

She laughed under her breath and took them back.
As she'd done countless times in the abbey, she smeared

the mixture across the firewood. The flame stirred to life with a faint hiss, licking through the dampness. Heat bloomed against her skin, chasing the chill from her limbs. Her coat still dripped from the rain, and her dress clung cold and wet to her knees.

Donald blinked at the fire, clearly impressed.

"How long were you in the Soto Forest before the abbey?" she asked.

"I don't know," Donald said and pointed at her with a pot in hand. "But I'm way better than Chris at this."

Sara chuckled. Around the fire, Donald had arranged thick roots like makeshift benches. A basket brimming with wild greens leaned against one of them.

"Are you seriously planning to eat that?" she asked, eyeing it with a mixture of curiosity and dread. The memory of Stuart's bitter, gooey broth returned unbidden.

"What? No! Of course not. I was just—"

She tilted her head and smiled, a faint curve of her lips that felt almost foreign. "Mind if I look for something edible? You'd be surprised how many wonders hide within these roots."

He handed over the pot without protest and sat on one of the roots, rubbing his hands near the flames.

It didn't take long before the aroma of mushrooms, herbs, and simmering earth drifted up from the bubbling pot. It was a scent that reminded Sara of peace.

"Oh, sweet gods," Donald said, closing his eyes. "It smells like heaven."

"Well, I hope it tastes half as good." She smirked.

"Though it's probably better than whatever you were planning."

"I am sure it is." He grabbed a stack of bowls from inside the tent. "And if I never eat whatever that goo was again, I'll count it as a win."

Sara stirred the soup slowly, enjoying the ritual of it. For a moment, she could pretend she wasn't broken.

"Your tent's... different," she said. "I've never seen one like it."

Donald's chest lifted with pride. "It's nothing special. Chris forced me to leave my real one in the desert—it was superb."

She smiled faintly, but conversation felt heavy. Her throat tightened with the weight of too much unsaid.

"The zhortas," Donald said with a somber tone, "they—you. Everyone at the abbey seemed familiar with my race. Did you ever meet one of us?"

Sara looked into the fire, fully aware that the Queen's settlement had no real idea what King Orson had been doing in Hune. The weight of Lily's secret—the one she'd been keeping from Donald—wouldn't stay buried much longer. The zhortas were gone, and with them, any real reason to protect the past. Guilt thudded through her chest. She didn't owe Lily her silence anymore.

"Well... I became close with one valsing. At least, I thought we were close. Until—"

The roots behind Donald shifted. Leaves crackled.

Chris appeared first, sliding over a root. "Gua! Donald didn't cook. This smells edible!"

He dropped his sword behind a branch, where it was

just out of Sara's sight. Across from him, John did the same.

They were disarming. That wasn't wise in reiser territory—but the message wasn't lost on Sara. Chris probably told John about her fear of soldiers.

"Or did you learn to cook in the library?" Chris asked.

"One day," Donald grumbled, "you'll be begging for my expertise." He tossed Chris a bowl. "You should already be grateful."

"Oh, I am," Chris said with a grin. "Grateful and deeply moved by your humility."

He ladled soup into a bowl and handed it to John.

"I don't believe we've been introduced," John said, his voice gentler than before.

"Right," Chris cut in. "Sara, meet Lieutenant John Monder. Call him 'John,' just to prevent you from giving him a higher rank than mine."

Chris offered her a bowl of soup, but she hesitated, unsure if her hands were steady enough to hold it.

He moved closer and put it on her lap, almost as if he understood.

"Thank you," she said."

"What do you mean?" John said after had eaten half of his soup. "And if you can, could you change my rank, please? General would do."

"General?" Chris said. "Really, John?"

Donald snorted. "I thought only royalty could be generals among humans."

"Exactly," Chris said. "John's delusional."

But John smiled at Sara—a warm, genuine smile—and she blinked, surprised by how much it disarmed her.

"General," he said. "Remember that one. Has a nice ring to it."

A woodchip hit him squarely in the head.

Chris raised a brow. "Watch it."

It wasn't a command, and this time John just rolled his eyes at Chris.

The pressure of being surrounded by soldiers kept her nerves at edge, and she needed to control herself. She took a deep breath and, although trembling, she met John's gaze. "I can't change your rank... but I can help with that bruise around your eye."

"My eye?" John touched his face and flinched. "Christopher!"

"You're lucky that's all I did," Chris muttered.

John looked back at Sara. "Please. I'd appreciate it."

Sara put her bowl down and gathered some moss. The same she used it on Chris's hand, back when they were—somewhere else.

"This won't hurt," she told John, mixing the paste on a leaf. "It'll reduce the swelling."

Donald nodded enthusiastically. "Natural medicine. Brilliant. And we're all grateful we don't have to look at your lurid face much longer."

The image of Lily, broken and bleeding, slammed into Sara without warning.

"Does it bother you?" she asked, voice sharp. "Looking at someone who's hurt?"

Donald looked stunned. "What? No! That's absurd.

I'm the royal medic for the valsing queen. Injuries don't bother me—or my people. We're not shallow."

"Hey," Chris said softly. "She was just asking."

Donald bowed his head. "Sorry. I just meant—we know that appearance isn't everything. Not when you've seen what I have."

Sara's voice dropped. "I met Lily, Donald. She is... my best friend. Or... she was."

"What do you mean 'was'?" Donald jumped up and tried to grab Sara by the shoulder. "What happened?"

John moved in front of her, protective.

Chris pulled Donald back. "You need to calm down."

"She knew Lily!" Donald shouted. "She knows something—"

"I do," Sara whispered, and her tears spilled freely now. "And I should have told you sooner."

Donald's voice cracked. "Where is she? Did the queen hurt her?"

Chris shoved him backward. "Look at her, Donald. This isn't the way."

Donald stepped back and took a deep breath, hands raised.

Sara flinched when John touched her shoulder.

"Sorry," he said gently. "Just checking on you."

Sara wanted to bolt into the forest and disappear. She couldn't bear the weight of that fear in her soul. But she owed Donald this. She'd promised herself she'd tell him —and then she'd leave. Rafael had asked her to save these people. She had. Now, she was free to go.

She took a shaky breath.

"I met Lily when her community moved close to the

abbey. Rafael told us they wouldn't stay long, but after weeks passed and they remained, he decided it was time to offer our help."

"No," Donald said, his voice tight. "That's not possible. We don't settle. How long did Orson stay there?"

"In the end... years," Sara replied. "Your king likes to defy your queen—and your traditions."

Donald snorted bitterly.

"We shared our food and knowledge of the forest. Lily started talking to me—claimed she was just curious. But we talked so much, eventually she had to admit we were friends. The valsings left for good over a year ago. After that, Lily only visited a few times."

She looked directly at Donald. "A couple of weeks ago, Lily came. Heartbroken. Hopeless."

Donald opened his mouth, but Chris placed a hand on his shoulder.

"Lily told me about you," Sara continued, "and what happened with the princess. She begged the queen to spare your life."

Donald's breathing quickened, eyes flashing with anger.

"The queen had to send Lily back to Orson. He gave her two options: marry Gale or live in exile."

"What the hell?" Donald began pacing. "That stupid, crowned bastard! Please tell me she didn't marry that loser."

Sara shook her head.

"So, what happened to her?"

John stepped closer. Chris remained near Donald. A

shiver ran down Sara's spine—they were bracing for whatever was coming next.

"Orson accused her of neglecting her mission, and—"

"What mission?" Donald interrupted.

Sara bit her lip. There was no point hiding it anymore. "The king sent her to gather information about the queen's war plans."

Donald's voice turned cold. "Lily was a spy?" His tone darkened. "She fooled me. I should have—"

"Don't." Sara cut him off, speaking quickly. "She loved you. She was ready to die for you. She denied knowing anything, so Orson ordered Gale to teach her a lesson..."

Donald clenched his fists, his jaw tightening. "Where is she now?"

Sara looked away. "She escaped. She tried to reach Tundra to speak with King Leonard. But the reisers had already burned the city. So she turned back—toward the battlefield."

"She thought the reisers' armor was too advanced," Sara went on. "She believed it had been designed by valsings. She feared Orson would support the reisers... by supplying them with weapons. Valsing weapons."

"What?" John shouted. "The valsings would *what*?"

Chris turned to Sara. "How do you know all this?"

But it was Donald who answered.

"She went to the abbey," he said, his voice hollow. "That's where she spoke to you. When did she leave? She wasn't there when the reisers—"

"She left the morning after you arrived," Sara said before he could finish.

Donald stepped back. "After? You mean before we got there. Why wouldn't she—"

He shut his eyes and sank to the ground.

"She didn't want me to see her," he muttered. "That's why you were asking about injured people. She thought I'd judge her... because those bastards hurt her."

"She was trying to help you, Donald," Sara whispered, her voice trembling.

"Help me?" Donald shouted. "By running off with the most *idiotic* idea possible? Going to the humans' king?"

Sara folded her arms, unsure what to say. She agreed with him. But to her surprise, it was Chris who spoke.

"Donald, she didn't reach Leonard. We know that much. So—"

"Not yet!" Donald pushed Chris aside and stepped toward Sara. "Why didn't you tell me this *days* ago? Lily is determined—she'll find your king. I thought you said she was your *friend*."

Sara stepped back. "I tried to stop her, but—"

"Well, you should've tried harder. Now, whatever happens to her... it's on *you*."

That was enough.

Sara turned and ran into the forest. Behind her, she heard Chris yell.

"Did you have to be such a jerk? Clearly, she cares about Lily!"

"Well, Lily's in danger!"

"Everyone is in freaking danger, Donald!" Chris

85

snapped. "But *you* more than anyone should know what a little empathy can do for someone who just lost *everything*. She saved your life, idiot. Or do you really think we could've made it out of the abbey without her?"

"I—no, I don't," Donald seemed to say, but Sara didn't care anymore.

She walked faster, letting the silence of the woods swallow her. She had nothing more to give. The roots would take her far away, and the forest would protect her. She jumped onto a root and glanced back.

No one followed.

An owl hooted in the distance. Her limbs felt heavy, too heavy to keep going. Instead of leaving, she sank to the ground, leaned back against the bark, and let its soft rhythm soothe her racing heart.

CHRIS MOVED A ROOT BY HIS HEAD AND mentally swore one more time when the fire from the torch burned his thumb. The wind hit his face, giving him goosebumps and threatening to extinguish his source of light. During his time in the abbey, he had forgotten how annoying those woods were, especially at night. Traveling through them felt like crawling under the scrubs of a normal forest, but with his eyes half-closed and carrying a bunch of stuff on his back while wearing wet clothes.

He pushed another branch out of his way, and the same empty roots he had been finding over the last hour filled his vision. The hair on the back of his neck stood up, and this time, the chill breeze had nothing to do with it. Sara had left too long ago, and he started to doubt he could find her.

The next root he moved bounced back and hit the back of his legs. He cursed out loud and turned to kick the stupid piece of wood, but didn't do it. To his relief, Sara was sitting on the ground against a nearby root. Her eyes were closed, but she wasn't asleep. She was holding her knees, and her head was resting on top of them.

Chris made sure the leaves cracked under his feet, but it wasn't until he was only a few steps away that she looked up. Her eyes reminded him of his mother's, empty and tired. Her skin was pale, and her cheeks and nose had the marks of the icy wind. He took his coat off and placed it over her shoulders.

"May I?" He pointed at her side, but she ignored the gesture.

"Are they gone for sure?" she said and covered her eyes with her hands. "The zhortas are they--sorry, it isn't your problem... I should have told you about Lily before."

Chris crouched in front of her and moved her hands to make sure she looked at him.

"Remember? It was my decision not to know, and you were right. It doesn't make any difference, not now or before, when we talked. Maybe if we had known years ago, but then neither of us would have been old enough to do something about it."

Sara's eyes shimmered, but she contained herself.

"As for the abbey," he continued, "it is important to me. I don't know for sure, but I have seen more than enough of what the reisers are capable of." He took a deep breath. "I'm very sorry for what happened, and I'm sorrier I could do nothing about it."

She looked down and covered her eyes again, making her hands wet. Chris let his knees fall to the ground, and hugged her. Her body was shaking, and for a second, he hesitated, thinking it could be because of her fear of soldiers, but she reached her arms around him and hid her face in his chest.

Chris brushed her hair, and the familiar sweet aroma surrounded him, until Sara calmed down, and he only heard her breathing in his arms.

An owl kept hooting in the distance, bringing vague memories of his visions. He wondered if there was a relation between them and Sara, but she moved back and took all his attention.

"I'm sorry." She wiped away her tears with the back of her hands and pulled her hair behind her ears. "I shouldn't—"

"Please, don't," Chris said and sat by her. "There is no reason to apologize. Not after all the things you have done for me."

Sara turned and tilted her head. "I don't think the soup was that much."

Chris chuckled, resting his arms on his knees. "Sara, you have no idea how good your soup was, but besides that." He inhaled and sighed. "I should start with you were right, and I'm sorry I didn't believe you then."

Sara frowned and was about to say something, but Chris didn't let her.

"Remember when I told you about my visions? Well,

they started years ago, not weeks, when you saved me from losing my mind and myself."

He turned to face her.

"You call them vivid dreams, but they are more than that. You can travel to places, meet people... I got myself in trouble with the army, and they punished me... I thought I was hallucinating when I met you."

Sara sat up and stared at him. Questions were written all over her face, ones he would try to answer.

"You told me you were real, and I didn't believe you." Chris rubbed the back of his neck. "I hurt you, and you promised me you would forget about me, and never—I can't believe I'm saying this out loud." He had to use all his will to not turn away from her gaze. "You told me you would never come to my dreams, which I called hallucinations for years. I assumed it was my self-control that stopped them, but I was wrong. It was you..."

Sara jerked back and covered her mouth. "No! That is not possible."

She looked at the trees and then back at him, and the only good thing was that she wasn't crying, running away, or yelling at him.

"I didn't dream—see you—for years, Sara. It wasn't until I met Gemli in the cave—I guess being tortured bring things back to your mind."

"Wait...Gemli? Who is...? Did you have visions of him, too?"

"Dear gods, no! No, Sara. You were—it was different. I saw you in Tundra, or by the forest. Most of the time by the ocean...the one we lost now. We talked about everything and nothing... We were—I thought —friends..."

She stood up, and when Chris was about to talk, she shook her head and stopped him.

"Weeks ago, you were in a cave? Very dark, even with hundreds of candles? There were horrible things on the wall. You were hurt. Injured—almost dying. Is Gemli tall, pale, very scary—"

"How do you know that?"

Gemli hadn't been part of his dreams with Sara. In fact, the sorcerer seeing her then had been one of Chris's biggest concerns.

"You killed me!" Sara said.

"What? No." Chris stood up. "No, I would never hurt you, Sara. I told you before, and I—While I was in that cave, I saw you in the ports of Laconia, but Gemli wasn't there."

"No, I was in a cave, and I saw you lying on the ground." She exhaled and played with her hands. "I don't understand. I didn't—before this—Years ago, did I know who you were? That you were a soldier?"

Chris pressed his mouth and shook his head. The first time he'd heard her name had been on the hill by the abbey. She had been a hallucination. His mind knew her, so what was the point of exchanging names?

"Right. So you had no idea I was a zhorta."

Chris nodded, though he had his doubts about it. She was so different, but he wasn't going to say it then, or maybe ever.

She exhaled and sat down on a root behind her.

"Why are you telling me this now? Do you even believe it?"

"I believe it now." Chris cleared his throat. "You lost everything, Sara. I realize this isn't even close to having a family or a real friend, but...I understand how lost feels. I want you to have something to hang on, even if it's as weird as this."

Sara shook her head and blocked her tears with her hands. "Your eyes...they seem so familiar."

"I may have been an idiot for not believing you years ago, and gods, it would have been so easy if I... I'm not making this up. I—I'm not that creative. I couldn't come up—"

"I don't think you are lying, but..."

Sara hugged herself and seemed to realize his coat was on her. She passed her fingers across the fabric and pulled it close to her face.

"You aren't alone, Sara. I remember you and our friendship."

"The only thing I remember is you in that cave and how hurt you were. Then your sword—your father's sword—killed me."

"Please, don't remember that," Chris said, and he took a step towards her. "It isn't a good memory, and you weren't there."

She looked at him and the pain in her eyes pinched his heart. Unable to do anything more, he hugged her again.

Sara rested her head on him and whispered, "How do you live without knowing what happened? Your family, your people, how do you go on?"

Chris took a deep breath and rested his head on top of hers. "Don't assume the worst."

She pushed back and stared at him.

"It won't do you any good to picture the zhortas— your family murdered," Chris said. "We don't know what happened, and though you need to be prepared for the worst, you don't need to think about it."

"What else could have happened?"

Chris paused and frowned. Giving false hope was dangerous, but over-imagining things wasn't any better.

"They could have escaped or been taken prisoner. They could be dead, or... Just don't torment yourself."

She nodded and moved back. Chris wished he hadn't lost so many years with her.

"I don't know if I should go back," she said. "I'm sure Donald hates me, and John, too."

Chris grinned. "John can be an idiot, but he doesn't hate you...and Donald is so sorry now. I want to see him apologize. You know, a diplomatic one."

Sara bit her bottom lip and nodded, but she didn't move.

"Also, I have no idea where the camp is."

That drew a shy smile on her face. It wasn't even close to Chris's favorite one, but it was better than nothing.

She walked towards the roots. After a few steps, she turned and waited for him.

CHAPTER TEN

The desert had never bothered Hayden—neither the heat nor the sand. In fact, he preferred it to the cold and dampness of the fortress. But this time, he was eager to get back.

Not long after leaving the fortress, he'd received a message from Murllen. The general wanted prisoners—not just soldiers, but any humans they encountered.

Hayden had opposed the order from the start. Prisoners slowed their progress and brought too many risks. They were desperate, unpredictable. Worse, he knew what Murllen wanted with them. If it were up to him, he would've wiped out the army and left the rest behind.

Humans were strange creatures—so unlike the reisers. They claimed to value their people, but always had favorites. A strange concept called love governed their actions, even when it endangered the group. Their stupidity fascinated him. The last battle had proven it.

The humans' commander had lost control of his own civilians. Instead of waiting for orders, they'd screamed and scattered, directionless. It had made Hayden's job embarrassingly easy—hardly a victory.

He shook his head as he ducked into his tent. No reiser would have acted like that. Reisers were trained to survive, not to live. They obeyed. They adapted.

Still, he had his preferences. Some humans intrigued him, especially the females. They looked and smelled better, but more than that, they behaved differently. Like Riddley's mother. She'd been aggressive and fearless, even furious. Claimed her son had died and never returned to Tundra. Somehow, she'd convinced the humans around her to follow the lie.

Then there were the civilians. He preferred them over the soldiers, who posed too much of a threat. Hayden had seen too many massacres carried out by human warriors. A caged enemy was the most dangerous kind.

And the worst of them was their king.

Hayden would've loved to kill Leonard. But Murllen had ordered otherwise. Alive. Unharmed.

Hayden wasn't a scholar of humans, but even he knew Leonard was a disgrace. Arrogant, pampered, weak. When his people were trapped, Leonard hadn't shown up until it was too late. And when he finally did, he had the gall to strike one of Hayden's guards. A tantrum from a man who couldn't win a fight against a child.

Throwing him down had been satisfying. Watching the fear in his eyes as reisers closed in around him, even more so. He didn't even realize how much his people hated him. They were ready to tear him apart the moment Hayden gave them the chance.

Humans thought reisers didn't listen, didn't pay

attention to their gossip. That amused Hayden. From their whispers, he'd learned plenty—like how the Armament Major had tried to kill Leonard the night of the battle. She'd once been one of their elite soldiers before being injured and reassigned to protect the king.

Her story should've ended in mercy. And Hayden had tried. But each time he saw her, something stopped him. A feeling—faint, but persistent—like he'd forgotten something important. Something that made his claw hesitate.

So instead, he healed her.

"Colonel," Sergeant Paul Torrents called from outside, "we've received another message from General Murllen."

Hayden kneeled beside the major, checking her temperature. Unconscious—but not feverish. He spoke only when he was certain she couldn't hear them.

"What does he want now?"

"He's requesting half the squadron meet him in Tundra. Immediately."

Hayden groaned. Another change. Another whim. Sending half his force away didn't bother him much, but the unpredictability did.

"Did he explain why?"

"Of course not. Just said to move immediately."

"Fine. We'll wait until morning."

He stepped outside to find Major Dunstan Miller, but Paul hesitated behind him.

"Colonel?"

Hayden turned. "Sergeant?"

Paul hesitated. "I—no, it's nothing. Sorry, sir."

Hayden didn't move. He studied the younger reiser, sensing the lie. He'd known something was off with Paul ever since they left the fortress. Murllen was involved—no doubt. And that meant trouble.

"Very well," Hayden said calmly. "When that 'nothing' turns into something, let me know. I may be able to help."

MAJOR DUNSTAN WAS WAITING BY THE LINE OF wagons when Hayden arrived to check on the prisoners and the next day's route. For as long as Hayden could remember, Dunstan had been there. They'd grown up and trained together at the fortress, fought the war side by side in the same squadron.

Reisers didn't have what humans called family. They had squadrons. Hayden had no idea who his parents were—no reiser did.

The asylum—a cold, sterile wing deep within the fortress—cared for young ones until they were skilled enough to fight. None of them remembered anything from their time inside, neither from before they left nor when they returned later, as a reward for preserving their race.

"Major," Hayden said, aware of how much he trusted Dunstan—more than any other reiser.

"Colonel," Dunstan replied. "So far, nothing new to report. The humans are tired, but most can move at the same speed. They've kept the short humans in the wagons, along with the injured ones, which prevents delays."

"You mean their offspring?" Hayden chuckled at Dunstan's startled expression. "Where else would they keep them, Major? They don't have an asylum like we do."

"Well, that's stupid," Dunstan muttered, shaking his head. "But then again, if they had one, it'd belong to us by now too."

Hayden nodded, a wave of relief washing over him. His offspring were far from this madness. Safe. That was something to be thankful for.

"Like you asked," Dunstan continued, "I kept watch on the little female. She's been helping humans all along the line. As soon as we stopped, she moved to the soldiers' line."

A small smile touched Hayden's lips. Another curious human. This one had almost made him believe all females were reckless and maddening. Thankfully, he'd figured out quickly that he'd just ended up with one of *those*.

A thousand times, she'd told him her name—Jean. He'd remembered it the first time, but teasing her had become a kind of entertainment. She was rash. She acted like she had nothing to lose.

He'd nearly killed her the first time she yelled at him, but King Leonard had dared to order him to proceed with no mercy, so Hayden let her be. He'd let her yell, made a few concessions. He didn't regret listening to Jean, not yet at least. Sometimes she needed to be reminded who was in charge—but she amused him.

"Colonel," a reiser said. "It's the human king."

Hayden and Dunstan hurried back. Dozens of scenarios raced through his mind, but none were as satisfying as what he found.

A broad grin split Hayden's face.

Leonard was on the ground, curled up, shielding his head. Alleta Riddley stood over him, furiously swinging a wooden cane. Jean tried to hold her back, but Alleta wasn't stopping. The woman had finally found a place to pour all her anger—and Hayden, if not bound by orders, would've let her beat Leonard into the sand.

"Well, well," Hayden said, strolling closer. "Had enough fun for today?"

He plucked the cane from her and gently pushed her back, careful not to hurt her.

"Teach that bitch a lesson!" Leonard spat.

"Absolutely," Hayden said smoothly, then turned to Alleta. "Next time you hit this bastard, make sure none of my reisers catch you before you finish the job."

He slammed the cane into the ground beside Leonard's head. The king shrieked and curled tighter.

"Isn't that a fine lesson, Leonard?" Hayden said. "Or should I give her a sword next time—let her effort have a better result?"

THE NEXT MORNING, HAYDEN ORDERED ALLETA moved to the front to walk beside the humans' commander. Though last night's spectacle had lifted his mood, he couldn't risk further chaos.

Inside his tent, the injured major lay awake. Her fever had broken. She looked healthier.

And still, the feeling gnawed at him—like he was forgetting something vital. That itch had followed him since the beginning of this cursed mission.

"Colonel," Dunstan said, entering, "did you send for me?"

Hayden moved away from the wounded human.

"Murllen wants half the squadron in Tundra. You'll take them."

Dunstan said nothing at first. His shoulders fell before he replied.

"When do we leave?"

"Today. Right after the caravan moves out."

"Yes, sir."

Dunstan turned, but Hayden stopped him.

"If there's anything I need to know... I'd appreciate you telling me."

Dunstan hesitated, then shook his head. "Nothing to report, Colonel."

Hayden nodded, but something tugged at him again.

"Major," he said.

Dunstan paused at the tent's opening.

Hayden didn't voice the real question. He didn't *want* to ask it. Didn't want to believe Dunstan would follow Murllen's orders blindly. But Murllen *was* their leader. Reisers didn't question commands.

"Before you go, put the human in the front wagon."

Dunstan nodded and move back to carry her.

Hayden didn't wait. Murllen had hated him for a

101

long time. Soon, he'd find out just how deep that hatred ran.

WITH HALF HIS REISERS GONE, THEY HAD TO move slower. Hayden stayed closer to the front now, wanting the mission—and the war—done.

He didn't want to see the world Murllen would build. For the first time, he didn't want to follow orders.

"Leave her alone, you coward!" the humans' commander yelled.

Trouble. Again. Before midday.

Murllen had given Leonard absurd privileges— freedom from ropes, his own wagon, the ability to walk around. That would end *now*.

When Hayden reached the wagon, Leonard held a bloody knife. Alleta lay motionless in the sand. The commander strained against his ropes to block Leonard. The human major tried to climb down, but she was too weak.

"Enough!" Hayden barked. The caravan halted.

Dark blood soaked the sand beneath Alleta. From here, she looked dead.

"I told you she needed a lesson," Leonard said.

Hayden's fingers twitched. He couldn't kill Leonard —Murllen's orders had been clear. Leonard must stay alive and "content."

But *this*?

"You're a coward," Leonard sneered. "I'm not."

Hayden kicked him hard. The king flew into the side of the wagon, hit his head, and slumped unconscious.

"Put the bastard back in his wagon and tie him up," Hayden snapped. "Gag him. If we don't hear him whine, he must be happy."

He dropped to Alleta's side. Her forehead was cut, but not deep. Her hand had several stab wounds, and her dress was soaked through with blood at the hip.

"Get Jean. Now!" he barked.

He pressed against the bleeding and didn't move. Alleta couldn't die—not under his watch. Not Riddley's mother. His whole squadron would pay for it.

And though he told himself he was only protecting his men... he wasn't sure that was true.

The commander strained toward them. "Is she alive?"

The major in the wagon echoed the question. Then Jean arrived.

She let out a gasp, barely muffling a scream behind trembling hands. Tears streamed down her cheeks.

"No, no, no..." she whispered, kneeling beside Alleta. "Alleta, please..."

"Jean," Hayden said, forcing her to meet his eyes. "Wrap her wounds. Check for broken bones. Clean her face."

Jean nodded numbly and got to work. But Hayden noticed something else—Charlie wasn't looking at Alleta anymore.

He was watching Jean.

Their connection had gone unnoticed before. Jean

might matter more than Alleta if Riddley was truly dead. Hayden didn't like that realization.

"I think—hope—she'll be okay," Jean whispered after a long silence.

She looked up at him briefly, then lowered her gaze, arms folded tightly around herself. Her face was stained with tears and dust.

Hayden saw the truth—Jean was an enemy. He could do nothing for her or Alleta.

And for the first time, he felt like a monster.

"Good," he said flatly. "Then we can move her faster."

Jean stood, ready to protest. He cut her off.

"If you want her dead," he said, "I can leave her with you. Let the king finish what he started."

She stopped, stunned, and stepped back, tears still falling.

Hayden turned to one of his reisers. "Take her to the fortress. She's valuable. If she dies, you die."

He didn't believe it would help Alleta, but at least she wouldn't die under his command.

As Alleta disappeared into the distance, Jean cried silently. She wouldn't see her again—not in this life. Hayden looked away and left her with the commander.

"Colonel," the human major said quietly from the wagon. "May I have a word?"

He approached.

"You need to watch your back."

"Is that a threat?" he snapped. "Don't forget, I saved—"

"It's not a threat. And I won't forget. Ever." She

lowered her voice. "The reisers... they have orders to kill you."

He stared at her.

"He told me," she whispered. "Before he left. Said I should warn you."

Hayden exhaled slowly. His suspicions were right.

Murllen had crossed every line. But knowing Dunstan was still loyal gave him a flicker of hope.

"I saved your life," he said. "There are worse things than death. Where we're going... you may wish for it."

"I agree," she replied. "But today, you saved me. Thank you. I'll let you know if I change my mind."

Hayden smiled faintly and tapped the wagon to move forward.

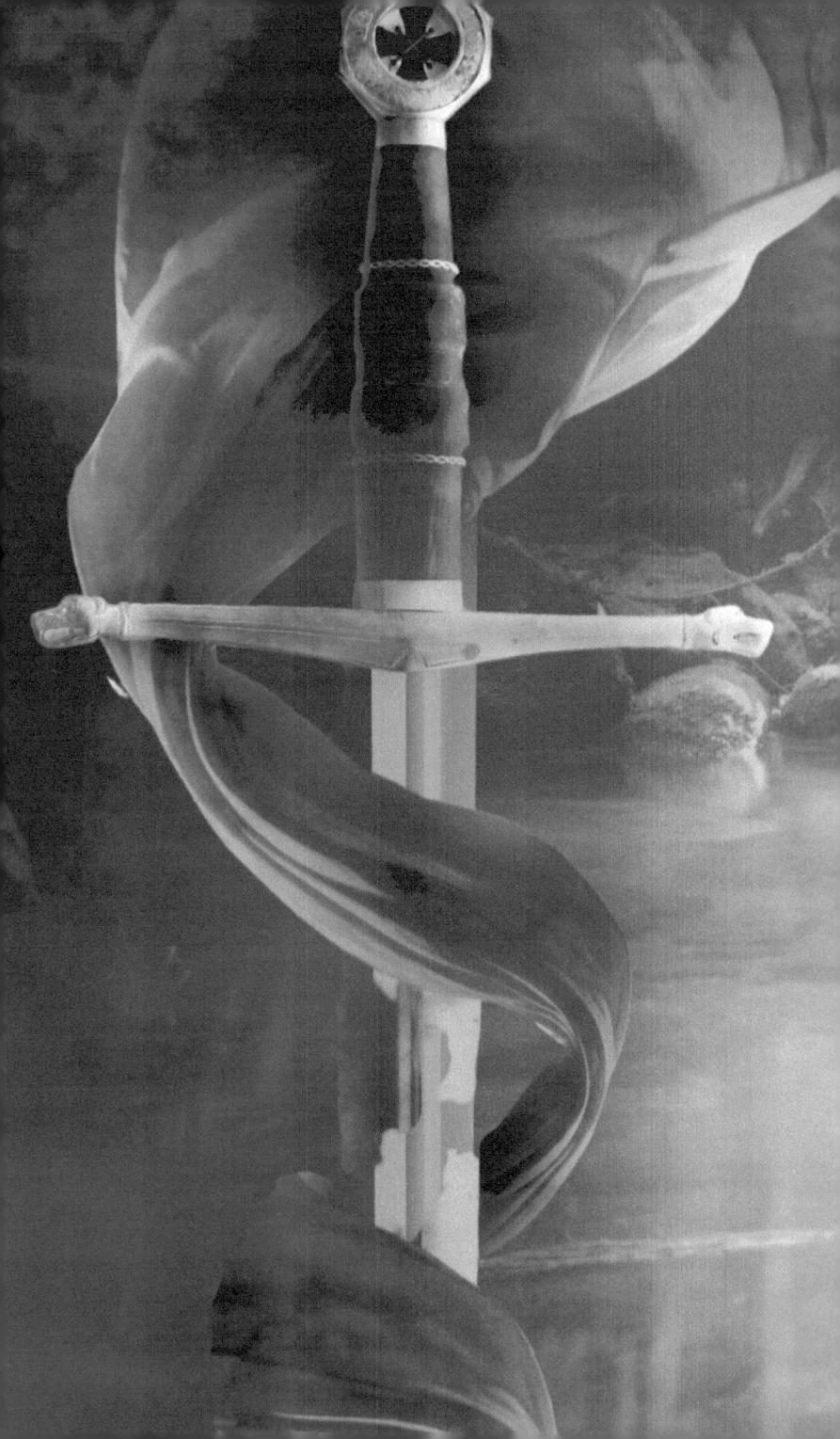

CHAPTER ELEVEN

L ily felt her fingers slip from the wet bark and screamed as her feet lost their grip on the root. The ground slammed into her back, knocking the air from her lungs, and her head struck a branch, turning her vision to a blur.

She didn't know how long she lay there, but when she managed to sit up, her entire body protested, and another cry escaped her lips. Miraculously, her bones remained intact, and only minor scratches covered her skin and clothing. Blood coated her hand from a gash at the back of her head, but beyond that, she was alive.

It took her a moment to realize the blue above her was the sky, and the trees hadn't shrunk—she had fallen beyond the northern edge of the Soto Forest. Tears welled in her eyes.

Something terrible must have happened. Days ago, those towering trees had pulled her from the edge of the desert and brought her here. They would never have moved that fast without a reason.

Sara had once explained how the zhortas could shift the Soto Forest's trees when necessary—typically to repair parts of the abbey or the scaffoldings. But it was rarely done. The consequences, Sara had warned, could be catastrophic.

Lily leaned back against a tree and looked around.

A sharp wind cut through her coat, making her wrap it tighter. Long ago, Sara had told her the height of the Soto Forest's trees blocked the brunt of the wind, giving it the best weather in all of Hune. She'd been right—and the memory made Lily giggle. The ache in her chest, though, deepened at the thought of her friend.

She used to be so sure of herself. Now, she missed that certainty. The chance to see Donald, lost. The things she'd said to Sara, unthinkable. Regret was unfamiliar, and she didn't like it.

She'd been lying to herself for days. She hadn't lashed out at Sara just to protect her, nor had she stayed away from Donald because she wasn't ready. The truth was, just the thought of facing him made her heart race—and the things she'd uncovered about Sara's life made her sick.

Sara was the key to saving Hune. And helping her would risk the one person Lily loved most.

She remembered the first time she saw her. Sara had been a short mess of tangled hair, drowning in oversized zhortas clothes, wary of everyone. Lily should've kept her distance. But something about her had drawn her in— made her feel lighter, better.

Over time, their bond had deepened in ways Lily never expected. Sara matched her wit, her fire. She had become the sister Lily never had—a chosen family where blood had failed. Lily treasured her empathy, the way she always saw the best in people. It was a kindness Lily lacked.

And it broke her heart.

In the abbey, Lily had spent hours reading ancient scrolls and scripts. They all spoke of a wise and justice one—someone destined to save Hune. It hadn't taken long to realize they meant Sara. And that truth shattered her.

Yes, Rafael had tried to protect Sara. But protection had come at a cost. He and the other zhortas had taken her, imprisoned her in the forest's depths, called it love—but it was still a cage.

Sara never had a childhood among her own kind. Not when she was small, not even now as a capable woman. They told her she belonged. But she didn't. They had stolen her life and wrapped it in comfort—and Sara, in her boundless compassion, had loved them for it.

The truth would destroy her. And for that, Lily wanted to kill Rafael.

But she had no proof. So she'd tried to force Sara to see—challenging her beliefs, wounding her pride. In the end, all she'd done was tear her down when she needed strength most.

The wind stung Lily's face, pushing her to move. She clutched her coat and sobbed harder, aching for the safety of Donald's arms. When Sara told her he was at the abbey, it had unleashed a storm of guilt and longing.

Donald had changed her.

His kindness, his decency—they made her want to be

better. He'd shown her the settlement, welcomed her without suspicion, taught her the harm in how her people had divided the race. And she—she had spied on him, nearly doomed everything he had built.

She hadn't followed through with Orson's orders. She'd stopped. But only because she'd met Donald. She hadn't questioned the mission or doubted the harm it would cause. She hadn't even thought about it— until him.

Donald had made her see.

He'd shown her a world that could be different. That should be different. He had trusted her.

And she had been ready to betray him.

Even his compassion couldn't excuse what she'd done. She had to become someone worthy of him. The day he arrived at the abbey, she hadn't been ready. Not even close.

A RUMBLE, DEEP AND THUNDEROUS, ECHOED through the earth.

The ground shook beneath Lily's feet, knocking her off balance as a growing shadow spread across the forest floor. She looked up—just in time to see the tops of the Soto Forest trees parting. A massive dark trunk descended from the sky like a falling tower.

She had no chance of outrunning it.

Instead, she scanned the clearing and spotted a cluster of jagged rocks. Sprinting toward them, she dodged tumbling branches as thousands of leaves rained down around her in a golden-green storm. In a desperate leap, she dove behind the rocks, bracing herself just as the trunk struck the earth with a force that launched her briefly into the air.

The silence that followed was unnatural. Eerie. Lily pressed a hand to her chest, trying to calm the frantic beat of her heart. Around her, broken trees lay scattered in ruin. The impact had carved open the edge of the Soto Forest.

Then came a sound—metal grinding against metal. Her mind recognized it. A battle.

Screams tore through the stillness.

Lily gasped and slapped a hand over her mouth. She slipped down from the trunk and dashed toward the trees, seeking cover. But the screams grew louder—closer.

She froze.

These weren't soldiers. Soldiers didn't scream like that.

They were people.

And they were dying.

Each step she took, the cries surged tenfold. Panic clawed at her throat as a thick, foul odor rolled over her— wet, heavy, putrid. She gagged.

She turned to run, but something cold and slick brushed her ankle.

"They're coming."

Lily looked down and recoiled.

A valsing dragged himself out of a bush, his face streaked with blood, a hollow carved brutally into his shoulder. She dropped to her knees, but he shoved her away.

"Run!"

Behind them, footsteps thundered through the trees.

The valsing choked on blood as it poured from his mouth. His head struck a rock with a sickening crack, and he moved no more.

Lily staggered backward, losing her balance. The footsteps shifted—heading toward her. Leaves and branches flew into the air, clearing a path as something massive approached.

She scrambled under a bush and held her breath.

Any second now, she expected to see the grotesque form of a reiser looming over her.

Instead, a short valsing stepped out of the trees, bloodied sword in hand, grinning at the corpse beside Lily.

"Too cowardly to stay and have fun?" the woman said, jamming the blade deep into the dead valsing's skull.

Lily choked on a scream, pressing both hands over her ears. The valsing twisted her sword, still smiling. A shrill, manic laugh echoed around them.

Even with her ears covered, the screams rang out—sharp, raw, unending.

The stench was unbearable now, turning sour at the back of Lily's throat. Her whole body shook as she cried, breath hitching uncontrollably. The sounds and the smells blurred together into something inhuman.

She rose on unsteady legs and stumbled toward the Soto Forest. She didn't want to believe it—but there was no denying it now.

King Orson was attacking the Queen's settlement.

Her people were killing their own kind.

A soft whimpering sound stopped her.

A valsing guy dashed past, weeping.

Moments later, a massive reiser stormed through the underbrush. With one claw, he seized the valsing's hair. The other lifted a blood-slick sword.

Lily dropped into a crouch and wrapped her arms tightly around her knees. She closed her eyes. She didn't move. Couldn't. She wished her hands were free so she could block out the sickening crack that followed.

Suddenly, a firm hand gripped her shoulder.

Another clamped over her mouth, muffling her cry.

"Don't move," a voice growled low beside her ear.

Branches rustled as the reiser searched the underbrush. Lily's pulse pounded so loudly in her head, she was sure it would give her away. Her thoughts scattered. For the first time in her life, fear erased everything else.

"I'm going to let you go," the voice said. "Follow me. Quiet and fast."

She turned—and relief washed through her at the sight of a human soldier.

She crawled after him, every breath shallow, every movement trembling.

The forest floor was wet beneath her hands, but it didn't feel cold. She glanced down. Her palm came away coated in blood.

Her stomach lurched.

"Don't think about it," the soldier whispered. "Just keep moving."

It stunned her that he was waiting for her, guiding her.

He didn't have to help her.

But he was.

Behind her, the screams pressed closer, spurring her on.

At last, they reached a fallen tree with gnarled roots arched like ribs above a hollow in the earth.

"Stay here," he said.

In any other life, she'd never have crawled into a hole like that. It reeked of rot and mold, spiderwebs stretched across the bark, insects squirmed between moss and decay.

But now, she didn't hesitate.

She shoved herself deep into the hiding space, clutching her knees to her chest.

"Some other valsings are nearby," the soldier said. "We're trying to get them out. If not me, one of us will come for you."

He placed branches over the entrance like a makeshift veil and turned back toward the danger—toward the reisers, toward the madness.

He had no reason to risk his life for her.

No reason to help her kind.

And yet... he did.

CHAPTER TWELVE

Time became a tricky thing to measure. Lily wasn't sure whether she wanted to stay in that hole forever or escape in the next breath. The screams of her kind echoed in her mind, and the stench of rot, mingled with the salt of her own tears, stuck to the back of her throat.

A weight pressed down from above, shaking her hiding place. Dirt rained down on her hair.

"I told you it would be fun," said a deep voice overhead.

Lily pulled her legs closer to her chest, unsure what she feared more—the cave collapsing or the monsters finding her.

Then came the laugh. The one that had haunted her nightmares for weeks.

"I just wasn't sure my people would pull this off," King Orson said. "Valsings were never known to be hunters."

Another laugh followed, deeper and colder, and

Lily's heart pounded so hard she thought it might give her away.

"That's why my reisers are here, Orson. I never doubted your people—they just needed to taste power. Nothing changes a creature faster than fear. Make them run, prove they were right to fear you... and they'll never forget who made them feel it."

"General Murllen!" someone shouted. "We've found the queen!"

"Excellent," Murllen said, his voice curling with dark satisfaction.

More dirt spilled into Lily's makeshift shelter as the bark above her shifted.

"For the gods' sake," Orson muttered. "I can't wait to see that stupid bitch's face."

Lily covered her face with her hands. Her worst fear had been confirmed: Orson had joined the war. If he gave the reisers weapons, the humans wouldn't stand a chance. And Sara—Sara had been right all along. Lily should have warned Donald how bad things were going to get.

The air around her suddenly changed. A sour, metallic tang burned her nose, and warmth spread unnaturally through the forest.

"Murllen, is *this* the important thing you were doing?"

The voice was unfamiliar, but Lily's skin prickled at its tone. She held her breath.

The forest went silent. No screams. No crackling fire. No cries for mercy.

Maybe it wouldn't be so bad to stay here forever.

"Oh, come on, Gemli," Murllen replied. "You always ruin the fun. We were just enjoying ourselves."

"You think hunting valsings is a priority?" the new voice—Gemli—said sharply. "Do you think the war is over just because your pet king joined it?"

"I'm not playing, Gemli," Murllen said. "Besides, I thought you'd be celebrating at the abbey with your *ex*-friends. Guess that didn't go as planned?"

"Oh, it did," Gemli said. "But now we have a new problem."

"Of course we do!" Murllen groaned. Something heavy crashed nearby, shaking the earth. "Orson, my friend, it seems our hunt has been interrupted. Go enjoy your queen. Just don't kill her... yet."

"Absolutely," Orson replied, though the tremble in his voice betrayed him.

Lily clutched her arms tighter. Whoever Gemli was, he scared *Orson*. That truth rooted itself in her chest like a stone.

"Dear Gemli, I expected better. What happened?" Murllen asked.

Gemli laughed—low, measured, cruel. "The useless people weren't the problem," he said. "By the way... making new friends, are you?"

"Gemli, come on—"

Something hit the ground hard. The forest trembled. A growl rose through the trees—not like the valsings' terrified cries, but something worse. Something ancient.

When Murllen spoke again, his voice had dropped, almost weak. "You're jealous."

"Jealous?" Gemli's laugh chilled Lily to her core. "No one's ever felt jealous of you, Murllen. No one ever will."

Then he added, "Let's talk about stupidity. Rafael let her escape."

Lily's breath caught.

"How?" Murllen snarled.

"Turns out Colonel Green was right. Your reisers aren't what they used to be. And the zhortas had watchers in Soto Forest."

"That *bastard!*" Murllen roared. "I told you he was weak. The way he looked at Sara should've told you everything. Did you kill him?"

"Better. He's waiting for you at the fortress."

A wicked pleasure filled Lily's chest. She wasn't proud of it—but it was there.

"Well, that *does* brighten my day. But how did she escape?"

A long silence followed. Lily almost believed they were gone.

Far off, she heard the valsings scream again. Her stomach turned.

"She had help," Gemli finally said.

Murllen's sharp snort almost made her scream.

"No kidding! Who would've guessed someone might help a scared girl over a malicious sorcerer?"

"There's nothing funny about this," Gemli snapped. "If she can escape me—"

Footsteps stopped right outside Lily's hiding place. The branches covering her trembled.

Through the leaves, she saw a pale, long-fingered hand.

"I know where she went, Gemli," Murllen said.

The fingers slipped away, and Lily exhaled—her first breath in minutes.

"You've told me every time we talked about her. She's going to find the saber. Once she has it, where do you think she'll go to use it?"

"Smart," Gemli said, voice rich with patronizing approval. "Very smart, Murllen."

Though she couldn't see him, Lily knew that tone. It was the one all valsings used when they thought other races didn't understand the game being played.

""See, Gemli? There is nothing to be worried about."

AFTER A WHILE, THE FOREST CAME BACK TO life. Birds and crickets sang again, joined by insects chirping far too close to Lily's head. No tears remained in her eyes, and her body had grown too tired to keep shivering from fear or cold.

"Are you still there?" a soldier whispered outside the cave.

Lily took a deep breath and crawled out, glancing around cautiously before stepping into the open.

"I think they're gone, little one," the soldier said gently, "but we need to get out of here before anything else happens."

"Where are we—?" Lily began, but her voice faltered when she looked around.

The forest had been transformed into a graveyard. Smashed vegetation created a small clearing. The crushed leaves and broken branches were dark with blood, and from the few trees still standing hung torn cloth and flesh —remnants of the valsings. In the distance, smoke curled from the ruins of the queen's settlement, now nothing but ash and scattered bodies.

She hadn't realized she'd stopped walking until the soldier stepped in front of her and grabbed her shoulders.

"We need to move. Now."

He didn't wait. He pulled her toward Soto Forest, and Lily stumbled after him. More soldiers moved in the same direction, a few valsings among them. Once the tall trees wrapped around them like sheltering arms, she noticed more valsings hidden among the shadows. She didn't recognize these; they were from Donald's community. But after visiting them, she was sure more than half were missing.

"Please, tell me he's all right!" a valsing woman said, grabbing Lily's arm.

Lily jerked in surprise and tried to twist free, but the woman's grip only tightened, nails digging into her skin.

"Please, I don't—" Lily began, then blinked. "Queen Vanessa? How— I thought you were—Orson—"

"Is he all right?" the queen asked, breathless. "Donald. Where is he? I need to talk to him."

Lily shook her head, and Vanessa dropped to her knees.

"Then it's over," the queen whispered.

Lily had never liked the queen. From the moment they met, Vanessa had carried herself with the same arrogant bearing as Orson, only with better manners. That queen had destroyed Lily's life without a second thought.

Even the scar on her face—branding her as disgraceful—was Vanessa's fault.

And yet, in that moment, Lily saw something human beneath the mask: a woman who had lost someone, too.

"He's with Sara," Lily said quietly. "Or... at least, that's what I hope."

"Sara? Who is she?"

Lily hesitated. She didn't trust anyone here enough to tell the whole truth.

"She's my friend. She lived at the abbey where Donald—"

"Thank the gods," Vanessa exhaled, relief softening her face. "And thank *you*, too, Major Baker. More of my people would be dead if it weren't for your soldiers' help."

Her voice broke, and she covered her mouth with trembling fingers to muffle the sob rising in her throat.

She tried to stand, but her legs buckled. Lily reached out to catch her, but the queen was too heavy, and they both nearly fell. The major caught her instead, lifting her with ease and barking orders to the soldiers around them.

Lily straightened and looked around. The sight stirred the same hollow ache she'd felt when she saw Tundra after the reisers burn it. Only a few worn, nearly useless tents remained. Soldiers and civilians moved among the roots in a small clearing—more a dent in the vegetation than a proper camp. Most of the humans weren't even in uniform.

And among them stood the surviving valsings. Watching her.

Lily hadn't hurt them personally, but her community

had. That truth pressed down on her, heavy as stone, and she lowered her head under the weight of it.

She clenched her fists, uncertain what else to do, and followed the major into a nearby tent.

Inside, a strange sensation made her glance down at her hands. Blood. The queen's blood. It dripped from her fingers and soaked the front of her dress, which had already been ruined beyond recognition.

She tried to wipe her hands clean, but there was too much.

"I'm sorry, Major," a soldier said softly.

It took a moment for Lily's eyes to adjust. When they did, she saw Queen Vanessa lying on a cot. The major stood nearby, his shoulders rigid, while another soldier knelt beside the queen, inspecting her wounds.

"There has to be something you can do," Major Baker said, his voice tight.

"I can try to make her comfortable," the medic said, "but... it's bad. I've never seen anything like this before."

"What do you mean?" the major snapped. "We've been fighting these bastards for years. What more could they— What the hell is going on, Lieutenant?"

"The king's community joined the war," Lily said. "And King Orson is giving new weapons to the reisers."

Both men turned to her, and Lily saw the flicker of realization in their eyes.

"In the gods' name," the major whispered. "Why would he do that?"

Lily shook her head, helpless. Orson had wanted to outrage Vanessa, to wage war against her as if it were a game. He never should have joined the fight—especially not against his own race, and certainly not with his own hands.

There had to be a reason.

But whatever it was, it was beyond her understanding.

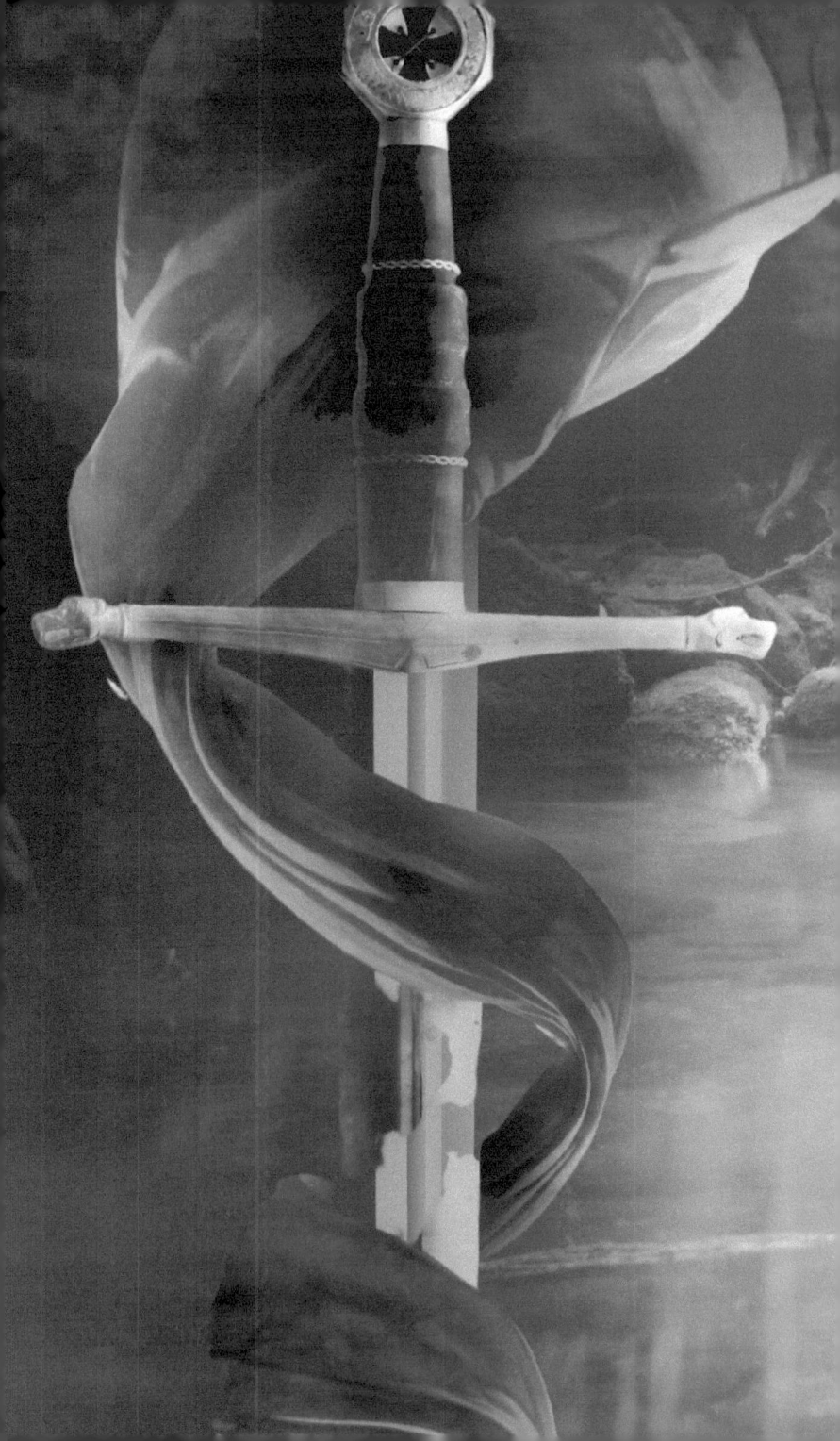

CHAPTER THIRTEEN

During the next few hours, humans and valsings went in and out of the tent, carrying water, bandages, medicine—anything they could find to help the queen—while Lily sat in a corner. She overheard voices but made little sense of them. In her mind, the only important conversation was the one between Murllen and Gemli.

Rafael being a traitor made her blood boil. She wanted to kill him. Yet, according to Gemli, he had helped Sara escape—and that meant everything to Lily. Murllen's rage left no doubt the zhorta had betrayed the reisers, but it raised more questions. If they knew where Sara was, why hadn't they taken her before? What had changed that made them search for her now? More importantly, why were they so sure she would find the saber?

As far as Lily understood, Sara was the weapon. Or so she thought.

"Are you all right, little one?" Major Baker asked, making Lily jump. "Sorry. I didn't mean to scare you."

He sat down beside her and closed his eyes, resting his head against the tent wall.

"I don't think your queen will survive."

Lily hid her hands in the damp fabric of her dress. She'd washed them, but the warm sensation of Vanessa's blood clung to her skin.

"What's your name?"

She looked at him. His smile was wide and open—no judgment in it.

"Lilian Granite. But everyone calls me Lily."

"I couldn't imagine a more appropriate name for someone like you."

Lily lifted an eyebrow.

"A small name for a small girl. That's very strong, you know."

Her face warmed, and she looked down.

"You remind me of someone I dearly cared for," he added, his tone quieting. The silence that followed told Lily the rest.

"I'm sorry," she said softly. "I can't think of anything else to say."

"Sorry is fine, Lily. We've all lost someone... or more."

The queen's voice broke their moment. "Lily, please."

Lily stood and hurried to her side.

"Is he alive? What happened to him?"

She knelt so Vanessa could see her better, and to her surprise, the queen reached for her hand. A few valsings stepped into the tent but stopped at the entrance, their eyes fixed on Lily.

"Your Highness," she said, "Donald reached the abbey with a human soldier."

Vanessa's smile brightened her pale face. "Christopher... Riddley."

Behind her, Major Baker straightened and stepped closer.

"As long as they are together," Vanessa whispered, "there's still hope."

"Your Highness," one valsing said gently, "let me check your—"

Lily tried to step back, but the queen tightened her grip.

"Listen to me," she said, addressing the others now. "It is my command that all of my faithful valsings help and serve Commander Christopher Riddley in his quest."

The queen looked up at Major Baker, and after a deep breath, she continued, her voice louder.

"I can only hope my people will aid you and the human army, Joseph."

Apprehension flickered in the major's eyes. "There's no need for that, Your Excellency. We can protect your people. There's no need to put them—"

Vanessa lifted a frail hand, and he stopped.

"In the past, I failed to offer Christopher our support —our resources."

Lily looked at the floor. Vanessa kept mentioning Christopher but not Sara. That, to Lily, was a mistake. It wasn't the commander who would save Hune—it was her friend.

"We may not be fighters, but our knowledge could help..."

She began coughing—blood trickled from her lips. Lily rushed to clean her face and offered water, but Vanessa waved her off.

"I hurt you so much, Lily," Vanessa said, sitting as straight as she could. "Have you found my daughter?"

One valsing at the door shook his head.

Vanessa turned away, but Lily caught the tears in her eyes.

"I just... Her father is a monster," the queen murmured, "but she is his daughter. Hopefully, she won't suffer his punishment."

Lily shivered, remembering how Orson had spoken of Princess Cassandra after her affair with a human. She hated the princess for what she'd done to Donald and to her—but not enough to wish her a reunion with her father.

"Lily," Vanessa said gently, "Donald is dear to me. His love for you must mean you're worthy of that privilege."

Lily lowered her eyes.

"I'm sorry for what I did to you... and for what I must do now." The queen touched Lily's cheek. "This is the only way I can save you."

Before Lily could respond, Vanessa drew a breath, and though her voice trembled, her authority didn't.

"Until you find my congressman and royal medic, Donald Terrance, this valsing, Lilian Granite, will be my successor. Once Donald returns, he will rule—for all valsings. Our survivors must stand together, whether from my community or deserters from Orson's. We must forget and seek what peace remains in this war."

The queen's coughing worsened, more blood staining her lips. Lily tried to help, but Vanessa pushed her aside.

"Major Baker... please take care of Lily. Some valsings may protest this proclamation, but Major—help my people. And tell Christopher—I would have supported him sooner... even with what my daughter did. I should've... but I was so mad... please... protect my..."

Her pupils widened—then lost their shine.

There was no time for a response. Her plea remained unfinished.

Lily cleaned the queen's face and closed her eyes. A knot tightened in her throat, but she didn't want to cry. In seconds, her life had changed in ways she never imagined.

Vanessa had taken the throne from her daughter. Was that why Donald's engagement had existed at all? Would the queen really entrust everything to Lily just to secure Donald's rule?

Lily stood and looked behind her. Vanessa's words echoed.

Inside the tent, not one valsing met her gaze with welcome. She was sure the ones outside felt the same.

"The queen said what?" someone said from the back.

"There's no way I'll follow this failure of a valsing as my ruler," said another, only steps away.

"She's disgraced!" another voice shouted.

Lily became acutely aware of everything wrong with her: the torn clothes, the stains on her hands, her missing curls, and the scar down her cheek. Everyone knew she was the reason Donald hadn't married the princess. Worse—she was a valsing from the king's community. The same people who had just slaughtered their friends.

"We have to find the princess. She's the rightful heir!"

"But the queen just said—" one tried to respond.

"What's wrong with you? Our queen is dead! We need to grieve before we—"

Major Baker stepped forward and put a hand on Lily's shoulder. "There's no point in arguing here," he said. "This is your queen's last will. Follow it—or leave my camp."

Some valsings murmured and turned away. Most stared at the ground.

"What do you want to do, Lily?" Major Baker asked.

The warmth of his hand and the certainty in his voice steadied her thoughts.

She brushed her dress. "I understand why none of you like this."

Even to herself, she sounded unsure. She cleared her throat again and forced her voice stronger. It was her first time speaking as a leader, and the weight of that pressed on every word.

"I don't like the queen's will either. But this isn't permanent. Until we find Donald, we have priorities."

There were many things they couldn't fix. But others... they could.

"We need to find the survivors, help the wounded, and get to safety."

She turned to the major. His smile steadied her.

"No offense, Major Baker, but your camp isn't exactly a hidden gem." She turned back to the valsings, letting their pride bolster her own.

"You're looking at the best space designers in Hune. I know you'll come up with something better."

ONLY HOURS LATER, THE VALSINGS HAD MOVED their settlement to the far edge of the Northern Forest. It lay near enough to the Soto Forest to offer an escape route if needed, but not so close that the monumental trees could crush their new tents again.

The site impressed Lily, though many of the valsings remained unsatisfied. Lacking proper materials, tools, and labor, they'd only managed what they called a "decent shelter." To Lily, it seemed smaller than their previous community, but compared to the settlements she had grown up in, it was an immense improvement.

Major Baker and the human survivors couldn't have been happier. Their new tents stayed dry, the wind no longer stole their warmth, and the lighting alone had earned the place the name "village."

"Lily!" Major Baker called, interrupting her walk. "I'm certain we found everyone we could. Besides the small bunch... I'm sorry, little one. There wasn't much hope from the beginning."

The human soldiers had joined the valsings in combing the forest. They'd found more bodies than survivors—and among the living, most of the injured wouldn't recover.

"I understand. And I appreciate you and your men," Lily said, lifting her gaze toward the sky. "It's just... more than half of the queen's community is gone."

"What about yours?" the major asked gently. "Are there any here?"

She nodded but didn't trust her voice. The papers in her hands made a good excuse to look away, so she studied them instead.

"Some valsings are talking about forming a new council," she offered. "I think it's a good idea—"

"Lily," Major Baker interrupted, "you can't blame yourself for what the people you used to live with did."

"I know, but... how could they? We weren't friends, but we didn't hate each other either. The monarchs did. Most of us didn't care."

The major inclined his head. "Sometimes fear makes people do strange things, little one."

"Fear?"

"Yes, Lily," a valsing voice said from behind her.

She turned, hand to her heart, the other rising to cover her mouth. Two soldiers were dragging a valsing between them. The sword at his belt marked him as one of her old community.

She took a step back as they forced him to his knees.

"We just found this one near the perimeter, Major," one soldier said.

"Damn it. I'll send a watch to sweep the area—"

"There's no one else," the valsing said quickly. "I'm alone. Lily, please—you know me. I would never have—"

She leaned forward, unsure how he knew her. But a second glance at his dark eyes unlocked a memory: a quiet boy from her early studies.

"Liam Gabbro? No. That can't be... How did you—? What did you do? Why...?"

"You said it yourself, Lily." Tears carved pale tracks down Liam's face. "Fear. Orson joined the reisers and— Lily, their leader is a monster. I couldn't say no. I couldn't take the pain anymore..."

Major Baker signaled to his men, who let Liam fall forward, weeping into the earth.

"I'm so sorry. Please forgive me. I—"

Lily stepped forward, but the major gently blocked her path.

"Tell me what Orson did," she said, her voice steady even as her memories clashed with the broken figure before her. "What did you do?"

Liam sat back on his heels, eyes lowered.

"We arrived with the reisers just before sunrise. It was still dark, but Vanessa went straight to Orson. He slapped her so hard she fell." His hands trembled. "It was that monster—Murllen, their leader—who stopped Orson from killing her on the spot. I didn't know what I expected, Lily, but it wasn't that."

His breath hitched. He tried twice to speak again, but his voice fractured under guilt and grief.

"The valsings here said Orson ordered the fire," Lily said. "That's why the queen ran."

"No." Liam looked up at her. "Murllen grabbed her guards and threw them into one of the big cabins. Then he set it on fire. He told the reisers to block the exits... and told the queen he'd leave them there until she ran."

Lily covered her mouth and shook her head. Major Baker stood stunned, jaw tight, staring at Liam.

"Orson just laughed," Liam whispered. "It wasn't until a reiser tried to grab another valsing that the queen bolted. Then we—we burned everything. One of them put a sword in my hand, Lily. I said no. But the pain... Every time I refused..."

Lily moved closer, reaching to examine his back—but had to turn away. His shirt hung in ribbons, fused with strips of flayed skin.

"They did that to all of you?" she asked. "The reisers forced our people to kill each other?"

Liam shook his head. "Some, yes. But most of the killing... it came from Orson's guard. And a few of our own valsings."

Lily backed away, sick with fury and disbelief. She didn't need to hear more. Orson wasn't just cruel—he was unstable, and now he had an army.

"Major," Lily said, clearing her throat, "could your soldiers help Liam? I don't think the valsings would..."

"Of course, Lily."

She nodded, unable to speak. Around her, voices of humans and valsings mixed as they worked side by side to finish the camp.

She remembered the time Orson had received the human envoys—the day Princess Cassandra had turned their visit into a spectacle. No one had talked about the humans' real petition, not even Lily. But now she understood how important it must have been.

Apparently, they needed a greater enemy—one big enough, dangerous enough, to force humans and valsings to unite. Even Donald must have been in serious trouble to be sent as support to the commander.

Her thoughts returned to Sara. The conversation between Gemli and Murllen still echoed in her mind. Sara had escaped... but that didn't mean she was safe. Lily owed it to her friend to find out what had really happened to the abbey.

She walked to the camp's edge and stared toward the Soto Forest. The zhortas were gone—but maybe, just maybe, their books and parchments had survived.

CHAPTER FOURTEEN

G emli sat inside Murllen's tent, watching as Orson vented his frustration with his valsings. The king kept railing about the ineptitude of his people for mistaking his daughter for the queen—a petty complaint, considering he had upended their peaceful ways in mere days.

The valsings had never interested Gemli. He'd met many over the years, but found little worth in them. Murllen's newfound appreciation for them, however, was... curious.

"Those idiots!" Orson snapped. "I'll teach them how to recognize—"

"It isn't that bad, Orson," Murllen interrupted. "You can always use her as leverage with your ex-wife."

Orson flung his arms up with a dramatic sigh. "I cannot, Murllen. Neither of us can stand Cassandra."

Gemli chuckled, making Orson flinch.

"No wonder you like him, Murllen," Gemli muttered. "Cynical and shameless."

The king straightened to his full height, holding Gemli's gaze until the sorcerer grinned. Then Orson turned away, pretending interest in his wine.

"In any case, I will make them find her."

Murllen leaned forward. "Orson, our plans have changed."

Gemli turned sharply toward the general, not bothering to hide his annoyance.

"What do you mean? I need to find her! Vanessa must pay for her stupidity!"

"I understand," Murllen said calmly. "And she will. But... Gemli's news is urgent. We must reach the fortress."

The color drained from Orson's already pale face. The fortress had become a myth during the war—none of its stories ended well. Gemli chuckled again. The place was worse than legend, and Orson's trembling hands showed he believed it.

"Murllen, I don't mean to upset you, but—"

"Then don't," Murllen said, standing. "We'll find your queen. You'll have your time with her. But first, we finish what we started: you earning my forgiveness."

Orson's shoulders slumped in defeat. Murllen took it as surrender. Gemli wasn't so sure.

"Come on, Orson," Murllen added. "Your stay in my home won't be long. Laconia is close. You and your people could move there."

Murllen stepped out of the tent. Orson didn't follow.

Instead, he turned to Gemli. "I know your kind well, sorcerer."

Gemli raised an eyebrow. "Do you?"

"You're clever and powerful. You seek justice—not law, but personal justice. Just like me. We could help each other rather than block one another's goals."

"Just like me?" Gemli stepped closer, lowering himself to Orson's eye level. "I don't doubt your intelligence, valsing. I'm sure you've maneuvered your goals for some time. But no, Orson—we are not alike," Gemli smiled. "If I wanted you dead, you'd be dead. If I wanted your pathetic secrets, you'd spill them now."

He didn't need magic. Orson's shallow breaths and sudden sweat proved the point.

"You were right about one thing," Gemli said, standing tall again. "Don't block my objectives. You won't get far."

He swept from the tent and into the cold night, pulling up his hood—then lowering it again. Old habits. He had no reason to hide, and he didn't need to use his cloak like his former fellows in the Soto Forest.

Destroying the zhortas had satisfied something in him. Just as he'd imagined. But the victory stirred memories better left buried. Murllen's presence, for once, offered a distraction.

"Why do most of Hune not see beyond themselves?" Murllen asked beside him.

Gemli kept walking. "Are you counting yourself among them? If so, you know the answer. If not, there's no point explaining."

He had chosen Murllen not just for his love of violence, but for his rare reasoning. Murllen nodded—understanding the point. It was a shame he'd have to die.

"I appreciate your love for questions, Gemli," Murllen said. "So, how is it possible that Sara escaped from you?"

Gemli stared into Murllen's too-bright eyes. Blue—so vivid against such a dark soul.

"I don't think I'm the only one with surprises," Murllen added.

"The valsings aren't surprises," Gemli muttered. "Just annoyances. You'll learn that soon."

Murllen opened his mouth, but Gemli cut him off. "As for your niece..."

The memory rose sharp and clear. He knew what she'd done. He also couldn't help admiring it.

"Long ago, the zhortas compiled certain ingredients to command the trees. She had those seeds—and she used them."

Murllen laughed. "She bewitched the trees to hide behind them?"

"Like you use swamp mud to win battles?" Gemli shot back.

Murllen stopped laughing.

"It's near impossible to find anyone there, especially someone who understands those woods. She grew up in that strangeness—and learned how to use it."

Murllen's smile held a trace of pride. "Then our family reunion will be interesting. Unless this... becomes a problem." He leaned in. "Do you think Rafael was smart enough to teach her—?"

In a blink, Murllen collapsed, gasping, clutching his stomach.

Inside Gemli's mind, he felt the reiser's organs scream

as he twisted them—not enough to kill, but enough to remind.

"Rafael is as stupid as you," Gemli said calmly. "He didn't see my plan for Sara. Just as you think I can't see how you're plotting with Orson."

He let go, just for a moment, and crouched in front of Murllen.

"Don't make me regret the side I chose, Murllen. A miracle is necessary for you to defeat me. But remember." He stroked Murllen's hair and whispered in his ear, "Without me, Commander Christopher Riddley will defeat you."

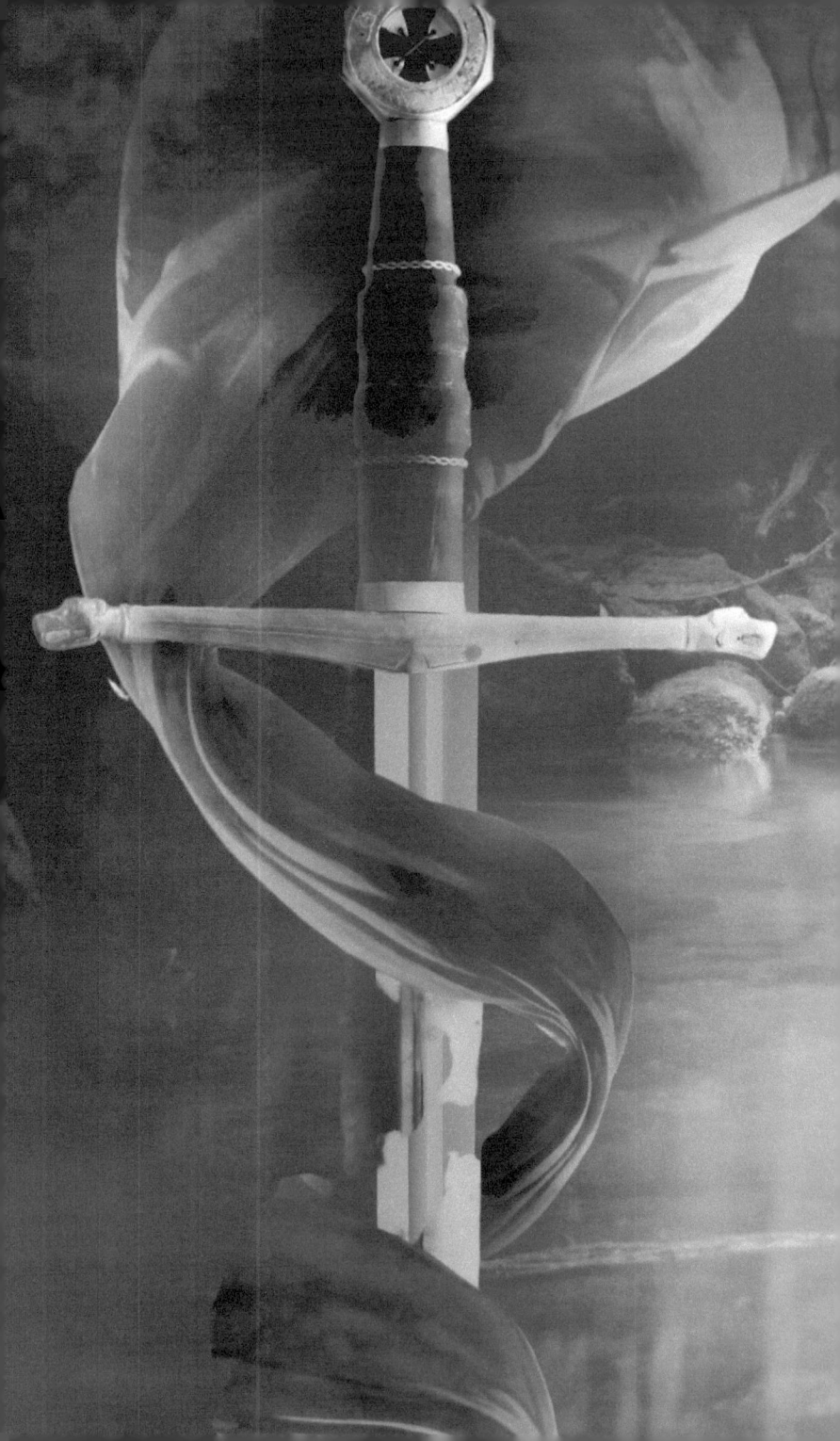

CHAPTER FIFTEEN

The voices around the camp woke Chris, and the indulgent aroma of food gave him the motivation to leave the tent. After what had happened the day before at the abbey, they needed to stay vigilant. John's physical and emotional state had made Chris take the longer night shift—something he hadn't done since becoming a major, and hadn't missed.

He'd spent most of the night questioning what to do next. The only decision he'd made was that he wouldn't give up. Leonard would pay for what he'd done, and he would find Charlie and the rest of his soldiers. The problem was how.

Sara had become a constant in his mind. Talking to her had cleared his thoughts, but now he was too aware of how special she was. Now that he admitted she was vital to saving Hune, he feared for her future. He wanted to find a safe place for her—but in his world, such places no longer existed.

"Well, it's about time you woke up!" John called. "My superiors never let me sleep this long."

"Privileges of being your superior," Chris said, yawning. "And by the way, the sun is barely up."

Donald chuckled and pointed to the pot over the fire. "There's some food left."

Chris moved closer and glanced around the camp.

"Sara made it," Donald added.

He didn't need the clarification. The smell told him enough. It didn't, however, tell him where she was.

"She left to get some supplies," John said, reading his expression. "Or at least, that's what she said."

Chris stared into his bowl, wondering if he'd ever stop worrying about her leaving. She had every reason to. Maybe the conversation last night had pushed her away. Maybe she'd gone back to the abbey now that her reasons for helping Hune were gone. Or maybe she just didn't want to deal with soldiers anymore. To stop himself from spiraling, he asked, "Supplies? I doubt there's anything here we could—"

"Pointless," Donald muttered. "This is ridiculous and pointless."

Chris looked up at him, already regretting it.

"There's nothing in these pages about a saber or any weapon. I can't figure out what Lily might have found in them."

"Lily found?" Chris asked.

"Oh yes," John said. "While you slept for hours, Sara already explained everything Lily told her—at least twice. Let's just say I don't blame her for going off to find something. Anything to get away from this guy. I'm not joking

—if we ever need someone for interrogations, Donald is your man."

Chris rolled his eyes. "I was awake. Very awake until John was nice enough to take over his shift—hours later."

"It wasn't hours," John said. "Just a few minutes. And only because you didn't wake me."

"Minutes? Sure."

Chris took another bite, letting the flavor linger. One of the few pleasures left, and he intended to enjoy it.

"So," he said, "what did you two figure out overnight?"

"Nothing," Donald grumbled. "There's nothing else to follow."

Chris had come to the same conclusion. Nothing felt clear. Not even chasing the saber.

"All right, Chris," John said. "In your own words. What've we got so far?"

Chris laughed, but he got it. Donald could wear anyone down.

"Let's see," he began. "I got the king's letter sending me to St. Peter's Abbey. Charlie and I agreed it was safer to leave the guard at Tundra and go alone."

"Charlie told me it was all your idea," John said. "If it had been up to him, he would've sent the letter back to the king with his best wishes."

Chris grinned. "He was right. Just don't tell him."

"Of course not," John said. "No need to boost his ego—yours is bad enough."

Donald rolled his eyes and returned to the papers.

"I ran into a reiser watch," Chris went on, "but a sandstorm forced them to retreat."

It had been the first time he'd sensed the flower's presence—though not with Sara. That time, the vision had been of the valsings' queen.

"That's why your horse made it back to Tundra," John said. "Lucky storm."

Chris snorted. "Lucky for the horse. Not so much for me, getting ambushed, drugged, and hauled through the desert for days? Not ideal."

"What the hell?" John asked. "Who—"

"I told you already," Donald said. "I didn't mean to keep you unconscious for so long."

"You drugged him?" John laughed. "You?"

Chris glared at Donald. "Still drugged me."

Donald sniffed. "I wasn't risking my life arguing with you. My queen wanted to see you—so I made it happen."

Chris waved him off. "Anyway. Queen Vanessa had a letter from the High Council, addressed to me, telling me to retrieve our first king's journal."

John snorted again but quieted when Chris didn't join in.

"You're serious? Why would the High Council send a letter to the valsings? Don't they know what you did? How much the queen hated you?"

Donald laughed this time, but John ignored him.

"Why now? Why you?"

Chris had wondered the same. Vanessa's letter had led him to the journal—and to Gemli. If the council was involved with Leonard, he might've made a huge mistake by following their orders.

"Maybe Leonard was behind that letter, too," Donald said. "Pretending to be the council. That would explain everything."

"It's possible," Chris admitted. "But why complicate it? Leonard could've just taken the journal. Or sent someone else."

John sighed. "You can't forget the armament. They didn't think Leonard knew anything about those letters."

A sound behind them made Chris turn, his hand instinctively going to his sword. But when he saw Sara emerge from the roots, his breath caught. She was balancing a mess of branches and roots in her arms, with the sack Rafael had given her slung across her shoulder.

He couldn't even greet her.

"What are you carrying?" Donald asked. "Those branches look exactly like the ones we already have."

"They're not," Sara said, setting everything down. "We're in the northern part of the Soto Forest. It's better to stock up when you can."

"Right," John said. "Because we need more roots and dry leaves."

Sara chuckled as she took off the sack and sat.

"The northern woods aren't as fertile," she said, sorting the roots. "I assume we're not staying here, and we'll need food for the road to the Northern Forest. Well, if that's where we're going. But I can always leave this and forage along the way."

"No, no," Donald said quickly. "We've already tried what not to eat. Right, Chris?"

Chris scowled, but his chest warmed when Sara answered for him.

"At least he kept you alive. And didn't poison you—by accident."

John choked. "Poison? Wait—you mean there are poisonous roots?"

"Oh, yes," Sara said. "You're all very lucky. Or the gods want you alive."

From her sack, she pulled out old parchment sheets and envelopes and pushed them toward the other papers.

"I hoped these might help."

Donald reached for them, hesitating as he opened the first. The edges crumbled in his hands, and the writing had faded with age.

"Where did you get these?" Chris asked, already dreading the answer.

"Rafael gave me the bag, remember?" she said. "I didn't see these until last night. I guess he thought they might help."

She picked up one envelope, running her fingers over it.

"They talk about a 'special person.' Just like Lily said... or what Rafael believed—" Sara stopped clearly trying to control her grief.

Chris set his bowl down and moved beside her.

"So, the High Council?" John said, mercifully changing the subject. "Do we think they're still alive? Do we even know who used to be on it?"

"As far as I know," Donald said, "it had members from all the races—sorcerers, zhortas, too—but I never knew their names. Queen Vanessa didn't say much, though she suspected the war started inside that group."

Sara tapped her mouth thoughtfully, then looked at Donald.

"Don't look at me," he said. "That's everything I know."

"Can I see the letter?" she asked Chris. "Vanessa's?"

He nodded and reached for his sack.

"What's your problem?" John shoved his shoulder. "You could've given it to me too."

"You didn't ask."

After handing it to Sara, Donald offered him one of the papers.

The second he focused, he saw why the valsing had passed it to him. The crisp, clear script. The direct instructions. Unlike the valsings' symbols, this was unmistakably written by a reiser.

"What is it?" John asked.

Chris handed him the sheet and picked up another. Same symbols.

"This is strange," Sara said, eyes still on Vanessa's letter. "She got this for you?"

"Yes," Chris said. "She knew the war would affect the valsings and wanted to help. She searched for the council's members. She didn't think they were all dead. This was the only help she found."

Sara stared at Donald.

"I'm telling you, that's all I know."

"Can I see that?" John asked, and she handed it to him.

"But this isn't—maybe even Vanessa missed the point," he said, frowning. "This asked you to protect the Great Wizard's descendant and legacy."

Donald scowled.

"What point could she miss? The letter's clear: what needed doing, not very clear and who to bring it to."

"Wait," Sara said, turning to Chris. "You followed the letter? I thought the king sent you to the abbey."

Chris sighed and rubbed the back of his neck. "Yes, he did. And I went—just after I—we lost..." He trailed off, then added, "It's a long story."

John threw the letter onto the pile. "So you betrayed the bastard after all."

"I didn't betray him," Chris said. "I just... delayed my response. And to be clear, I followed the higher command's order first."

CHRIS EXPLAINED THEIR VISIT TO REIGN Mountain—how they'd found the journal, faced the dragon, and met the sorcerer Gemli. As he spoke, the lie he'd told Gemli gnawed at him. The sorcerer still believed Chris had come seeking answers for someone else. And maybe that was true—at first. But Gemli's strange calm, that odd empathy, now felt like a performance. He hadn't seemed concerned about the saber itself, but about the one destined to wield it. Maybe he'd tried to mislead them, but maybe he knew more than the zhorta scholars ever did.

When Chris finished, silence fell. The wind brushed dry leaves across the gnarled roots around them.

John broke the quiet. "You do realize there's a reason he let you walk away alive, right?"

"Yes," Chris said, jaw tight. "That's why went to the abbey. I didn't want to keep chasing the saber or whoever. I didn't know Rafael would send me right back onto the same path."

Sara turned toward him. "Do you want to find the saber?"

He groaned and looked away. "Even if I did, it's not like we know where to go. These—" he gestured at the scattered papers, "—they're all dead ends. We spent days in the library, and nothing helped. Yesterday was the first time I heard something new, and it came from you. So no. I'm not sure."

Sara tilted her head, picking up one of the parchments.

"If Gemli said the blade was blessed by the gods, it has to be the one from reiser legend. I always thought it was just that—a myth. But if glacier orchids really help you speak with dragons..."

"What are you talking about?" Donald asked. "Reiser legends are all stories. Nothing concrete."

"Not for you," Sara said softly, "but in the abbey, we keep the histories of every race. We learn from all of them. The reisers were condemned by the gods, cast into Hune's most desolate lands. Hated. Humiliated. They've suffered—"

"They've *suffered*?" John snapped. "Are you out of your mind? They've been butchering our world for years."

"I know they're destroying Hune," Sara said. "They destroyed my home, too... But that doesn't mean we shouldn't—"

"No," Chris interrupted, his voice low and sharp. "Don't ask us to *understand* them. They're monsters. Heartless. They *deserve* what they got."

Sara nodded, lips tight, and began gathering the papers.

"You have no idea what it's like out there," John added. "They've done things that don't even belong on a battlefield."

"I never said they hadn't. But knowing their *reasons* matters. If you're ever going to end this war, you need to understand what led to it. Otherwise, you're just swinging blindly."

Chris's stomach twisted. Her words felt like blades.

"What do you know about war, Sara?" he asked. "You weren't there when they burned cities to ash. You never saw what they did to my men. To my father."

"I don't pretend to know what you or John have lived through," she said, gently offering a scroll. "And I'm not defending them. I was raised by zhortas, yes, but I'm still human. I don't side with our enemy. Still, if you want to fight for Hune's *future*, you have to understand its past."

He didn't take the scroll. He stared at her.

She stood, exhaled. "The gods banished the reisers to a cursed land, hoping they'd destroy each other. According to legend, a sword—maybe a dagger, a saber —was meant to cleanse the unworthy race from Hune."

Chris snatched the scroll, only to toss it onto the pile. "And let me guess—you want me to ask who *really* deserves to be erased?"

Her arms fell to her sides. "No, but I thought... It's

obvious to me the reisers' actions are unworthy of Hune. I have been in Andromeda. I saw what they left... Whether or not humans are worthy of Hune is a question I'm not trying to answer."

Donald picked up the scroll and studied it.

"You expect me to forgive them?" Chris asked, his voice low and rough.

Sara met his eyes, steady and unflinching. "Isn't that what you expect from me?"

His expression twisted. "What are you talking about?"

"Yesterday was the first time I saw a reiser," she said. "But it wasn't the first time I faced a monster."

She crossed her arms, but lifted her chin slightly, as if bracing against a storm only she could feel.

"I was almost five. The zhortas and I were delivering food and medicine to a camp—like we always did. Maybe the war had gotten worse. Maybe people were just looking for someone to blame. Someone started yelling. Called us traitors. Cowards. Then came the garbage. The rocks. Anything they could throw."

Donald went still beside her, head tilted slightly, listening like he'd never really *heard* her voice before.

"A dear zhorta named Marcus was with me. He saw the horses first. Big and loud, armored. He took my hand and told me help was coming. That they'd save us." Her voice cracked. "But he was wrong."

Her gaze drifted to a place far beyond the campfire.

"They chased us down. On horseback. I still remember the smells—burnt hair, blood, scorched skin

—but what I can't forget is the laughter. The chanting. From the people we were feeding."

She reached up and tugged her collar aside. A scar trailed from the base of her neck. Another ran under her collarbone, and a third curved faintly down her back. "One of them stabbed my shoulder. I still dream about the sound."

Chris's fist clenched at his side, nausea rising in his throat. The image of someone harming a child —*this* child—struck deeper than he expected.

"Marcus begged them to spare me," she said softly. "Told them I was just a little girl. That the robes weren't even mine. But they didn't care."

Her eyes shimmered, not with tears, but something fiercer. Older.

"I woke up beside him. He was dead. His hand still holding mine. I'm sure you can imagine what they did to him. To the others."

Chris took a step closer without thinking. She immediately stepped back, not in fear—but in defiance. Her eyes dared him to speak.

"You're right," she said. "I haven't seen what the reisers have done. I haven't stood on a battlefield. But I *have* seen horror. I've *lived* it. And the ones who caused it? Wore the same uniforms you and John do now."

Her voice lowered, calm again—but haunted. "The zhortas taught me something I never forgot. Forgiveness isn't for others. It's a gift you give yourself."

Chris didn't speak. Couldn't. The fire popped behind them, a soft crack that made everything else feel too loud.

Sara knelt slowly, gathering the scattered parchments and scrolls, her movements deliberate.

After a long, aching pause, she said, without looking at anyone, "We should go. There's a human refuge near the edge of the Northern Forest. If we leave now, we'll reach it by tomorrow evening. I won't travel after dark—not this close to the Ethereal Glaciers. Strange things happen when the roots get cold."

She rose again, meeting Chris's gaze. Something unreadable passed between them—grief, fury, longing. Maybe all three.

"From there," she said, voice like wind across glass, "you can do whatever you want."

CHAPTER SIXTEEN

From the very beginning, things had been complicated—but complications were the cost of meddling in other people's wars. Orson still believed the benefits outweighed the risk. Tolerating the reisers was a small price to pay for what he stood to gain, though he hated returning to the fortress, where everything he'd built could so easily unravel.

When the humans had failed to win his allegiance, his thirst for knowledge had driven him to investigate the war on his own. It hadn't taken long to uncover the truth. What he discovered—paired with his own long-buried history—gave him the motive he needed to act. He shielded it all behind his well-known hatred for his ex-wife, letting the world believe his old rivalry was what had driven him to choose a side.

But Vanessa's crown had never belonged to her. Orson's family were the rightful heirs by birth. Their arranged marriage had placed her on the throne—a union he'd despised from the moment the engagement was announced. He had never revealed his lineage to her, nor the dangerous secrets it carried.

Orson's ancestors had once defied the gods by aiding the reisers. In punishment, the gods cursed the valsings to walk the land without a home. But his family had turned that curse into an advantage. Over generations, they twisted the truth, teaching their descendants that the gods had gifted them freedom to roam Hune. Most valsings believed the lie. But Orson had grown tired of the wandering, tired of pretending.

He divided his people into communities, challenged the gods in quiet rebellion, and settled in Soto Forest to test their wrath. A year passed. Nothing happened. No divine punishment struck. That silence told him everything: the exile had never been enforced. It was choice, not curse, that kept them moving.

The Soto Forest was harsh, but its proximity to the abbey was a strategic gift. The zhortas were hardworking, resourceful, and naive enough to trust. Their peace-loving nature made them ideal allies—or easy tools. He decided to stay and he learned much from them. One zhorta in particular had become especially useful: Stuart.

Orson had met him on the edge of the desert just weeks ago. It hadn't taken much to uncover something dangerous hidden in Stuart's nerves. The zhorta was rattled. And then he mentioned a union—humans and valsings working together. Orson's blood ran cold. Lily, his valsing was the one who talked to Stuart, and she'd been a fool for it. She used to be irrelevant. But her betrayal had changed everything.

Now, he smiled at the thought of Murllen's punishments. When he found her, those lessons would be put to good use.

Still, Stuart's panic intrigued him. So Orson played his role. He served strong wine, offered warm bread, laughed easily. Friendship, real or feigned, loosened tongues. By the end of the night, he had what he came for.

Rafael had returned to Laconia without the king's permission and discovered an ancient script from the High Council—one that spoke of a weapon that could stop the reiser leader. Orson remembered the feeling clearly: satisfaction, thick and cold as blood. Without lifting a finger, he had stumbled upon the heart of the war. And its possible end.

According to Stuart, General Murllen had turned the reisers cruel, feeding their hatred and sharpening their thirst for vengeance. Once, they'd been creatures of survival. Now, they were beasts of retribution. Orson had seen the same poison at work among his own people.

Murllen, however, wasn't acting alone. He was protected by a powerful sorcerer—one whose magic was old and dangerous. That was why they needed the weapon. The cursed sword.

Only one person could wield it. Stuart hadn't said who. Perhaps he didn't know.

Orson, ever cautious, pressed further. Why hadn't Rafael told Leonard?

The zhorta hesitated—then admitted he didn't trust his superior. Orson didn't even need to ask. The answer came to him instantly, like a whisper from the forest: a frozen saber.

The next morning, Orson lied. Claimed he'd gotten too drunk to remember the night's conversation. He even apologized for his rambling about Vanessa, pretending he was still in love with her—one of his finest performances.

Stuart had smiled sympathetically and promised to keep the secret. As a zhorta, he would. That much Orson trusted.

Afterward, Orson searched his own collection of ancient texts. He found it: a legend about a cursed saber buried in ice.

The Eternal Glaciers had become his home for several grueling days. His fingers had gone numb. His head ached with every breath. But he endured. And then Gale returned—with a block of ice, and inside it, a sword.

It shimmered with something ancient and unkind. The ice wouldn't break.

He didn't have time to figure out why.

Gemli transported him and Murllen back to the fortress. Orson insisted Murllen force his daughter to travel on foot as punishment, though his true reason was simple: the saber had to be hidden, and far from prying eyes.

But he couldn't keep it forever.

He wanted to believe Murllen would honor his word and leave the valsings alone when the war was over. But Orson knew better.

He had only one option. As much as he longed to keep the weapon—and the chance to rise above the reisers—he couldn't afford it. Not if he wanted to live.

If he gave Murllen the saber, perhaps he could buy his life. Perhaps.

A knock sounded on his door.

"King Orson," a reiser called from outside the chamber. "General Murllen requests your presence."

Orson's hands went clammy. A bitter burn rose in his throat.

"I'll be right there."

Compared to the abbey, the fortress was in magnificent shape. The reisers had kept it surprisingly orderly and clean, considering the hostile land they inhabited. The building was utilitarian in design—small window slits barely allowed any light to penetrate the gloom, and the rooms were stripped of decoration and warmth. Despite this, a quiet pride echoed from the cold stone walls, as if the place itself stood defiant against the world.

The swamp's bitter cold seeped into the bones and nested there. The stench—wet moss, rot, and stagnant air—scorched the throat and dulled all flavor. Orson had eaten just enough to stay alive, and even then, he'd nearly vomited every time.

He no longer questioned why his ancestors had answered the reisers' plea centuries ago. Their hatred for humans now made perfect sense. They weren't predators, he realized—not anymore. They were wounded beasts, snarling from pain. All except Murllen. There was something wrong about him. Something that didn't belong in this world.

"Murllen will meet you here," a reiser said, stopping at a heavy iron door.

Orson pressed his palm to the frozen handle. His pulse thundered. He inhaled twice, deeply, praying that Murllen would believe in his carefully constructed ignorance about the saber—a dangerous pretense for a valsing.

The room was cold, lit by a single torch. In the far corner sat Murllen, his monstrous form relaxed in a carved stone chair. Suspended from a glowing, red-hot chain in the center of the room was Rafael.

Orson recognized him only by his face—everything else was ruin. The zhorta's clothing hung in tatters, exposing flesh flayed down to bone. None of the wounds looked fatal, but his ashen pallor suggested he was close.

"Orson, my friend," Murllen said, his voice disturbingly cheerful. "Thank you for coming. You never know how long a turncoat will stay conscious—or alive."

"It is the least I can do," Orson said, glancing at Rafael. "Though... this is disgusting."

"Of course it is." Murllen chuckled. "But I wasn't working with a handsome subject."

He sauntered closer to Rafael, whose bloodied eyes fluttered open. Beneath them, bruises bloomed like ink stains.

"Orson, let me introduce you—"

"Forgive me, Murllen," Orson cut in. "I met Rafael years ago."

Murllen tilted his head. "Ah yes, you lived near the

abbey for some time. Tell me—why would a powerful king like you choose such a place?"

Though the reiser smiled, Orson's every nerve sparked in alarm.

"It's complicated," he said. "But simply put—the zhortas."

Murllen narrowed his eyes.

"Yes, hard to believe," Orson went on smoothly. "But their knowledge of Hune is... alluring. As a valsing, I've always been drawn to forgotten things. Even our exile."

Before Murllen could ask more, Orson redirected his gaze to Rafael. "But enough of that. Please, tell me what this traitor shared. It's been years since we last spoke. I miss—"

"Bastard," Rafael wheezed. "I believed you were smarter than this—"

Orson laughed and turned to Murllen. "And that's why I left! No amount of hidden knowledge makes up for working with such limited minds."

Rafael tried to speak again, but Murllen silenced him by tearing a strip of skin from his back.

Orson swallowed bile, struggling to stay composed.

"That's enough, Rafael," Murllen said. "The rest of this conversation is between friends."

He gestured to a chair. "Please, Orson. Sit. Today is a lesson in persuasion... and strategy."

Orson forced his shoulders to relax. Just for a moment.

Then Murllen's smile deepened. "Now, a question. What do you know about my niece, Orson?"

Orson blinked, genuinely confused. "Your niece?"

Murllen leaned back. "You'll understand soon. We're allies now. So I'll trust you with a secret."

Orson hated secrets when they came at a cost. He said nothing.

"I was born a human. It was Gemli who transformed me."

Orson nodded, baffled. Even among reisers, Murllen was monstrous. His long, thick neck and oversized hands were wrong, grotesque. His face was a patchwork of scars, as if it had been broken and remade over and over. Only his eyes, piercing blue, resembled anything close to human—but even they radiated violence.

"I have enemies," Murllen continued. "But only one truly matters. My niece. I believe you met her at the abbey."

Realization hit Orson like a slap. The saber... and the girl meant to wield it... had been right under his nose.

"Sara," he whispered. "You share the same eyes."

Murllen smiled, almost tender. "My brother would've liked that. Our family's signature."

He paused, clearing his throat as if dislodging something painful.

"According to this one—" he gestured to Rafael, "—one of your valsings befriended her. I want to use that bond to find the girl."

Orson stiffened. Lily.

The bastard was talking about Lily.

Murllen turned sharply and kicked Rafael's knees. The crack of breaking bone echoed off the walls.

Orson flinched. The heat of panic crawled up his spine.

"Murllen, please," he said quickly. "Believe me—I want that stupid valsing just as much as you do."

Murllen's eyes locked onto his, and Orson froze. So this was what Vanessa had seen in the woods. The abyss.

He had to lie. Fast. Convincingly.

"Lily and I... we had a falling out," he said, voice steadier than he felt. "She betrayed me. But before she ran, she gave me something valuable. I had her spying on Vanessa. That's how I learned of her alliance with the humans."

Murllen moved to a wall rack, selecting a curved blade. Orson's stomach turned.

"Vanessa gave Lily a choice: exile or a disgraced valsing husband. Lily ran to the abbey and sought out your niece. A zhorta—Stuart, I believe—took pity on them both. He told me things even Rafael doesn't know."

Rafael lifted his battered head.

"Look at that," Murllen said. "He's still listening."

"Stuart," Orson said, "told me about a cursed saber. Said it could kill you."

Murllen laughed.

"You think I didn't already know that? I even know who the wielder—"

Orson interrupted boldly. "But do you know where it is? Because I do."

Murllen's eyes glittered.

"You coward," Rafael hissed. "Stuart would never have trusted you!"

"He didn't have to," Orson said. "He told me enough to let me find it."

"Fascinating," said Gemli from the doorway. "So what did you do with it?"

Murllen turned to him, but Orson rushed ahead.

"I apologize, Murllen. I intended it as a gift—to seal our alliance. But when we failed to capture Vanessa, I... lost control."

Gemli's eyes began to glow, red light bleeding from his pupils. A pounding filled Orson's skull.

He dropped to his knees, clutching his head as if it might burst.

"Where is it now?" Gemli demanded.

Orson couldn't move. A shadow loomed over him.

"Come on, Gemli," Murllen said. "He's telling the truth."

The pressure vanished. Orson sagged, panting.

"I regret it," he said weakly. "I was going to hand it over. My valsings still have it. I can get it."

Rafael's chains shook. Tears streamed down his bruised face.

"You have no idea who you're dealing with, valsing," he whispered.

For the first time, Orson sensed the power on the zhorta. And he was glad Murllen had him caged.

"Well, well," Murllen mused looking at Rafael. "You have a heart after all, old friend. Must be because of my little girl."

"She is not your girl!" Rafael shouted. "She'll destroy you all!"

Murllen turned to Gemli, eyes bright with anticipation.

"My sweet Rafael," Gemli said. "Just imagine her face

when she sees you again. That amazing girl... How many reisers did she allegedly killed, Murllen?"

"Three, I believe. But we weren't supposed to know that."

Gemli laughed, staring into Rafael's eyes.

"I wonder what she'll do when she learns the truth about you."

Murllen leaned back and looked at Orson.

"Curious, isn't it? Do you think she inherited our family's mercy? Or our rage? We share the same eyes, after all. Right, Orson?"

And for what felt like hours, Orson witnessed what true power looked like. It wasn't the throne. It wasn't the saber. It was the monsters who ruled Hune from the shadows—and believed themselves gods.

CHAPTER SEVENTEEN

After days of marching through the desert with the reisers, Jean had begun to believe Hune no longer existed. All that remained was sand and silence. Since the night Colonel Hayden had saved Alleta, she'd barely seen Charlie. And the few glimpses she caught of him were hollow—he moved like a ghost, distant, his expression flat. She told herself it was guilt, not her. But the sight of that dullness in his eyes cracked something deep inside her.

Maybe Hayden was right. Maybe death wouldn't be the worst thing anymore.

What kept her going wasn't goodwill—it had died long ago. What remained was a need to keep moving, to keep busy, to drown out the nights filled with regret. Helping the wounded, supporting the soldiers—it gave her a reason to breathe.

"What trouble are you causing today?" Colonel Hayden's voice startled her.

She jumped, earning a laugh from the reiser before he strode on.

Jean exhaled and tried to shake the nerves. Amanda's warning echoed in her mind. She didn't trust Hayden, but the thought of losing him unsettled her more. He wasn't kind—she'd seen him dispatch soldiers with terrifying ease—but he hadn't touched a single civilian. He annoyed her constantly, but somehow, his presence felt like protection.

Not that she was under any illusions. She wasn't special. He wouldn't hesitate to kill her if ordered. Her tattered clothes, aching muscles, and gnawing hunger were daily reminders that she was a prisoner. But the others respected him, and the fear of who might take over if he fell kept her quiet.

That night, after the camp settled, Jean couldn't bear another moment of loneliness. The ache in her chest had settled into a hollow space, and she didn't care if it deepened. She needed something—even sorrow—to fill the void.

Major Belk's recovery had been a surprise. The reisers had clearly given her something to fight the infection. She was walking again, thanks to a crude cane Jean had found, but Jean suspected Amanda's leg wouldn't last much longer. It was swollen, and Jean feared they were delaying the inevitable. The journey was unrelenting. No one knew when—or if—it would end.

Charlie, too, had changed. His right eye was almost certainly lost, and she hadn't found the courage to say it aloud. Yet he still stood tall, his steps steady, his jaw clenched with that familiar stubborn pride.

Jean made her way toward the front of the column. She decided she'd stay there through the night. Walking all the way back to where the rest of the captives slept was more than she could manage, and besides, it wouldn't be the first time.

"How are you feeling, Amanda?" she overheard Charlie ask gently—a tone she hadn't heard from him in days. It pierced her like a blade.

"Not so bad," Amanda rasped. "But look who's here."

"Good evening," Jean murmured, slowing her steps.

Her stomach twisted at the sight of Charlie. He was crouched beside Amanda, a tired smile lighting his face.

"Jean, I'm so—" he started, but the words never came. He slumped to the ground, his eyes falling shut.

Jean gasped and rushed to his side. The short distance between them had suddenly become endless. She knelt beside him, brushing his cheek. When she felt his breath, her body sagged with relief.

There were no wounds that she could see. His limbs trembled, his skin was soaked with sweat, but he had no fever.

"He didn't listen to me," Amanda muttered. "After the cane broke, that colossal idiot carried me for nearly an hour."

Jean turned to Amanda, whose face was pale and lined with pain. Her leg looked worse. Most likely, Charlie's foolish heroism had bought her time.

A hand gently touched her cheek.

Jean turned—and Charlie's eyes met hers.

"Hi, pretty," he whispered, smiling softly. "I missed you."

"Shh," she warned, glancing toward the shadows. "The reisers might hear—"

"I'm just stating facts," he said, his voice like warmth against a long winter. "You're pretty, and I missed you."

Her cheeks burned. She wasn't ready for this—this softness.

"It's not like I'm telling you how I can't stop thinking about you, or how much I love you, right?" he added with a grin.

She looked away, but the tears came anyway. His hand cupped her face.

"Please, don't," she said softly.

"Don't what?"

"Don't talk like it's goodbye. I can't—"

He pulled her into a quick embrace. She clung to him, just for a second.

"I'm not going anywhere," he promised. "At least not yet."

The sound of approaching footsteps made her freeze. She jerked away and sat beside Amanda, whose eyes were closed as she leaned against the wagon.

"Let me see your leg," Jean said quickly, hoping the reiser hadn't seen anything.

"I'm fine. Just need to rest."

Jean didn't wait. She pulled up Amanda's pant leg. The skin was red and swollen, but not bleeding. A small mercy. She exhaled and rested her forehead against Amanda's shoulder.

"See?" Charlie said, his voice weak but teasing. "This

colossal idiot actually helped. We'll get you another cane, and all will be well."

Jean looked around for something to use.

That's when the reiser came.

She didn't see his face—just claws and silence. He moved fast, pressing something over her mouth before she could cry out.

A sickly-sweet scent flooded her senses. She heard Charlie shout, but his voice was warped, distant. The world spun. Her limbs turned to lead.

Then—silence.

And darkness.

HAYDEN FINISHED HIS DAILY SUPERVISION AND stepped into his tent. He was smiling at the thought of walking through trees in the morning instead of sand—until he saw Major Dunstan's messenger waiting.

The young reiser informed him that by the time the squadron reached Tundra, Murllen had already left. The instructions were to remain in position until further notice.

Without a word, Hayden pointed to the door, swallowing the urge to growl or strike something. Once the soldier left, he paced. For a long time—against every principle his kind held—he had been questioning Murllen's priorities. This mission had only confirmed his doubts.

He hadn't spent much time around humans until now, but their grief was impossible to ignore. The weight of their losses, the danger, the pain—it all carved away at the human commander's soul, little by little. Hayden recognized it. He had felt the same in the early days of the war, back when losses outnumbered victories.

Murllen didn't carry that burden. As far as Hayden knew, the general never buried the dead. Never mourned. Never looked back.

Laconia and Andromeda had once been reiser cities, as had the small villages surrounding Hune's southern forests. All of them had remained lifeless since the war began. And now Tundra, newly conquered, would meet the same fate —swallowed by sand, void of purpose. They might be in charge of these humans, but it felt more like while they were imprisoning them, they also imprisoned themselves.

And now this—this abandonment enraged him more. Half his troops stood stranded in a dead city without supplies, waiting for a general who might never return. The rest were camped in the desert, equally vulnerable. Yes, they had shattered the human army—or so Murllen claimed—but Hayden knew better. Refugees still wandered. Camps still existed. And the humans' true commander was still unaccounted for.

"Colonel!" Sergeant Paul's voice broke his thoughts. "The king!"

"What the hell did he do now?"

Ever since Commander Riddley's mother had attacked Leonard, the coward had acted with more caution. But Hayden had no doubt the little bastard was planning something.

"He took off with the female soldier. The other human girl ran after them."

Hayden grabbed Paul by the front of his armor and pulled him in. "What kind of idiot are you?"

"I—I stopped the humans' commander. He tried to follow. I thought he was weak. I knocked him out and came straight to you."

Hayden stormed out of the tent, dragging Paul behind him. His stomach turned when he realized how much he looked like Murllen in that moment. He shoved the sergeant to the ground.

"You will be held accountable if I have to kill the king!"

Paul paled.

"Which way did they go?"

Without waiting for a response, Hayden barked an order at another reiser to guard the caravan and took off. There was no point in bringing backup. It was only the king. And it was time he learned just how dangerous Colonel Green could be.

Leonard clearly didn't know how to cover his trail. It didn't take long for Hayden to spot crushed brush leading into a narrow, improvised path in the forest right by the edge of the desert.

He reached for his sword just as something brushed the back of his neck—and then the backs of his knees.

He spun, but the ground buckled beneath him. His legs gave out. A flash of pain radiated from his lower back, sharp enough to make him gag. He fell, hands digging into wet soil that offered no support.

Nearby, dry leaves crackled. It took everything in him to turn his head. When he saw Paul step from the brush, sword drawn, dripping with a familiar dark liquid, something inside Hayden roared.

He deserved this. The human major had warned him. And he had known Murllen.

He let his sword fall from his grasp and stared at Paul, proud of him. The insecure sergeant had tricked him, and he was about to finish the job.

"Murllen will never accept it was you who—" Hayden said, but the effort almost made him throw up.

"Stop it!" Paul said, but not to him. It was then that Hayden heard a soft moan.

He moved his arm up, and a pinch in his stomach made him yell. The weight of his armor smashed the bush by him. He recognized the uniform.

The human major. She was wounded, but breathing.

"What the hell are you doing?" His voice cracked, but it still made Paul flinch.

"Colonel—no! Forgive me. I didn't know if you'd check my story. I had orders. General Murllen—" Paul's voice dropped. "He didn't want you back. I had no choice." He pressed his sword to Hayden's chest. "I'm sorry."

Branches rustled behind Paul.

Jean screamed as she launched herself at him. She slammed into him with more force than expected, knocking the sword from his hand.

Paul snarled and tossed her like she weighed nothing.

She hit a tree with a sickening crack and slumped, unconscious.

Paul turned toward her, not even bothering to reclaim his blade.

"Sergeant, wait—Murllen will kill you," Hayden warned.

Paul hesitated, his hand twitching toward his blade.

"You shouldn't kill her, Paul. She's too valuable." Hayden slid a shaky hand over the major, pulling nearby brush to conceal her.

"What? Why?" Paul narrowed his eyes. "She's just a human prisoner."

"She's the commander's partner," Hayden said, his vision blurring. Each breath scraped like fire. "Murllen wants her alive."

Paul stared at Jean for a moment, his frown deepening—then stepped back.

Hayden groaned. He could already see Murllen's satisfied smirk—pleased at how his plan had played out. And now, he'd get to add the murder of that poor human girl to his list. Enough.

He forced himself to turn over, the trees slipping from view as a burning agony surged up his throat. Gritting his teeth, he focused through the haze of pain and reached for a large rock beside him.

"I could've helped you," he said, just loud enough.

Paul's shoulders sagged. He closed his eyes.

None of Hayden's squadron would've let their guard down around a threat—especially not their colonel. He used that mistake.

With one last surge of strength, Hayden lunged and yanked Paul's legs out from under him.

The sergeant hit the ground hard, clutching his gut.

Hayden straddled him and wrapped his claws around

179

Paul's neck. He could have ended him easily. Instead, he leaned in and whispered:

"You're going to slow the caravan, bastard. And if you think Murllen is more dangerous than me, you're wrong. I *will* survive. I *will* find you. And you better keep her alive."

He slammed his forehead into Paul's face. Bone cracked. Paul screamed.

"Listen carefully," Hayden growled. "As far as you know, a tree fell on the human soldier and me."

Hayden took a deep breath and shook his head. Although he was about to betray his race, he was also going to end Murllen's madness. With a strength he thought he had lost, he stood and pulled the soldier up from the ground.

Jean would survive the walk, but without him, the king would kill the major.

CHAPTER EIGHTEEN

H ayden moved quickly, weaving through the trees with little care for noise. He had to put distance—miles, if possible—between himself and the caravan. Pain flared with every step. The wound behind his knee made him limp, and warm blood slid down his leg in thin, persistent trails.

He'd been lucky. Taller than Paul, the reiser's blade had only nicked the edge of his helmet. But it wasn't the cut that would kill him—it was the poison.

Stopping was dangerous, but when the shadows started to blur and he stumbled into brush more often than not, he had no choice. With a grunt, he lowered the soldier from his arms and collapsed to his knees. His hands trembled as he searched the hidden pocket in his armor. Reiser bodies weren't supposed to need the antidote. In fact, he'd never known one to need it—never imagined a reason why they would. Until now.

The liquid was thick and black, darker than the poison itself. Its stench rivaled the swamps that rotted behind the fortress walls. Still, he drank the full vial. It scorched down his throat and lit his stomach on fire. He couldn't stay upright. Gasping, he dropped onto the forest floor and shut his eyes.

His mind betrayed him.

A memory surfaced—an infirmary room with a tiny, cracked window. The taste in his mouth began to shift, bitter turning sweet, and for a moment, peace crept over him like fog. Was this death?

His stomach clenched violently, bile rising to his throat. With a ragged growl, he rolled to his side and opened his eyes.

The fire still burned inside him. It didn't work.

The antidote should've been enough. But Paul's blade had dripped with poison—far more than they had ever used in a blade before.

Hayden didn't know how much time he had. Forcing himself upright, he hoisted the human major back into his arms and pushed on. At least the antidote had dulled the edge of pain enough to move faster. This time, he covered his tracks.

Only when the world threatened to tilt into blackness did he stop again.

He laid her down carefully and checked for wounds. A bitter laugh escaped him. The poison had made him stupid. If Amanda had been mortally wounded, carrying her around would have been pointless. Fortunately for his ego, her pulse was steady, her injuries minor.

Relieved and thoroughly annoyed, he leaned back against a tree.

Some time passed before her eyes fluttered open. She stared at him, unmoving.

"You saved Jean's life," she murmured. "And mine. Again. Why?"

Hayden closed his eyes. "Does it matter?"

"It might," she said, voice soft but sharp. "Depends on your intentions. Because I'm not calling you colonel."

Her tone was defiant, but not cold.

He opened one eye and found her watching him, a faint smile tugging at her lips.

"Good," he muttered. "I'll call you colonel if you carry me from now on."

He let his eyes close again, and her laugh—warm and unexpected—echoed through the trees as the back of his mind tried to bring a memory before fading into silence.

THE WARMTH OF A FIRE STIRRED HAYDEN awake.

For a moment, he didn't move, unsure whether he was alive or reliving some trick of his mind. But the ache in his body felt real enough. So did the scent of smoke, sharp and earthy. And across the fire—*she* was still there.

The human had set the fire between them like a silent boundary, but her posture was calm, watchful. Not afraid. Not angry. There was something almost... familiar in the way she sat—quietly steady, like she belonged in moments like this.

"I thought you were dead," she said softly. "But... I wasn't going to check. Not yet."

A dry laugh caught in his throat, breaking into a cough that blurred his vision again. The poison still gnawed at his insides.

"What are we going to do now?" she asked.

"We?" he rasped. "I thought you'd be long gone."

Amanda gave a half-shrug. "I'm not in the habit of leaving wounded soldiers behind. Unless you tell me to go, I'm staying."

He blinked, thrown. He had heard that before—almost those exact words. Not from her. From another voice, one softer, laced with fire and defiance. A voice that once made him want to stand between her and Murllen, between her and his entire race if it came to that.

But who had she been?

The memory dissolved before he could reach it. Only the pull in his chest remained, sharp and hollow.

He should tell Amanda to leave. He didn't need her. But as the ache in his chest grew heavier, something more than physical pain stirred—he wasn't afraid to die. But reisers die in battle, by others. Somehow, the thought of dying alone triggered an old fear that he didn't want to face.

"I need to get back to my army," he said.

She poked at the fire with a stick, sparks jumping into the night.

"They tried to kill you."

Hayden snorted and winced as the motion jarred his ribs. "Some did. But not my squadron. It's time we fought a smarter enemy. Against our *real* enemy."

Amanda chuckled. "A smarter enemy? Sorry humans aren't enough of a challenge."

"*Hayden* will be appropriate for you," he muttered, "not colonel."

She glanced up. "Then *Amanda* should do. Especially since I'm not carrying you anywhere."

He almost laughed again—but then her smile faded.

"If we reach your army... what will they do to me?" she asked, her voice low.

"You're free," Hayden said quietly. "Now and then."

They fell into silence. The fire cracked and hissed between them.

He leaned back against a tree and let his eyes close again. For a moment, in the drifting quiet of half-sleep, he thought he felt someone else beside him—someone whose name he should know. A hand in his. A promise.

And then it came—the sensation of arms around him, not Amanda's, but another girl's embrace, warm and protective. It hit him like a memory that wasn't supposed to exist.

He stiffened.

Because more terrifying than dying... was the fear of *forgetting*.

Now, he could only wished he could survive to help his race.

CHAPTER NINETEEN

At least they had a fire and better food, Chris kept telling himself.

After Sara's vivid account of her childhood, he hadn't expected her to help them anymore. But of course, she was better than that. In silence, she had guided them through the more unfamiliar stretches of the Soto Forest, helped Donald light a fire, and cooked a warm meal—one she barely touched.

Chris took the second watch, hoping the exhaustion would help him sleep. It didn't. The walk had worn down his body, but his thoughts kept dragging him back to Sara. The entire day he had told himself she needed space, but if he was being honest, it was shame and avoidance that kept him away.

"You couldn't wait to see the stars?" John asked, shifting beside the fire.

"Stars?" Chris sat opposite him. "Funny what you forget exists in a place like this."

He looked up—no stars. Just a tight weave of roots, leaves, and massive, gnarled branches above them.

"Chris, you were closer," John said. "Please tell me she doesn't have— They killed the zhorta, but didn't try to—"

Chris shook his head and leaned forward, rubbing his palms together.

"It's a miracle she's alive, John. Hell, it's a miracle she's helping us at all."

His entire understanding of the war had cracked beneath Sara's story. They'd all blamed the zhortas for abandoning them. He had believed the lies, passed judgment. Now, he wondered how many truths had been buried right alongside their history.

"What the hell is wrong with some people?" John muttered. "I mean, yeah, I've said things about the zhortas, but... hurting a child? Even those scrawny people at the abbey—"

"It was a long time ago, John."

"Time changes nothing."

"Oh, it does. It means those bastards are dead, and I won't get the chance to teach them how to behave like proper soldiers."

John nudged a log deeper into the flames, sparks flaring upward.

"She'd be safer in the refuge," John said. "At least there, she can—"

"I don't think she plans to stay."

John frowned but didn't press. They both knew the army protected the refugees—too closely. Chris doubted

Sara would want to stay under their watch. He could already see her walking back into the forest, leaving no trace behind. That thought alone was enough to keep him wide awake.

At his feet, the ground shifted with a soft crack. When he looked, nothing seemed different. John noticed it too. Then came another snap—this one louder. Sara sat up immediately.

Chris grabbed his sword. John followed suit, but Sara lifted a hand.

"Don't move," she whispered. "This is bad."

He felt it then. The fire shrank as frost crystalized across the forest floor. Ice spread over roots and leaves like creeping veins. Cold breath marked the air between them. The branches overhead began to pale, brittle and unnatural.

Donald's snoring from the tent only made the moment more surreal. No one dared wake him. The last thing they wanted was to disturb the roots.

Then—crack!

A bird smashed into a root behind John. Chris flinched. The owl flapped away in a broken, looping flight, only to slam into another root behind the tent.

The instant the bird hit the ground, the roots lifted.

The ice shattered into glittering shards, and the trees groaned—*angry* now. The frozen roots ruptured, and the forest around them split apart.

"Sara!" Chris shouted, but he wasn't fast enough.

A root behind her rose, toppling her into a sinkhole opening beneath her. Chris lunged, but the roots thrashed and shoved him back. He fought to stay upright, catching only glimpses of John and the tent as they were tossed like leaves in a storm.

A deep, resonating boom cracked through the ground. Chris lost his footing, his face slamming into the frozen dirt.

When he raised his head again, the roots were withdrawing—leaving behind a vast, icy wasteland.

Dizzy, he climbed to his knees, his palms burning with cold. Beside him, John groaned and rolled onto his back. Without the fire, visibility plummeted. It was hard to make out anything but pale outlines.

Chris forced himself upright, ignoring the vertigo. His breath fogged the air.

The Soto Forest was gone.

Only shattered trees and slick sheets of ice remained.

"Sara! Donald!" he yelled.

He stumbled forward, slipping on the uneven surface. Behind him, John called Sara and Donald's names as he searched in the opposite direction.

A silver light fell across the landscape—the moon. Chris stopped. They had to be in the Eternal Glaciers now. Ice stretched endlessly to the horizon, webbed with deep cracks.

He approached one and peered down. Darkness swallowed everything below.

"John, you better walk carefully—"

He caught sight of something in the distance and ran toward it, sliding with each step. A lump of fabric— **Donald's coat**. Chris dropped beside the still form and rolled him gently onto his back.

"Donald?"

The valsing groaned, a deep cut running across his head.

"Don't move," Chris said, pressing his neckerchief to the wound. Donald barely stirred, which worried him more than anything.

"I'll look for Sara," John said, arriving beside him.

"Sara?" Donald mumbled, his gaze struggling to focus. "I can help... Where is she?"

"We don't know yet," Chris replied. "We'll find her. John, watch for—"

A hoot echoed through the night.

Chris turned. The owl sat atop a dead root at the edge of a nearby fissure. Both men ran toward it, slowing as the cracking ice grew louder beneath them.

Chris dropped flat, crawling to the ledge. The canyon dropped steeply, but not far off, it leveled out.

There—Sara's coat, snagged on an icicle halfway down. And below that... her body.

"Sara!" he shouted. She didn't move.

Sliding back from the edge, he began searching for a path downward.

"I think I can make it," he said. "Getting back up is the hard part."

They spread out, finding a gentler slope. At the base, Chris took John's neckerchief. Then, from his own pocket, he pulled something smaller—Sara's blue ribbon. The one she had wrapped around his palm so long ago.

As he wound it around his other hand, a truth he'd avoided settled heavily in his chest.

He cared for her. Deeply.

"This isn't good," he said. "Donald might have a concussion—or worse. And we *have* to get Sara out of here. I don't know when the sun's coming back. If it even matters in this place."

"I'll stay with Donald," John said. "Try to start a fire—"

"No. Keep him safe, but we need a rope. Donald's tent was tossed—our supplies should be nearby."

John nodded, but didn't move.

"What are you waiting for?"

"I'll wait till you get to her. You can climb back up without a rope if she's—"

"Don't say it."

Chris descended.

He didn't want to think how long Sara had been down there, how far she'd fallen. Didn't want to imagine climbing back up without her.

His boot slipped. His hands lost their grip.

He crashed against the wall, bouncing off it until he landed hard at the bottom.

"Are you all right?" John called.

Chris didn't answer. He pushed himself to his feet and searched—desperate now.

Clouds blanketed the moon. Darkness swallowed the canyon. He cursed his timing, his luck.

Then—a hoot.

He turned toward the sound, prepared to kill the bird. But in the moonlight returning just then, he saw her.

Sara.

He ran, kneeling by her side. Her eyes were shut, skin nearly translucent. A fine mist from her breath hovered in the air—she was alive.

He cradled her carefully, her head on his leg. Her skin was nearly as cold as the ice, her lips tinged blue. One arm hung limply, wrist bent at a wrong angle. Blood marked her knuckles.

"Sara," he said gently, "can you hear me?"

Her eyes fluttered open. She tried to lift her head but faltered. Chris caught her.

"The roots," she whispered. "The cold... it froze them."

"It's all right," he said, brushing her hair from her face. "We'll get you out of here."

He stood. "John! We need the rope!"

A moment later, John's head appeared at the ledge. "Thank the gods. I'll search!"

Chris turned back. Sara had lost consciousness again. Her breathing was harder to detect. He needed warmth —*now*.

He walked a short distance but was soon blocked by a tall, scraped ice wall. At its base sat a large rock, and something about it set off alarms in his gut.

He knelt, brushing away loose ice. Beneath it —footprints.

Small. Multiple. Valsing.

Fresh.

Chris's heart pounded. Why would they be *here*? This wasn't a settlement—it was a grave.

He looked down at Sara. No more time.

He carried her to the rock and paused to look around

once more. Ice covered everything. There was no sign of help, and he couldn't perceive her breathing anymore.

"Sara, John's finding a rope. We'll get you out. Just stay with me."

As he laid her down, the ice walls rumbled.

He threw himself over her as the walls moved inward —sealing them inside a vault of frozen silence.

CHRIS WAS STILL TRYING TO UNDERSTAND what had happened when a voice echoed from behind.

"Dear goodness! You took long enough to bring her here. What were you thinking?"

Chris instinctively drew his sword. The familiar growl of a dragon shook the ice walls that now trapped them. He considered reaching for the glacier orchid in his pocket, but his trembling hands made even holding his weapon a challenge.

Another growl reverberated through the chamber, and Chris had to close his eyes to clear his vision. He stepped closer to Sara, unsure how to protect her when everything spun around him.

"Sweet gods, son! That sword won't be necessary."

Chris turned toward the voice. His head throbbed. A blurred figure approached, lantern in hand, its light briefly blinding him.

"You're scaring my poor dragons. They've suffered enough already," said the man, dressed in layers of tattered fabric, his voice full of wounded amusement. "They imprisoned my friends in this frozen hell. Can you imagine what it's like—being unable to protect the ones you love?"

Chris blinked and finally saw them—hundreds of dragons, frozen into the very walls and floor around him. Wings and tails, snouts and claws, all suspended in glacial stillness. His mind flashed to the dragon he'd seen in the mountain, and he shivered at the idea of a legion of those beasts—alive.

Unconsciously, he stepped back and bumped into the rock where Sara lay.

The old man stepped closer. "But what matters now is that we bring her deeper inside to warm up. Come on."

Chris didn't lower his weapon.

"Who the hell are you? And what is this place?"

The man's shoulders slumped. "My prison. And I... am no one anymore." He forced a brittle smile. "But I can help her—and I'd rather not let her die."

Chris turned to Sara. The frost clinging to her lashes, the bluish tint of her lips, and the paleness of her skin chilled him more than the ice.

The stranger took another step. Chris raised his sword.

"Let me bring her back to my home. She doesn't deserve to die here."

"No, she doesn't. But I'm not letting you touch her." He narrowed his eyes. "Last chance. Who are you?"

The man raised his hands. "Very well. If it pleases you —Cielthos. I was once a sorcerer. Now, I'm just a fool locked in the ruins of my mistakes. But listen: you're already being affected by the curse. We need to leave this place—before it's too late."

"I don't trust sorcerers."

"Me neither," Cielthos said with a weary smile. "But what are your options? Let her die here?"

Chris's grip faltered. The sword felt heavier by the second. His ears buzzed.

"Every second she stays out here brings her closer to death. I can save her. And you too."

Cielthos walked deep into the vault. As the light of his lantern grew smaller, the cold by Chris increased, leaving the sensation of hundreds of needles poking his skin.

"Well? Come on! Sara matters more than your doubts."

Chris's mind throbbed in his skull, making it difficult to understand his own thoughts. He hated being unsure of what to do or even remembering if he had told Cielthos Sara's name. Another sorcerer had trapped him in a cave once. It hadn't ended well.

But when he turned to Sara, her lips were cracked and bleeding, and her breath so shallow he could barely see her chest rise.

He picked her up. Her body was ice.

He followed.

As he walked into the cave, the ceiling of the vault dropped but remained at a comfortable height. The walls enclosed the space, making the ice blocks look like an icehouse. Cielthos disappeared into a small opening, which, Chris soon discovered, was a room.

"Come on in. Come, come!" Cielthos said as a light illuminated the room.

Similar to Queen Vanessa's tent, the room was full of

cushions and carpets, and under other circumstances, it would have been nice to rest on them. Chris's muscles relaxed from the heat of the hot rocks at the center, which was the reason the only chairs in the chamber encircled the pit. Hundreds of crystals and mirrors hung from the walls, but aside from those, they were bare. No books, cups, or even food, which made Chris uneasy.

"They reflect the light from outside," Cielthos said, and he gestured to a cushioned chair. "Please, here. She needs to get warmer."

He moved back, giving Chris space to walk with Sara.

"The cave's small skylight lets the stars and sun through—when it's clear. But right now, this is our best hope."

Chris laid Sara on the chair, shielding her from view.

"I'm sure she has a broken arm, and"—Chris rubbed his face—"broken arm, and I'm not sure if she has more injuries..." He groaned and held his head. "What did you—?"

"I did nothing, son. Like I said, you two are being affected by the curse."

Chris shook his head and had to sit down in a chair by Sara. "What curse?"

Cielthos moved impossibly fast and kneeled by him. His face was so close that his nose almost touched Chris's.

Chris noticed how his eyes had no pupils and only a light blue broke the white in his eyeballs. "The saber's curse...well, its remains now. With the sword gone, the curse is more powerful, and it's trying to possess you two."

As fast as he moved before, Cielthos stood up and looked at Sara. He placed his hand on top of her forehead but didn't touch it. The air warmed instantly, and Chris's memories flooded with a forgotten comfort—his mother's shawl wrapped around him on a cold night.

"What the hell is that?" he whispered.

"Longing," Cielthos murmured. "True warmth comes from inside. I'm helping her find a safe place in her mind. It's easing you, too." The old man brushed Sara's hair from her face. He picked up her arm and rested it at her side. "I'll get to her arm, too."

Chris thought of Gemli's very different idea of longing. He eyed Cielthos warily but said nothing as he saw Sara's breathing steady.

"I'm glad to see she has someone who cares for her," said Cielthos.

Chris stared at him. "I don't give a damn what you are glad of."

The old man nodded "Of course, not. But since you are doing my job, I'm happy to see it's getting done."

Almost losing his own balance, Chris shoved him back. "What job were you talking about?"

Cielthos's smile faded.

"I was chosen to protect her. I was supposed to raise her, teach her, keep her safe. The Great Wizard's orders."

Chris snorted. "Right, and this huge wizard also told you all about the prophecy, the letters, the war, Leonard's betrayal, and the reisers taking over Hune? You must know how—"

Cielthos sat back, as the color drained from his face. "They took over Hune? When? What about Leonard?

Letters? I know nothing about—no, it can't be. No, no."
He rested back on a chair.

"Son, they imprisoned me in this cave for years. I had
no idea how bad...how far it had gone. We had a plan. I
thought you replaced me, that he chose you after Gemli
trapped me... We failed."

"What plan?" Chris took a step forward. "Who the
hell decided to do what?"

In the back of his mind, he thought how wrong it
was to attack that defeated man, but he didn't want to
stop. In front of him was someone who claimed to have
been able to save Hune. It was time to make someone pay
for all their losses.

He took his sword out again, and the frozen dragons
growled. This time, though, Chris didn't care.

"The anger you feel is the curse around here. You
need to—"

"I need? You can't tell me what to do." He
jumped, blocking Sara. "You just told me all of this is
your fault, and you think your fake tears will touch
me? That they will make me pity you? My entire world
shattered, my friends are dead, my people are prisoners,
and the reisers massacred my father. They destroyed
my mother's soul. You freaking bastard are going to
pay—"

He raised the sword but a cold brush on his arm
stopped him.

When he turned, Sara was awake and trying to say
something.

He lowered the sword and dropped to his knees.
"Sara? What is it?"

As she gasped for air, he held her hand and stroked her cheek.

"Don't hurt him..." she managed. "He isn't..."

Chris turned. Cielthos sat still, hands clasped, eyes full of sorrow—like the dragon in the mountain.

"Chris," Sara whispered, "don't act like one of them..."

Chris stepped back, her words like a slap. He understood all too well, and though his anger kept making his blood boil, he tried to contain himself.

Cielthos bowed his head. "Dear Sara... I have been looking to meet you since the day you were born."

Chris clenched his fists at his side, but didn't move and say nothing.

"Who are you?" Sara said. "Is that a dragon?"

"Yes, yes! It is my little Maximus." Cielthos sighed as he looked at the wall behind him. "My poor family suffered a horrible attack and got imprisoned in here. Maximus and the others were with me, but Brutus...he had a task to follow."

He turned to Sara, his head down and the lines around his eyes running deep into his skin. "He was supposed to bring you to safety."

Chris stared at the dragon, thinking of the one he'd met at the mountain and what it had shown him: the streets of Laconia along the piers, the city burning, and a mother with her baby.

The eyes of the frozen dragon opened, and a thin fog covered the ice by his mouth, making Chris jump back.

"Are you the master of the dragons?" Sara said as Cielthos helped her to sit up.

"At your service." He bowed again. "I'm pleased to know you have done some studies."

Sara looked back. Her gaze wandered off toward the dragons' walls.

"Dear gods!" Cielthos said. "That must hurt you. Let me see it."

CHAPTER TWENTY

"I told you it was broken," Chris said not caring to hide his anger towards the sorcerer.

Cielthos smiled, "Yes, you did son. I'm on it now."

Chris—even in his confused state of mind—couldn't help noticing the way Sara kept avoiding looking at him. He deserved it. Still, it hit harder than expected. She flinched at his voice but leaned into the strange old man's touch with quiet trust.

She trusted this *dragon-person* more than she trusted him. That truth hollowed him out in a way no battlefield ever had.

"If your stupid dragon Brutus was supposed to save Sara," Chris snapped, bitterness in his voice, "how come that beast is working for Gemli now?"

Cielthos froze mid-motion. His fingers went rigid on Sara's wrist. For the briefest second, something ancient and wild flickered behind his eyes—fire, unmistakable.

"No," he whispered. "He would never—"

Without another word, Cielthos turned and swept out of the chamber.

A roar split the silence a heartbeat later. It tore through the vault, shaking the walls and making the icicles tremble. Sara gasped and covered her head. Chris threw himself over her, shielding her just as several shards of ice crashed down around them.

The storm outside raged—glass shattering, metal screaming, footsteps like thunder—then fell into eerie silence. Moments later, Cielthos returned, his arms full of blankets, jars, and an old book that pulsed faintly with hidden magic.

"Could you tell me," the old man said, dropping everything unceremoniously at Sara's feet, "how you came up with such a barbaric notion, son?"

Chris rose slowly, tension simmering. "It isn't barbaric. It's the truth. And don't call me 'son.' My name is Commander Christopher Riddley. I may not speak to dragons or cast spells, but I've earned your respect—or I'll *teach* you how to behave if I have to."

Sara's gaze flicked to him. She bit her lip, trying—and failing—to hide her dismay.

"Very well, Commander," Cielthos said evenly. He shoved a blanket into Chris's arms. "But you must understand—what you're feeling right now isn't *you*. The curse feeds on your doubt and fear. If you don't fight it, you *will* kill us all."

"I might kill *you*," Chris growled, "but I would never hurt Sara."

"Good." Cielthos nodded. "At least we agree on who matters."

The sorcerer crouched and sifted through the pile, brushing aside broken jars until he retrieved the battered book. Time had not been kind to it—its spine had crumbled, and its once-blue cover was now smeared with ash and frost.

He blew gently across the surface. Instead of dust, fine frost curled into the air like breath from a sleeping beast. The book shimmered faintly with magic.

"This is for you, Sara," he said, holding it out. "It will help you understand—"

Chris snatched it away and tossed it onto a nearby chair. "I'll be damned if I let you hand her anything from this cursed place. You say I'm under a spell—how do I know this isn't part of it too?"

"I told you," Cielthos said, his voice growing firmer, "we have the same task. *He* chose us. You and me. To protect Sara, to help her fulfill her purpose—"

Chris grabbed the front of the old man's robes and slammed him against the ice wall. "I haven't been *chosen* by anyone."

"Yes, you have!" Cielthos's voice boomed, and for a second, the ice glowed with dragon-fire. "The Great Wizard gave us this duty. Sara must free the Saber from its curse. She is the key. And you—"

Chris shoved harder, cutting off his breath. "The Great Wizard has *nothing* to do with me. I protect *Hune*, not some ancient magic fairy tale."

The cave resonated with the growls of dragons, making the walls tremble.

"To protect Hune..." Cielthos gasped, managing to

lower Chris's grip. "You'll have to do more than swing a sword."

Chris shoved him again, choking him against the wall. "I don't care about your riddles or your dragon stories."

Sara pushed Chris.

Seeing her right there caught him off guard, and he took a step back. She put herself between the old man and him.

"Stop," she said, out of breath, "please don't... Listen this time. I beg you...listen to him."

Chris looked at Cielthos again, and rage traveled through his veins. But Sara was right there. Her skin still lacked all its color, and her lips were broken by the cold. The worst was the light in her eyes imploring him, the same way they did the last time he saw her in his visions. The time she asked him to believe she was real.

He helped her back on the chair, aware of how much he'd hurt her then and unwilling to do it again. He left his sword by her and walked as far away as that room allowed him.

Cielthos cleared his throat, still rubbing his neck. "The Great Wizard loved the people of Hune as much as you do, Christopher. That's why he tried to stop the war. Too late, he saw what Gemli was planning. He loved Sara's family, and he swore to protect her. That promise extended to you."

Chris turned away, fists clenched. The rage hadn't left—it just shifted, coiled inside his chest like a waiting storm.

"Gemli created a reiser with human origins—something twisted, born from magic meant to unbalance the world," Cielthos said quietly. "To defeat it, the Saber had to be cursed. But the curse... the curse needed someone of her blood to break it."

Chris caught a glimpse of Sara through the reflection in the ice—her arm now wrapped, her shoulders hunched beneath the blanket. The weight of it all pressed down on her, and yet, she didn't look away.

"Gemli trapped me here," Cielthos went on, "and drained my strength. Like you, I believed my anger was mine, that I could use it—but it only devours. Don't let it win."

His eyes glowed faintly again, like banked embers.

"I dream of facing that traitor and showing him why dragons are feared," the old man said. "Brutus... if he's aligned with Gemli, it means he believes we're all gone."

Chris hesitated. "He showed me—Brutus showed me Laconia in his memories. He believes Gemli is the only sorcerer left."

Cielthos's face paled. "My poor boy. If Brutus thinks that, he has no reason to resist. I wish he knew."

Sara touched his arm gently. The way Cielthos looked at her—like a soul reborn—tightened Chris's throat.

"I could go to Reign Mountain," she said softly. "Find him. Tell him the truth."

Chris stepped forward, but Cielthos stopped her with a trembling hand. "No, child. You have more important work than chasing ghosts... ghosts who might not remember your face."

He draped a heavier blanket over her shoulders and looked to Chris. "We must awaken her power."

"Her *what?*" Chris snapped. "You've spent all this time saying you want to protect her. Now you want to *use* her?"

"Christopher, it's not like that. Sara is the single most important thread in the weave of magic left in this world."

Chris ran a hand through his hair, dread curling like smoke in his chest. "Don't."

"It's the truth. You're a brilliant soldier, but Sara—"

"Sara *what?* Are you going to tell me she defeated three reisers when she was a kid?"

Cielthos laughed. "Who could believe something so absurd?"

Sara looked down, clutching the blanket tighter.

Misreading her reaction, Cielthos quickly added, "Just because you didn't kill anyone, my dear, it doesn't mean you're weak. In fact, you carry part of the Great Wizard's power."

Sara's eyes snapped up. "Excuse me—I carry *what?*"

"It was meant to be taught slowly, carefully. But time ran out. Your uncle... he was chosen by Gemli. The bloodline... it matters."

Chris's breath caught. His whole body tensed.

Sara looked at him, fear and confusion clouding her pale features. "How do you know who my uncle is? I don't even know who my *parents* were."

Cielthos's expression softened. "Because I met them. They were brave, beautiful people. It was an *honor* to know them."

He picked up the weathered book and tapped it. "The Great Wizard and I suspected Gemli would choose your uncle. The blood tie between you—it has the power to break the curse... or so we hoped."

"You *think*?" Chris barked. "You're gambling her life on guesses?"

Sara turned to him. "You remember the letter from the High Council, Chris. The one the queen had."

Cielthos looked stunned. "A letter? From the *High Council*? We haven't been together since, uff, I can't even remember. What did the letter say?"

Chris closed his fists and only answered because Sara seemed to want the sorcerer's answers.

"I had to find the journal of the First King. Then your stupid dragon took me to Gemli, and he deleted whatever was in there. I left the—"

"Thanks to the gods!" Cielthos said. "If Gemli didn't —no, couldn't destroy the journal, it means we still have hope."

Sara leaned forward. "What do you mean?"

The sorcerer stood, placing both hands gently on her cheeks. "We need to *see* what happened."

Chris saw the old man's intent a second too late. On his first step, he was back in the streets of Laconia.

IN THE DISTANCE, THE WATERFALL ROARED with life, its spray catching light like scattered stars. The nearby streets, lined with flower-laden porches and green fences, were tranquil—untouched by war. People walked by with idle smiles, unaware of the silent figure drifting among them. Chris couldn't touch them or be seen. He was merely a witness trapped in someone else's memory.

A woman's soft singing drew him. Her voice was bright and warm, wrapping the moment in peace. She sat on a small porch, her hands resting gently on her swollen belly. That wooden house with its flower boxes—he'd seen it before. The dragon had shown it to him.

When the woman stood, something about her struck him—her posture, the gentleness of her face. She looked like Sara, but her hair was lighter, and her eyes were darker. Still, the smile was unmistakable—the same one Chris had come to love.

A carriage pulled up by the gate, and he knew. He had been one those before—a young messenger from the army. His heart clenched. He turned, searching for Sara or even Cielthos, but found only the vision.

Sara's mom wrapped her arms around herself and walked down to the gate. A group of soldiers wearing the Laconian uniform made a formation and saluted her. Chris couldn't understand why so many high-ranking soldiers were there, until he saw the insignia one commander gave her.

Her hands shook, and the silver and dark gray star fell on the ground. The commander had to hold Sara's mom as her soul cracked into pieces. From the star on the ground, a black and a white ribbon fluttered in the breeze. All doubt left Chris, along with the hope of being wrong. He knew who Sara's father was, and a bitter taste filled his throat.

He searched the streets again, desperate to spare Sara from this. But the memory rushed on.

The thrum of ceremonial drums followed, dragging him to a cemetery. Sara's mother sat alone, hollowed by grief. In her lap, she cradled a baby wrapped in soft cloth. Her skin had paled; her eyes stared forward but didn't see. Her hands still moved—rocking the baby gently—but her soul was already half-gone.

Chris's chest tightened. His mind flashed to his own mother. Her quiet strength, her fading laughter. He had to look away.

Then came the moment that shattered him.

He should have been ready for it. Among the crowd of soldiers, his father stood. Younger. Sharper. Hopeful. That murder had been a major event in Hune, and his father had traveled all the way to Laconia for it.

The sight burned. Seeing him there, full of belief, a commander just beginning to carry burdens... it reopened wounds. And when the man disappeared again, Chris was left with a grief that felt too raw.

The scene shifted quickly.

Now night draped the streets. Sara's mother, cloaked in a hood, clutched baby Sara close. Blood dripped in her wake. She leaned on the walls as she walked, trembling. Chris had seen soldiers move like that—bleeding out, too proud or too desperate to fall.

A dark alley swallowed her.

Three hooded men stepped from the shadows. Chris's stomach turned.

"Let's just be done with this," one said.

The voice sent an electric jolt through Chris. His

traitor king, Leonard the III younger and somehow more arrogant.

A chill ran down Chris's spine as the bitter voice of Gemli answered, "I told you before. It'll only mean more complications."

The sorcerer grabbed baby Sara, and her cry filled the alley. Her mother screamed at them, but Leonard kicked her in the stomach. He took the baby from Gemli, and set her down on the wet street, just out of her mom's reach.

Chris felt his nails digging into his palms.

"We keep her alive until we found the saber. Then, if she survives, you can do whatever you want with her."

Sara's mom had bruises all over her face, along with blood on her head and lips. Her missing shoes revealed the deep cuts on the soles of her feet. Still, the woman crawled up crying, trying to reach her baby while Leonard kept kicking her and Gemli laughed.

Between the baby's cries, Chris thought he heard an owl singing. That's when the third hooded man approached them.

He crouched down and moved the baby closer so she could touch her infant. "That is a peculiar blessing."

This time, Chris felt numb as he turned around.

"Please, save her," Sara's mom said, and somehow, he knew she was also shocked to find a younger, leaner, and less white-bearded version of Zhorta Rafael.

The memory slowly faded as if he were looking through a window covered with raindrops. He saw Sara's mom take off a pendant and put it around her baby's wrist. He couldn't hear what she said, but he could read her lips.

"I love you, Sara."

Ice walls formed around him, and Sara was there—huddled on the ground, arms around her knees, sobs shaking her shoulders. He slid toward her, ignoring the sting of frozen stone on his hands.

He wrapped his arms around her.

Fury twisted in his gut. He wanted to kill Cielthos. Rip Rafael apart. Take Sara away from all of this.

"What kind of monster are you?" Chris said. "Do you even understand what this means to her?"

"I do," Cielthos answered, voice quiet. "I've lost loved ones, too. I know it hurts. But she already knew they were gone. I just—"

"You bastard!" Chris snapped. "You think that makes it okay? You think because she *knew* they were dead, she deserved to *see* it? To watch what those bastards did?"

Cielthos paled. "I didn't know. I *didn't know* who raised her."

His voice cracked, and he looked at Sara. His eyes turned red.

"They'll pay for what they've done to your family, child. For what they've done to *you*."

Sara pulled away from Chris and wiped her eyes.

"It doesn't matter. It's done."

"No, Sara." Cielthos stepped forward, grabbing her hands. "This is the curse. Trying to make you give up. But it isn't done."

His voice dropped to a whisper. "Your mother's name was Elizabeth. She was kindness itself. She made your father a better man. He was a close friend of the Great Wizard."

"Then why?" Sara asked. "Why did this happen? Why the Great Wizard abandoned her?"

"There was no other way. Your father was dead. You were the only one left. Gemli picked your uncle to replace him, but—"

"My mother's brother?"

"No," Cielthos said. "Your father's. Your uncle is a complicated soul, and Gemli twisted him even more. Hate and anger are powerful. That's how they corrupted Hune."

Chris swallowed hard.

Cielthos threw herbs onto the hot stones, the heat rising like smoke.

"You have part of the Great Wizard's power, Sara. Only you can break the curse. Only you can stop Gemli."

Sara's eyes widened. "That's not possible. I don't have any magic. Not even like a zhorta."

"You lived in Soto Forest. Its magic hid you. It protected you. Haven't your dreams always felt *real*? Haven't you always found what you needed, even when no one else could? Did you ever get lost in that forest?"

He smiled, mournful and proud. "I wish I could have taught you. But there's no time. You must defeat the curse. That's the only way."

He helped Sara on her feet.

Chris shook his head. "That's it? Just that?" His voice rose. "You expect her to carry all of this?"

"I do," Cielthos said softly. "Because if she doesn't... we all die."

The sorcerer placed a book in Sara's hands. His expression was final. "Take care of her, Christopher." He pushed his sword in his hand.

Cielthos grabbed Sara's shoulders and gently but firm pushed her into Chris's arms.

The walls around them melted. A cold wind whipped through the cave, stealing Chris's breath. He coughed, blinked—then blinked again.

And all changed. They were out of the glaciers and the trees surrounded them weren't the roots of the Soto forest. The frozen world was gone.

Sara dropped on her knees, barely moving. Chris knelt and gently lifted her chin. Her eyes were raw, shadowed by the memories she'd seen.

"Sara? Did he hurt you? Are you—"

"Chris! Chris, thank the gods!"

He turned. John was helping Donald limp toward them.

"What the hell happened?" John asked. "One second, I'm looking for a rope—next thing I know, I'm in a forest."

Chris's eyes locked on him.

"How long ago? How many *days* have you been here?"

John blinked. "What do you mean? You just shouted at me to get a rope."

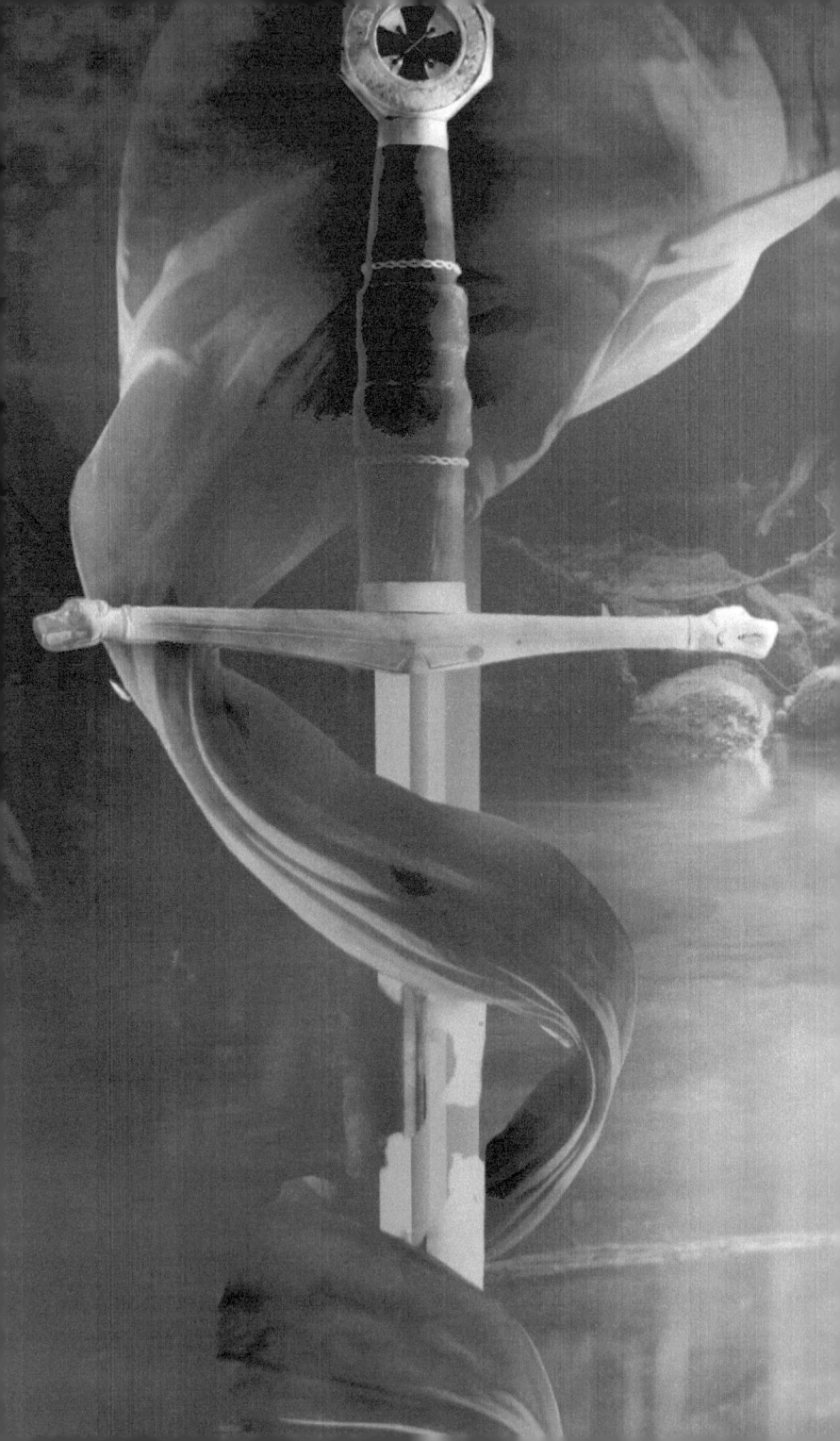

CHAPTER TWENTY-ONE

Chris understood how it was going to be a different journey from here.

Not only had they lost all their belongings somewhere between Soto Forest and the Eternal Glaciers, but he wasn't willing—or ready—to follow the path Cielthos had told him.

There was no doubt Sara was special. It made sense she had some kind of power. He'd seen it himself—not just when they'd walked through the roots, but even back in the vault during his punishment. Still, that didn't mean he was ready to watch her stand against someone like Gemli... or Murllen.

Magic or not, she was human. She wasn't trained as a soldier, let alone a sorcerer. Letting her face that darkness would be madness. And yet... he couldn't think of another option.

The way Sara explained the prophecy changed how he understood it. It wasn't about fate anymore—it was about choice. Taking control of the losses they'd endured.

But Chris didn't know what to do next.

Worse, after the way he'd acted with Cielthos, he wasn't even sure Sara would speak to him again.

She was checking on Donald while John, after building a fire, had fallen asleep. That way, he could take the second watch.

FROM TIME TO TIME, SHE GLANCED UP AT THE trees—as if she still didn't trust the sky above her. No roots. No whispering leaves. Just silence.

He guessed they were somewhere in the Northern Forest, but until daylight returned, he wouldn't be able to tell how far they'd come. One thing was certain: the Soto Forest was gone.

Fabric rustled. Light footsteps approached. He looked up.

Sara walked toward the fire, a blanket from Cielthos still wrapped around her shoulders. She stood, holding her hands closer to the heat, eyes fixed on the flames.

"Will he be all right?" Chris asked.

"I hope so," she said, tugging the blanket higher.

Chris still didn't understand how Cielthos had managed to shove a blanket into his hands—and two around Sara—but it was something to be grateful for.

"He doesn't seem to have broken anything," she said. "Just hit his head too hard. I think he needs rest, but otherwise..."

"How's your arm?"

She lifted her shoulders slightly but didn't meet his gaze. Chris stayed quiet.

To his surprise, she sat beside him and leaned her head against his shoulder.

"So," she said after a moment, her voice soft, "my father was a soldier?"

Chris nodded, hardly daring to breathe. "Not just any soldier. He was the colonel of Laconia's army. Before the war."

She pulled back and turned to look at him. Up close, he could see the tiny freckles scattered over her nose, the way the firelight reflected in the darker shades of her eyes. The bruised shadows beneath them reminded him what was at stake.

"What happened?" she asked.

He looked away, clearing his throat. Not long ago, he'd shattered his mother's heart by revealing a truth like this. He didn't want to do it again—to her, especially.

"Please," she said. "I know it won't be good... but I want to know."

Chris rubbed his face and leaned forward. "Commander Thornton White murdered Colonel Landford White. Your father."

Sara stilled.

Chris stared into the fire. "Both were from Laconia's army. Brothers."

"So... Thornton started the war?"

He hesitated. "Maybe. The murder happened years before the war. Back then, it was treated like... like a terrible tragedy. But no one saw the connection until now."

He remembered whispers in his childhood—adults speaking in hushed voices, training instructors mentioning it with haunted eyes. Colonel White had suffered unimaginable cruelty: flayed skin, burns, mutilation. In the end, he'd drowned in a puddle of his own blood.

And Thornton had boasted about it.

"I grew up hearing stories about both men," Chris said quietly. "Your father was strict, but respected. His brother was feared. Ruthless. Everyone believed Thornton did it. But he vanished. The army searched, but... he was gone."

He paused. "I wouldn't be surprised if Leonard had a hand in that, too."

Sara covered her face with her hands, then tucked her hair behind her ears.

"Your dad," she said, her voice catching, "he was there because of my..."

Her voice cracked. Chris gently reached for her hand.

"Our families knew each other," he said. "My dad was there because of your father's rank, but I know he grieved that death. So did my mother."

He would never know why Sara's mother hadn't left with his father to Tundra. Or why she'd been alone in that alley. He could ask his mom—but maybe it didn't matter now. They were dead, and no one could change the past.

"I'm sorry," Sara whispered. "It must've been hard for you to see him again."

Chris nodded, exhaling.

After a moment, Sara broke the silence.

"I just don't understand why Gemli needed a reiser," she said. "He already had power—plenty of people doing his bidding. And Rafael? Why would he..."

Chris shook his head. "He's lucky I don't have a way to question him myself."

Sara reached into her collar and pulled a chain from her neck.

"He gave me this," she said. "I think it's the one my..." She inhaled, fingers closing around it. "The one she gave me."

"May I?"

She handed it to him, and for the first time since they'd left the glacier, Chris felt a flicker of joy.

"I'm sure this is the pendant your mother gave you," he said.

She turned to him, one eyebrow raised—a look that made her seem skeptical, a little stubborn, and somehow completely endearing.

He smiled.

"The waterfall is Laconia's symbol. The lines on the back with the star? That's a kind of map. My mom has one, too. It's a tradition in Hune."

He flipped it carefully.

"When a woman marries, her family gives her a pendant like this. The map marks her childhood home. The star reminds her that she'll always be welcome back."

He brushed her fingers against the engraving.

"My mom's says A.R.—Alleta Riddley. This one says E.W." He looked up. "Elizabeth White. I think your mom tried to mark it for you, too."

Faint, roughly etched letters—S and W—had been scratched into the metal.

"Unless... you made them yourself?"

Sara closed her hand around it, pressing it to her heart.

Chris noticed the swelling in her hand—the same one he thought it was broken. Purple bruises marred her knuckles.

"Is it hurting you again?"

Sara shook her head, extending the arm slowly, then let out a breath and rested her head on his shoulder once more.

"I'm mad at you, Chris."

He stilled. "I'm sorry. For what I said in the forest. For everything that happened to you. I didn't understand how horrible it was—what you lived through. Then in the cave, I—"

"Not because of that."

She sat up, staring into the fire.

"I don't even understand what happened in there. But Cielthos was right. If he hadn't pulled us out... I wouldn't have survived it."

Chris tried to meet her eyes, but she looked away.

"When I jumped on you outside the abbey," she said, voice thin, "I didn't know what kind of soldier you were. What you might have done to me."

"Sara, I would never—"

"This time, when I stood in front of Cielthos I *did* know. And I was still looking forward it. Everything just felt so heavy. I didn't want to keep fighting. I wanted it to stop."

Chris took her hand, threading their fingers together.

"If Gemli is right—and justice is an illusion—and if forgiveness, like you said, is something we do for ourselves..." He met her gaze. "Then revenge is what I'll give you. For every bruise. Every scar. For every time they hurt you."

He pressed a kiss to her temple and drew her close.

"I'll probably regret this, but... if that's not why you're mad at me, then why?"

Sara didn't pull away.

"You didn't believe I was real," she said. "You thought I was a hallucination. But we *lived* all of that, Chris. We walked. Swim. You got soaked in the rain. We spent hours talking. We—"

Chris turned to her, eyes wide. "You remember that? All of it? I thought—"

"Cielthos," she said, nodding. "He helped. I was so cold, and then I saw places. I felt... happy. It's all blurry still. Just fragments. But *you* were there."

She smiled. Chris felt something in his chest unclench.

"I'm mad at you," she whispered. "But I'm glad to see you again."

She leaned into him, closing her eyes.

"Please don't leave me again."

Everything came back—Cielthos's warning, the truth in the visions, the choice still before them.

And still, Chris's answer was simple.

"I promised you, Sara."

He kissed her forehead and rested his head against hers.

"I won't leave you."

Not long after, Sara fell asleep in his arms. Chris stayed awake, holding her as if the warmth of the fire and his body could protect her from everything waiting in the dark.

He only hoped it wouldn't be the last night she slept safely.

CHAPTER TWENTY-TWO

The light of the day and the darkness of the night became mixed in Hayden's mind. It should have only been days since Paul had poisoned him, because he was still alive, but if Amanda had told him a year had passed, he would have believed it.

It surprised him how much pain, tiredness, and suffering his body had tolerated. The reason for his survival must have been his stubbornness and concern for his race. Only he could be in a position where dying wasn't the major problem. He needed to reach Tundra to convince Dunstan and his squadron to betray their leader.

Like him, they didn't like Murllen, but that didn't mean they would turn against their race. He wasn't even sure how or when he'd decided to do it. Nevertheless, he had no doubt he'd made the right choice.

All his life, he'd fought to have the capital of Hune in the reisers' hands. The stupidity of owning the city and never stepping in it explained a lot about Murllen and his actual intentions.

"Let me help you," Amanda said, pointing at his sword.

For a moment, he just looked at her. "Are you going to kill me, or just steal my awesome sword?"

Amanda shook her head, but her voice was firm when she answered, "I won't kill you. Not yet."

Hayden tried to stand tall, but his gut shrieked, and he had to bend down while holding his abdomen.

"Didn't you say death wasn't the worst option?" she said. "You aren't ready to go, still...I got your point."

She reached to grab his sword, but Hayden caught her hand to stop her.

Amanda groaned and pulled away. However, he didn't let her walk too far.

"You need to be careful with this." His wrist shook as he took the weapon from his scabbard. "It has poison on it."

In her hands, the sword looked huge and heavy, but she had no trouble hanging it on her back. He was glad they'd never fought. It would have been a shame to have to kill her.

During their walk, he didn't say much, and Amanda didn't fill the silence. It was easy to be with someone as quiet as her. Jean would have driven him insane. He chuckled, realizing maybe he would have killed himself then. Still, a strange pinch in his chest bothered him when he thought that Paul might have killed her.

Yet the quiet between him and Amanda wasn't hollow. Something about her presence eased the pressure in his chest, even as his thoughts spun in too many directions.

Once, a long time ago—or had it been a dream?—someone had spoken to him like this, with this strange mixture of fire and gentleness. He couldn't picture a face, but the sense lingered like a taste he couldn't name.

"What will you do when I die?" he said to clear his mind.

Amanda stared at him for a second and then kept walking.

"Do you have something to tell me?"

Hayden snorted. "No, I don't. I'm just curious. How would you say all this will end?"

Amanda shook her head, and this time, she stopped and turned to face him. The way she played with her hands made his interest grow.

"I have a plan, so you better survive this one."

"Really?" Hayden laughed, but he had to stop before he threw up. "I can't wait to find out about it."

She looked heavenward, and for a second, Hayden noticed the weight of the responsibility she carried in her eyes—too similar to his.

"I'll try to convince you and your squadron to join my army."

Many sarcastic ideas came to him, but before he said anything, his mind analyzed the idea. It might have been the poison, but it sounded interesting, if not brilliant.

"The problem is, you don't have an army, Amanda. I may be dying, but last I learned, your kind lost everything. Your cities, your guards, your people... Soon you will have to respond to another king."

This time, Amanda was the one who chuckled. "You really think we are done?"

Hayden smiled, amused at his own wisdom. He had known someone important was missing, and he'd tried to point it out as a priority, but Murllen didn't care about him.

"Your commander, Christopher Riddley, is working on—"

Amanda's face drained of all its color, and her eyes opened wide as she stared at him. She looked just like Paul with Murllen.

"Don't worry," he said. "I will die before I say a word of it... and I can tell you, Murllen doesn't care about him."

"How do you—?" She leaned against a tree and sighed. "During the time I enjoyed traveling with your reisers, I learned some stuff. They made me question things I assumed were...different."

Hayden sat down and held his head while the nausea went away. "Like the vicious abominations we are?"

Amanda looked away, making Hayden want to have the strength to push something.

"Despise your own crimes," he said. "Hune privileged you humans. Do you have any idea how we lived? Where we live? The things we have to do just to find food? You have your children with you. You raise them at your side. I have never seen ours. They can't live without our armor, so we keep them hiding from everything... prisoners until they can fight for our race. We have no options. We must fight to survive, not to live."

Amanda tried to say something, but he stopped her.

"I'm sure you are convinced you are fighting to save Hune, but have you wondered what are *we* fighting for? We aren't valsings, but we aren't stupid, either. Hune is our home. Why would we destroy it?"

"What about the ocean in Tundra? The desert, the drought, the fires in the forest. That was—"

"You did it!" Hayden said, but then he shook his head. "Of course, it wasn't either of our races. Why would you destroy your...?" He groaned, and this time, he hit the ground, which made him groan again but for a different reason. "Gods damn him! Why did your king betray you?"

Amanda rested her elbows on her knees. For a while, she remained quiet, and this time, the silence weighed around them.

"The real question is, why start a war and not form an alliance... He was already king. What could he potentially gain by taking our supposed enemy's side? I had options when I joined my army, but I wanted to help my people." Her eyes drifted away. "I was too young to question what was happening, and when I became old enough to understand it, I didn't want to—I had to be wrong..."

Hayden didn't say it, but it sounded too familiar.

"My king wasn't working for our best interest," Amanda said. "I was a coward and did nothing. It was easier pretending not to notice it."

He looked up, remembering the many times Murllen had done nothing for the reisers' well-being. He wanted to blame his principles, but it had been denial and cowardice that had stopped him.

"I don't understand why your leader tried to kill you, Hayden. It doesn't make sense. I learned about your reputation and saw you fighting. After being around you for a while, I noticed the respect the reisers have for you. You act like our former colonel."

"My reputation?" Hayden said. "I like how this sounds. Can you talk more about it?"

Amanda rolled her eyes but kept talking. "For a superior to want to kill one of their best elements? It's often because they represent a threat to them."

Hayden knew Murllen had always hated him, but he'd blamed his attitude towards him and his lack of fear for Gemli. Maybe Amanda was right, though.

In the past, when the time was right, their leaders stepped down, and a physical confrontation chose the new leader. He wasn't sure how they picked their contingents, but he was certain it had to do with the asylum.

Murllen had gotten his position that way. Hayden remembered watching the fight as a young soldier in training. His leader possessed excellent skills, but time had passed. Now he was certain that if Gemli didn't intervene, he could defeat Murllen.

The same infirmary room flashed in his mind, along with the idea that he was the reisers' rightful leader. The back of his mind tried to tell him more, but his head pounded against his ears, and everything turned into a blur.

As Amanda sat quietly, he felt the oddest sense of déjà vu—like someone *like her* belonged in the missing pieces of his memory. Not as an enemy. Not even as a soldier. But something else. A human, perhaps, but one whose eyes caught the light like stars. Someone who mattered.

"It doesn't matter now," he said. "I won't make it far, and Amanda, although I see you as a friend, I don't think my squadron will even listen to you... or any human."

The image of Murllen winning hurt more than the poison in his blood because he'd just realized the danger his race was facing.

"Hayden," Amanda said, "you are not gone yet. We can reach—"

As Amanda stopped talking, the silence of the forest around them woke all his senses. He moved to the bushes and hid.

WHILE AMANDA SURVEYED THE FOREST, SHE thought—not for the first time—how much her beliefs had changed.

Charlie had told her Hayden had protected her from Leonard. He'd even saved her from a painful death. Her enemy's colonel had allowed Jean to tend to their people, and when Leonard had attacked Jean's mother, she'd seen real concern in Hayden's eyes.

It was already hard not to look at the reisers differently. But after listening to Hayden, she realized just how blind and naive she'd been. The picture she'd carried— monsters destroying everything—no longer fit. Yes, they had fought and killed each other. But maybe the reisers had lost just as much. Maybe more.

She no longer wanted to hate them. And she definitely couldn't wish the worst for them.

Somewhere nearby, Hayden was hunting trouble too. A sharp pinch twisted in her gut as she remembered his deteriorating state—his limping steps, the way he stood half bent, his breathing shallow with constant pain. She longed to repay him for what he'd done for her, but healing him was beyond her hands.

Her thoughts shattered when she spotted a clear path threading through the trees.

Long ago, these woods had served as trade routes between Laconia and Tundra. Now, they were the domain of the lost or the lawless. She crouched behind a bush, waiting to see who was coming.

She narrowed her eyes.

Not a swarm of brutish reisers—but a ragged group of valsings trudging out of line. On any other day, she might've let them pass. Their races had no history of tension. But these valsings gripped swords and guarded a wagon dragging an enormous block of ice.

And behind them, another line of valsings limped in chains. Bloodied. Clothes torn. Their faces cut in jagged lines—a valsing's mark of humiliation.

Amanda swallowed back nausea.

She might not be able to help Hayden—but maybe she could help them.

Quietly, she drew his sword from her back and concealed it as best she could under her tattered coat. Then she stepped into the center of the path.

"Hey, you! What do you have there?"

Several valsings jumped. One even dropped his

weapon. They exchanged alarmed glances until one stepped forward. From his grip on the sword, Amanda guessed he didn't know how to fight.

"None of your business, human. Get out of the way before I hurt you."

Amanda grinned. "I don't like your attitude—or your broken face, idiot."

The prisoners leaned to the side, peering at the commotion. A valsing stepped out of line and placed a hand on the leader's shoulder.

"Gale, we've got bigger problems. Just let her go."

Amanda turned her face away as the stench of filth and blood struck her hard. Even after adapting to the reisers' decay, this was worse.

"I didn't know you were so nasty," she muttered, spotting the deep gashes on their faces.

"None of your business. Now go, or—"

She'd heard enough.

In a flash, Amanda seized Gale's arm, spun him around, and pressed Hayden's sword to his neck. He trembled in her grasp.

"Not so brave after all," she murmured, then barked to the group, "Let them go!"

There was no question in her tone. She had commanded soldiers before—and it showed.

The valsings moved. Blades sliced ropes, freeing the captives. Amanda dragged Gale closer, the sword's tip brushing his skin.

"Now tell me what the hell is in that wagon."

Gale's body shook harder, but he didn't answer.

"This is a reiser's blade, valsing," she said coldly. "One nick, and the poison kills."

"A what?" he squeaked. "It's ice—"

Amanda pressed the blade in a fraction deeper.

"Wait! I can't tell—"

A reiser leapt from the bushes beside the wagon. Gale exhaled in relief, but Amanda braced.

"Let him go," the reiser said.

Leaves rustled as two more emerged.

"You heard him, bitch!" Gale spat. "Let me go!"

Of all the thoughts racing through her mind, two rose above the rest:

She would not be taken again.

And she was done listening to that valsing.

Amanda tightened her grip, ready to push the blade—

But a flicker of movement behind the first reiser caught her eye.

With effort, she held her smile and slowly eased the sword away.

Gale bolted three steps before spinning back. "You're an abhorrent—"

Hayden hopped out from the trees and grabbed the reiser's neck with his claw. The reisers looked at each other, which gave Amanda the second she needed. She lifted the sword, and the relief that washed over her when she didn't recognize them surprised her. Hayden's action of ripping the head off his captive confirmed they weren't part of his squadron.

One of the reisers ran at Hayden, while Amanda attacked the other one. Hayden's sword cut the reiser's head clean off with a minimal effort. She should have been ready for this; after all, it was their colonel's sword, but she took a step back and looked at it.

Her hesitation gave the other valsings time to pull Gale towards the wagon.

"Leave her alone, Gale. We have enough problems already. What do you think Orson is going to say?"

"Daniel, I am trying to—"

"Shut up! The princess escaped, moron. We are all doomed. Even you."

The valsing called Daniel knocked a sword from Gale's hand and pushed him into the wagon.

"You should have let me finish killing her," Gale said while the wagon moved away.

Amanda turned to Hayden and realized his sword was lying on the ground by her feet. The trees by her seemed to spin, upsetting her stomach. She dropped to her hands and knees and closed her eyes. Her skin seemed to be burning her insides, but she was freezing.

The lake outside the small hospital filled her thoughts. She squeezed her eyes shut and reached for John's voice in her memory. But the ache in her chest grew sharper.

If she died here, John would never know how much she loved him. How much she missed him.

"Don't move," Hayden said.

She screamed as sharp pressure crushed her leg just below the knee.

"Amanda! Stay with me!" a voice called—distant, desperate.

A cold claw cupped the back of her head.

"Drink this."

Something wet touched her lips. Bitter. She gagged.

"Amanda, drink!" Hayden's voice, now.

He tilted the bottle. She swallowed, but the liquid scorched her throat.

"Gods damned," Hayden cursed. He lowered her gently. "I'm sorry. This will be worse. You're too weak to drink..."

He lifted her leg.

The pain shattered her vision.

And then—

Nothing.

HAYDEN DIDN'T UNDERSTAND WHY THERE WERE reisers traveling with valsings, but he wasn't about to stick around and find out. Whatever political mess was unfolding back there, he didn't have the time—or the strength—for it. Murllen could be nearby, possibly with the rest of his personal guard. As much as Hayden would have liked to end it all with a blade to Murllen's throat, the odds weren't in his favor. Killing those three had already sent a clear message: the war had shifted. And now, it was personal.

Amanda was another reason to hurry.

He should have known that freaking valsing would do something else, but he needed the antidote. After killing the second reiser, he'd noticed Amanda using his sword. He appreciated how fast she was, but he'd underestimated the valsing's audacity.

After drinking a bottle, he saw Amanda fall. The valsing's wagon moved away, and one of the valsings tossed away one of the other reisers' sword.

She collapsed before he could reach her. The antidote she'd taken hadn't been enough. He'd poured more over the wound, but that alone wouldn't save her. He bound her leg with a tight tourniquet, cursing under his breath. Human wounds were harder—slower to treat, slower to heal. She wasn't a reiser; he couldn't just slice off the infected limb and burn the flesh. She seemed too fragile for that.

The skin around the wound was turning dark, and her muscle had seized up, pulling away from the bone. He gritted his teeth. If she were one of his, he'd have acted already. But she wasn't. She was Amanda. And somehow, that made it harder.

Thunder cracked overhead, and Hayden swore again. The last thing they needed was rain. He lifted her into his arms carefully, trying not to jostle her leg. Her eyes fluttered open, and she gave him a tired smile, just one corner of her mouth lifting.

"What are you going to do when I die?" she whispered between coughs.

"I don't know," he said honestly. "But I've got a plan. So you'd better not die."

Her head rested against his armor. "You called me friend. I think I like you better as a friend than as an enemy."

He didn't reply—just walked faster. His chest ached, but it wasn't from exertion. It was the way her body felt too light in his arms, the way he couldn't stop her pain.

And for the first time in his life, Hayden wished for a miracle.

A while later, her lips moved again, barely forming the word: "John."

Hayden's brow furrowed. Did she have a partner, like Jean? A lover? Someone lost to war or death or the camps? The name stirred something—distant and weightless—like a door swinging open in the back of his mind.

The asylum flashed before him. The locked door. The windowless infirmary. And the girl—not Amanda, but someone with a voice like wind through trees, someone whose eyes held the stars. He didn't remember her name. He wasn't even sure she'd existed. But the yearning in his chest, sharp and sudden, made him want to go back.

Back to that dark place.

Back to the place he fear the most.

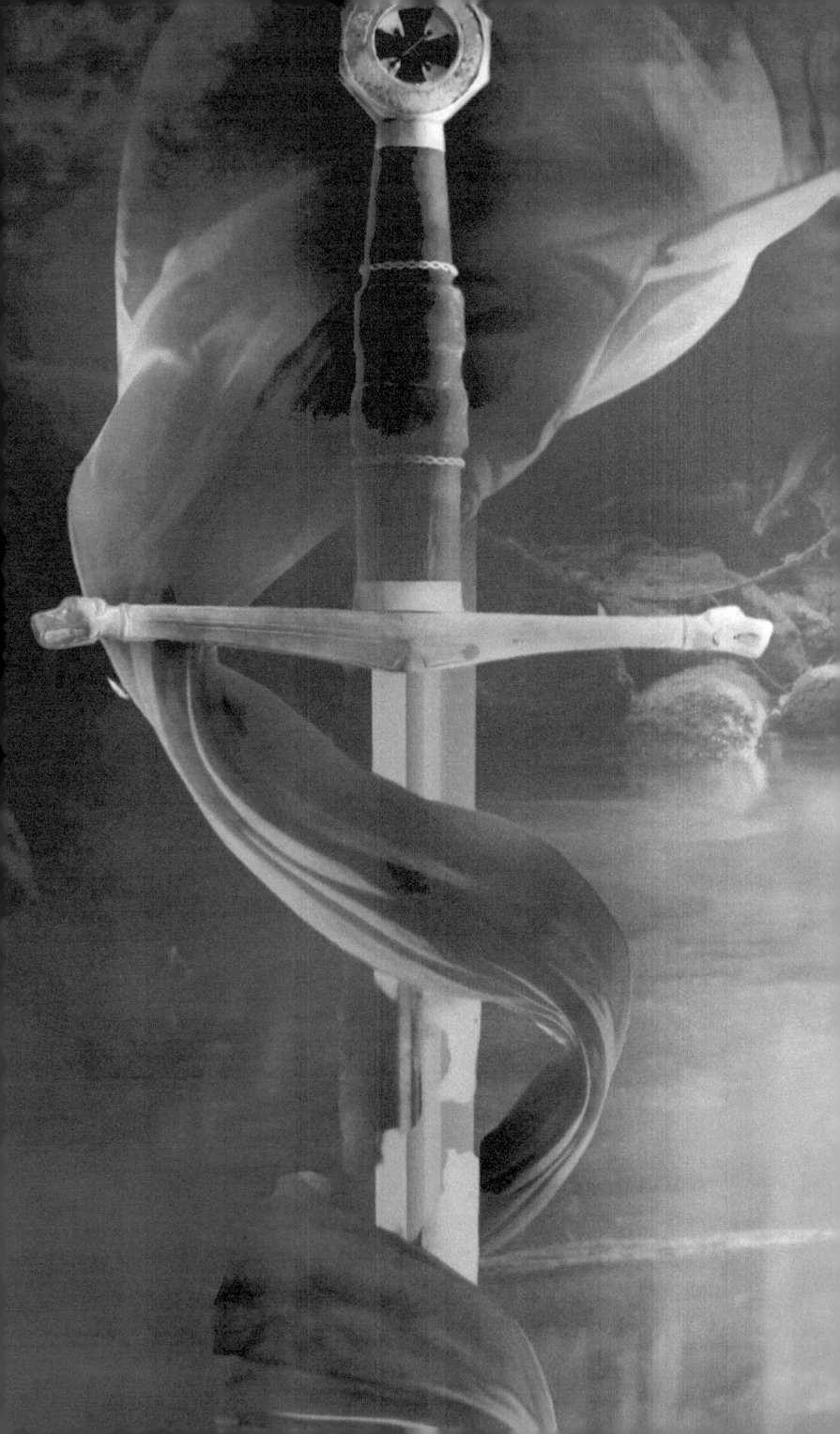

CHAPTER TWENTY-THREE

C hris had trained in the Northern Forest. He'd camped there with Charlie and the others in their youth, learning everything he knew about war, survival, and the enemy who haunted their future. For years, he'd walked these woods, protecting the trails that wove between villages and cities. The terrain felt familiar, comforting even. From the way the moss clung to bark and the distant cry of carrion birds, he knew Tundra lay to the south. The desert—its worst stretch—waited between.

As he walked, thoughts of his home city on fire kept crawling into his mind. He was certain there was nothing there, but the loss weighed more than he had imagined it would. The lack of rest didn't help, nor did his constant concern about the road ahead.

Donald, stubborn as ever, claimed he only had a headache that morning. Chris didn't believe him. The valsing's slow pace, and his silence—it all pointed to deeper wounds.

Sara stayed close, though she looked no better. The swelling in her arm and hand had gone down, and the cuts on her lips were fading, but her eyes stayed shadowed. Not just with exhaustion or the dark rings of pain, but something deeper—something missing.

Chris's gaze drifted back to John, who had been trailing behind for a while, his jaw tight with frustration. Eventually, the man sighed.

"I realize you don't need me to ask this," John muttered, "but I need to—"

"John, don't," Chris said sharply, already bracing.

John groaned and quickened his pace until he stepped in front of him.

"We need to help our people, Chris. I'm all for finding a way, but that *Cielthos* gave us nothing useful. The stupid sword—*saber*—is gone. The only concrete lead we have is what I told you."

Chris folded his arms. "Let's recap: you said the reisers attacked the guard outside Andromeda, near the canyons. You believed what Major Belk said about them taking prisoners, but you didn't actually see it happen, right? So you have *no* idea where they're being taken or who the hell is going to fight with us to get them back."

"I don't know," John admitted. "But I can't just keep wandering this forest like an idiot hoping for a sign."

He gestured toward Sara. "What if she were the one taken? How long would you wait before trying something—anything?"

Chris's eyes narrowed. "I'm not *waiting*, John. But to attempt a rescue, we need more soldiers. Even with them, we'd still need a—"

"Don't say it!" John shouted, spinning toward the sky. "We just need to *find her—them*. They have to be—"

"*Find her*?" Chris asked slowly. "What are you talking about?"

John dropped into a crouch, gripping his head. When he looked up again, his voice shook.

"They took my wife, Chris. And I don't know if that bastard Leonard—"

Chris blinked. "Wife? You're—"

"Oh yes," John snapped bitterly. "Married for years. You met her a few times. I should've gone with you to the armament camps. You took Charlie. I could've asked to join. But no—I was a damn coward. Now she may be dead. She was *looking* for you, Chris. She believed you could do something. She *saved* me. Sent me to find you. And now—what's the point?"

Chris sat hard on a fallen log. His mind connected the dots just before the name came out.

"Amanda?" he asked. "Amanda Belk?"

John nodded.

Chris exhaled slowly. He hadn't known Amanda well, but her reputation had preceded her. She'd always been calm, focused. His father had praised her often, used her as an example when Chris had still resented every lesson thrown his way. He remembered standing in the throne room beside her, both of them pretending not to hear the king's rambling speeches.

"Please tell me you didn't leave her because she joined the armament."

John winced. "Of course not. I mean... sort of. She's the one who left *me*. That's why I never told you."

Thunder rumbled above them. Dark clouds churned low across the sky, wind rustling the canopy like a warning. Chris looked back. Sara was helping Donald settle against a fallen tree, the pair of them still too far to overhear.

He turned to John. "Tell me the whole story."

John hesitated, then nodded. They sat close under the trees, as rain began to fall in thin, cold lines. As John spoke, Chris listened. Not just to the words, but to the weight in them. The heartbreak. The guilt. The unspoken hope still hiding behind John's fear.

By the time the last of John's story unraveled into silence, thunder and wind had swallowed the forest whole.

SARA QUICKENED HER PACE AS SHE RETRACED her steps to where she had left Donald. After seeing Chris's confusion—and the shock in his expression—she knew it would take time for them to sort it all out. But the rain had worsened, and the last thing she wanted was to be wet and cold. Especially cold again.

Cielthos had told her the Great Wizard's magic had helped her in the past. She hadn't believed it until, just a few minutes into walking through the strange forest, she'd stumbled across a perfect cave to shelter from the storm.

She didn't want to think about it, though. It was one thing to enjoy her dreams and find food. It was another to confront a cursed, evil sorcerer. Every time she pictured the dark wizard, she saw him torturing Chris. A shiver crawled down her spine and stayed there.

The clouds finally opened wide, and the rain poured down like a curtain of slate. The world turned dark gray, with only lightning to briefly illuminate her path—followed by rumbles of thunder that echoed like growling beasts.

She hated this place. The trees were short, exposing too much sky, and the open canopy made her feel small and defenseless.

For a moment, she stopped, almost wishing to be lost. If Cielthos had been wrong, maybe she wouldn't have to face what lay ahead. Nothing around her looked familiar, and for a heartbeat, that gave her hope. But then she saw them—faint silhouettes moving through the mist and rain, and her heart sank.

Chris and John were helping Donald walk.

She sighed and took a second to call them out, "Chris!"

Chris turned immediately and was at her side within seconds. He grabbed her shoulders, his face carved with worry.

"You were looking for a refugee?" he said. "What were you thinking, Sara? You haven't even been in these woods before."

"Refugee?" She blinked at him and shook her head. "I told Donald we needed to find shelter."

Chris leaned in, resting his forehead gently against hers. His eyes met hers—closer than ever before—and for the first time, they weren't just intense. They were pained. Protective.

She had to take a step back, breathless.

"I found a cave," she said quietly.

He nodded and turned to help Donald. "Do you remember where?"

She nodded again, unable to trust her voice. As they walked, she let the cold rain mingle with the tears she couldn't stop. The war had always felt like something far away, something that happened to others. Now, she wasn't just walking into it—she was supposed to be the key to stopping it.

She didn't know how Chris or John did it every day. Magic or not, her hands shook at the sight of a sword. Her heart thundered louder than the storm—and they weren't even in battle yet.

They reached the cave while she was still wrapped in her thoughts.

"Nice job, Sara," John said, making her jump.

She let Chris pass with Donald, then lingered outside just long enough to wipe her eyes and take a few calming breaths before stepping into the shelter.

John left again while Chris laid Donald against a large rock. The cave was bigger than she'd expected, with one section covered in sand and the other filled with dry leaves and branches—perfect for building a fire.

"Stay with Donald, please," Chris said. "I'm going to help John find logs—" He paused when he looked at her. "Are you all right? What happened?"

She opened her mouth, but Donald cut in before she could speak.

"I thought she said 'refugee,' Chris. I'm sorry. I didn't mean to cause concern—"

"It's all right, Donald," Chris said gently. "Just rest."

Then he leaned in, lowering his voice so Donald couldn't hear. "Don't tell him, but I miss his know-it-all self."

Sara smiled, but kept her eyes on the ground. Chris's hand brushed her arm, grounding her.

"Don't worry, Sara. I won't—" He glanced toward the cave entrance and sighed. "I'll be right back. We can talk then."

He stepped out and disappeared into the storm.

The rain pounded down harder, the sky black as night. Flashes of lightning lit the forest, followed by thunder that shook the cave walls.

"I told Chris we should've brought my tent and sacks, but no," Donald muttered. "He didn't want to listen. Travel light and fast."

"Donald, we lost everything when the trees froze in Soto Forest. Remember?"

He frowned. "Why in the hell did we bring a book, then?"

Sara blinked. The book. The one Cielthos had given her.

It sat beside Donald now, damp and resting on their few remaining blankets. She picked it up, half-expecting it to burn her fingers—and half-hoping it would just disappear.

Then she unfolded the blankets. Though damp, they weren't soaked.

"Cielthos gave us that book," she said.

She covered Donald's legs and checked his head. The light from the storm flickered unpredictably, but the swelling on his temple had gone down, and his pupils tracked her movement.

"Tell me I'm still as handsome as ever," he said weakly.

Sara laughed, though the wind chilled her arms and raised goosebumps. She wrapped her arms around herself.

"You don't have to worry about that, Donald. Though you might need to worry about your clothes. We lost—"

"Sara," Donald interrupted, pushing the blanket back. He glanced down at his pants. Muddy. Torn. Soaked through. "This is a catastrophe."

Then she heard it.

A strange sound outside the cave, just barely rising above the rain. A high-pitched squeak.

"What was that?" Donald asked.

"I don't..."

Something moved in a tree just beyond the entrance. Sara stepped closer. Lightning flashed—briefly illuminating the trees.

The wind dropped, and she saw it: an owl perched on a nearby branch. Hanging beside it was a canvas bag, swaying in the wind.

"I'll be right back, Donald."

She didn't wait for his response. The bag wasn't far. And as Donald had said, they needed supplies. Maybe Cielthos had sent it.

The rain slapped against her shoulders as the wind picked up again. A sharp squeak sounded in her ear, and she turned just as a heavy branch broke loose.

It struck her head.

Sara fell.

And the last thing she noticed before everything went black—was that the rain had suddenly stopped.

CHRIS COULDN'T FEEL THE TOPS OF HIS FINGERS anymore, and his legs were numb again. After all the time he'd spent in the desert, he'd grown to hate the heat—but now, he missed it. The cave Sara had found had some dry branches and leaves. Starting a fire shouldn't be a problem. Keeping it going was another story.

All of a sudden, the storm stopped.

It didn't feel natural. After everything he'd seen over the last few weeks, he couldn't shake the sense that Hune's magic was behind it. He picked up his pace, dread coiling in his gut. He hoped Sara had nothing to do with it.

He dropped the branches outside before stepping into the cave, careful not to drag water in. It was dark—so dark that the dim, gray light outside felt welcoming until his eyes adjusted.

Donald lay on the ground.

"Well," John said as he set down his own bundle of branches, "at least the storm's gone."

"Donald, where's Sara?" Chris asked, half-expecting a snarky remark—but the valsing sat up and looked at him in confusion.

"I don't know. She was here with me—"

Chris took a breath, biting back a sharp reply. But

before he could say anything, the rustle of branches outside snapped his attention to the trees. Silence fell around them, heavy and sudden.

They weren't alone.

Chris drew his sword, and John followed suit. Years of fighting together had taught them to move without a word.

The darkness made it hard to see, and knowing Sara might be nearby twisted his stomach. He strained to listen, hoping for the stench of decay to warn him if a reiser approached.

A twig snapped behind him, and he spun, raising his blade—only to freeze. The sword hovered at a reiser's throat, but something in his gut stopped him from striking.

John leapt beside him, sword lifted.

"Help me," the reiser rasped.

He had no weapon. He didn't move.

Something crawled along Chris's nerves. He blocked John's strike with his own sword.

"What the hell?" John said.

Before Chris could answer, the reiser collapsed.

"Let's take him to the cave," Chris said.

"Wait—what?"

Chris ignored him and grabbed the reiser's side. With a groan, John helped him carry the dying creature.

As they walked, fragments of Sara's story, and what Cielthos had told him, came rushing back. It could be a trap. But somehow... he didn't think so.

To his surprise, the cave's entrance glowed faintly. His heart jumped—until he saw Donald tending a small fire. Even though the comforting feeling was nice, he couldn't escape the disappointment of not finding Sara instead.

"Everything was soaked, Chris. It was almost impossible to—" Donald's words cut off when he saw the reiser.

They laid him down carefully, and Chris kept his sword ready. The reiser was breathing hard, coughing often. A large wound on the back of his leg had bled for a long time—but it was the thick, dark liquid oozing from it that was killing him.

The reiser opened his eyes and met Chris's.

"Help—" He coughed, dark blood trickling from his mouth. "Her. Help her."

Chris bolted outside.

It couldn't be Sara. It wasn't possible. But when he found a woman's form on the ground, he nearly dropped to his knees.

She wore an armament uniform.

He checked her carefully. The only visible injury was a makeshift tourniquet around her leg. Her breathing was so shallow, he feared she was already gone.

Her hair obscured her insignia—until Chris brushed it aside and saw the major's star.

There was only one major in the armament.

Amanda.

He scooped her up and ran back.

John was waiting at the entrance. The moment he saw her, his sword slipped from his hand.

"How is she here?" John choked. "Is she—?"

"She's alive," Chris said. He gently laid her by the fire. "Looks like the wound was wrapped, but—"

"Poison," the reiser said. "She was attacked and poisoned."

"You bastard," John growled. Chris held him back before he could strike.

The reiser groaned, ignoring the threat. "More antidote would help—but she's too weak to drink it." His coughing worsened. "I poured some over the wound. It wasn't—wasn't enough."

"You didn't save yourself?" Donald asked, incredulous.

Chris couldn't believe it either. The reiser had given up his own chance to live.

"Do you know her?" the reiser asked. "Can you save her?"

"Hayden," Amanda whispered, "I think I'm dead."

"Amanda." John dropped to his knees, tears spilling as he brushed the hair from her face.

"If you can feel pain," Hayden rasped, "you're still in this damned place."

Amanda smiled weakly and closed her eyes.

Donald knelt beside her leg, but froze, clutching his head. After a few seconds, he leaned in to examine the tourniquet. He barely brushed it, but Amanda gasped and nearly passed out.

Her skin had gone ghostly pale, her cheeks the only color left.

"This is bad," Donald said. "I don't—"

The reiser inched closer, groaning.

"Don't even think—" John started, but Amanda touched his scarred forehead.

"I didn't mean to cut that deep," she whispered.

"You saved my life," John murmured. "No complaints."

Donald ripped a piece of his shirt and tried to clean the wound. "The antidote worked. But the infection..." He winced. "If I had my equipment, maybe. As it is, it's her leg... or her life."

"No!" John shouted. "You're a valsing! There has to be another way. She can't—she can't lose her leg. You don't understand what that would mean to her."

Donald looked at Chris helplessly.

Chris stepped closer. The veins around the wound were dark and swollen, forming a black web under her skin. He didn't speak—just thrust his sword into the fire.

"Chris," John pleaded, "you can't let him do this. It'll destroy her."

Amanda sobbed in John's arms, trembling.

"Is that the only way?" Hayden asked softly.

Chris couldn't remember ever having a conversation with a reiser. Not like this. Just curses shouted in the chaos of battle. And now, here was one asking questions. Helping.

"Definitely," Donald said. "Even then, it might not be enough."

Chris checked the blade—hot, but not red enough.

"Is that what you want, Amanda?"

It wasn't only the use of her name, but his soft and understanding tone that surprised Chris and infuriated

John, who stood and grabbed his sword from the ground.

Amanda hesitated. "I don't... I don't want to die. The plan—I want to see it work, Hayden."

She sobbed harder and John lost it.

He raised his sword, "you bastard. This is all your fault!" Chris jumped in front of John and pushed him back, which gave Hayden the second he needed.

In that instant, Hayden crawled forward, pushed Donald aside, and with a single swipe of his claw, severed Amanda's leg just below the knee.

She gasped—then collapsed unconscious.

Donald and John rushed to her. Chris dragged Hayden to the cave wall and threw him down. Part of him wanted to kill the reiser. But deep down, he felt something else.

Relief.

Hayden had done what none of them had the strength to.

"She could bled to death," Chris muttered.

"She won't," Hayden said, slumping against the wall. "I sealed her wound, and I had no poison in me," Hayden said, slumping against the wall. "Should've done it sooner. I just wasn't sure if humans could survive it."

Chris tightened his grip on his sword. "Why?"

Hayden gave a rasping cough and looked at the blood on his claw.

"Believe me," he said, "I've been asking myself the same thing for a long, long time."

CHAPTER TWENTY-FOUR

Sara sat against a tree, holding her head and keeping her eyes shut. A dull throb pulsed in her temples, and a buzzing in her ears left her dizzy. She could feel her legs were fine, but she didn't want to stand—not yet. She was afraid she'd lose her balance or throw up.

Going out into the storm had been reckless. Even if her intentions were good, this wasn't the time for foolishness. Now, Chris was probably worried sick, or worse—Donald had taken a turn for the worse, and she wasn't there to help him.

She wrapped her arms around her knees and let her head fall forward. All her life, she'd thought of herself as strong. But lately, all she wanted was to sit under that tree and wait for Chris to find her.

Tears welled in her eyes, and a knot tightened in her throat. Now that the memories had begun to return—fragmented but vivid—she ached to fall back into those dreams. Back to the realm where time moved gently, where laughter echoed like spells and stolen glances held the weight of unspoken promises. A world where nothing bad could touch them, where they weren't fugitives or keys to ancient wars, just two souls tangled in something soft and secret. There, she could forget the cold, the fear, the prophecy.

"My poor child," a deep voice said, startling her upright. "Please don't cry. It breaks my heart, sweetie. I never wanted to hurt you, but..."

She touched her aching head, trying to locate the voice.

"Not just your head."

The owl from earlier landed on a branch in front of her, tilting its head.

"Your mom would've killed me for doing that. But you have to understand—manipulating objects as a bird is... difficult. And judging how hard to hit something? Practically impossible."

Sara stared, blinking through the fog in her mind. "How... You can't—"

"Can't talk? I'm not, technically. I'm projecting thoughts. Like dragons do."

The owl flew down, landing on her knees.

She leaned back cautiously. The talons were sharp, and she didn't want to test them.

"Don't be afraid, Sara," the bird said gently. "Not of me. Please."

His feathers were black and white, speckled like frost on stone. But it was his eyes that caught her breath—blue. The exact shade of her own.

"Let's talk."

The flap of his wings made her flinch, and when she opened her eyes, the forest was gone.

She now sat in a familiar prairie. The scent of glacier orchids filled the air, and the sound of a river nearby brought memories that stirred something deep within. She touched the grass, and then saw her hand was bruise-free and her clothes were spotless.

"Hope it's okay with you," a voice said. "It breaks my heart to see you hurt."

She looked up. No owl. A man stood there, tall and smiling, twirling a hat in his hands. His dark hair curled at the ends like hers, and his uniform was unfamiliar—military, but not threatening. And strangely, she wasn't afraid.

"Am I dead?"

His laugh was full and warm. "No. I just couldn't stay away anymore."

She looked around, and something about the place tugged at a buried memory—Zhorta Marcus, and the last time she had seen him. The shadows clung to the trees like ghosts, and her hands began to tremble. A phantom sound of hooves echoed in her ears, rhythmic and relentless, as if galloping through her bones. She forced herself to breathe slowly, to remember this wasn't real—wasn't happening again. But her mind betrayed her, unspooling more pieces of that day she had long tried to forget. The smell of smoke, the flash of steel, the look in Marcus's eyes... images she had buried deep, now clawing their way back to the surface.

"Sara, look at my eyes and focus on the flowers next to you."

She shook her head and pulled her legs closer to her chest. The only thing she wanted to do was run away, but she didn't dare move.

The blue in his eyes shone, and the flowers from the prairie filled the air with a nicer aroma. He didn't approach her, but he never stopped looking at her.

"I used a lot of my magic that day, Sara." He exhaled, looking heavenward. "A lot of what Thornton taught me came in handy when I reached up to those...soldiers."

"You killed them?" Sara's voice sounded strange to her, but she was glad that at least it worked.

"Nobody was going to hurt you and live to tell the story, sweetie."

She stood, taking a small step back. "Are you the Great Wizard?"

His face lit up with quiet pride. "That's one of my titles, yes."

She looked around, unease gnawing at her. "Why this —why me?"

"Because of Gemli." His expression darkened. "I couldn't risk being seen while he was watching. He let Rafael take you, but if he had known I was alive... it would've changed everything."

"You're alive? But I thought wizards... they're neither alive nor dead."

"I'm the *Great* Wizard. There are... loopholes."

There was something in his voice that felt kind and peaceful. Easy to talk to him. She wiped her face and tried to steady her voice. "Cielthos said I'm important, that I might have some kind of magic. Magic from you but...

I'm scared. I don't understand what I'm supposed to do."

He stepped closer, slowly, gently. "I'm so sorry, Sara. I had no choice. Your mother's prayer bound me, gave me a duty. It was the only way to keep you safe."

She noticed his hand reaching out to her, but he stopped midway, and the years weighed in his eyes.

"I fell in love. With your mother. The moment I met Elizabeth, I knew. I gave up everything to be with her—my title, my power, my role as the Great Wizard. I was happy with my human life, followed my family legacy and became a colonel. I thought I could protect her that way."

Emotion thickened his voice. "But I underestimated my brother. Thornton—Murllen. He aligned with Gemli."

He paused, fists clenched, and exhaled through his nose.

"I love my brother, but his soul... it's corrupted. I tried to stop him. But Gemli was faster. I had to disappear and reclaim what I had once given up... to protect you both."

Sara stumbled backward against the tree. "You mean... you're my... Are you saying you're my father?"

"Yes, Sara. I'm your father. And the Great Wizard." A soft smile lifted his face. "Though I always hoped you'd call me 'Dad.' Or even 'Daddy'"

Sara sank to the ground, trying to slow her thoughts.

He knelt beside her. "I know it's a lot. I felt the same way when I learned the truth about myself. Although, I didn't get it from family. I guess, Hune made the choice."

She stared at him, sure this was all an illusion.

But when he touched her forehead, his hand felt real. "I wish I could heal it. But that magic's beyond me now."

"What happened to you?" she whispered. "Did Murllen try to kill you?"

"He nearly did. I only survived by touching the foundation of Hune's magic at the last moment. But to do that... I had to give up my body."

"That's why you're an owl?"

"Your mother loved owls."

She reached for his hand. He kissed it and didn't let go.

"I saw her grief. I was outside when they told her I'd died. That's when I learned she was pregnant. I was devastated. I wanted to go to her, but I knew I'd put her in more danger."

"I had no idea Leonard or Rafael were involved. Cielthos was supposed to help me, but he became a prisoner, and Brutus didn't make it on time. I was a half-dying bird in the middle of a forest when I heard your mother's prayer. It took all my strength just to fly towards her. I couldn't see you then...but I heard you crying... So I gave everything I had to you, Sara. You are my successor."

Tears streamed down his cheeks. She hugged him, and his arms wrapped around her like she'd always imagined a father's would.

"I had hoped to reclaim that power, to take your place and face Gemli myself. But I won't ever be strong enough again. You will have to do it."

He pulled back and looked into her eyes.

"I'm so sorry, my little girl. You don't deserve this. You should have grown up with your mother in a peaceful Hune... not this broken world."

The weight of his words settled heavily on her shoulders.

"Now, listen," he said, his voice suddenly firm. "No one can know. Your mother was the only one who knew who I really was. Not even Chris, understand?"

Her heart twisted. "You don't trust him?"

"I do. That's why I sent those letters."

"You... sent them?"

"It was meant to guide him to Cielthos, and then to you. I never imagined Brutus would take him to Gemli instead."

His expression turned serious.

"I trust Chris, but I'm aware of how he feels about magic...and I can imagine what he'd do if he thought your life was at risk."

"Because of what happened with Cielthos?"

"Cielthos? Did Chris kill him?"

Sara shook her head, but as the memory came back, she remembered how close it had been for Chris to change that.

Her father's voice turned quiet. "The saber is more than a sword. It's a conduit to Hune's core magic. Created to heal the land—but also cursed for its danger. I don't know what releasing it would take."

He took Sara's hand and brushed her hair.

"I'm not sure what it would take to free that sword. And I still don't understand the magic in you. You are different, and I just don't—"

"Would I die?"

"I don't know, Sara. I believe there is a chance, and I'll keep looking around, but...I'm not sure."

Sara's stomach turned, and her hands grew sweaty while her blood traveled faster, making it hard to breathe.

"Sara, your mother's prayer was to save you. I won't give up, and you shouldn't, either. More importantly, don't forget about living. I chose to give away my powers so I could live with your mom. And I loved every day I spent with her. My only regret is that I wasn't able to save her...to meet you."

She clutched her mother's necklace. "Will I see you again?"

"I've been with you for a long time. Flying around. I'm not going anywhere. But this way... it costs me. And I'm afraid of Gemli noticing."

He kissed her forehead.

When Sara opened her eyes, she was back on the wet forest floor. The rain had stopped, but the wind still rustled the branches above.

An owl hooted once from a nearby tree, then flew into the sky.

For a moment, she thought it had all been a dream. Then she noticed Chris's sack sitting carefully beside her.

She picked it up and stood, whispering as she looked up into the dark canopy.

"Thank you... dad."

The cave's warm light glowed through the trees, and this time, her steps didn't falter.

As she approached the cave, the sound of raised voices reached her over the wind and rain.

"He didn't have the right, Donald," John shouted. "Best choice or not, he should've stayed out of it. It wasn't his problem."

"I understand that, but you need to calm down," Donald replied, his voice tight with restraint. "You're acting like an idiot. He saved her life."

"Saved her life? He ruined it."

"You think this is what she needs?" Donald asked. "She would've died if we'd used Chris's sword—"

Sara shifted the sack higher on her shoulder and slowed, her steps cautious. John swore under his breath.

"Listen, John," Donald said, voice low. "I would do anything to have Lily here. And if she were—I'd be right by her side. Or... does this change how you feel?"

"Of course not," John snapped. "I love Amanda no matter what."

"Then show her. Let Chris worry about the other one out there."

Sara paused, uncertain, and her confusion deepened as she noticed the dark bulk by the cave entrance. Her chest tightened with a memory—the foul stench, the thick reiser armor.

As she drew nearer, she saw the creature clearly now. The layers of skin and metal were grotesque, and the way the dark armor clung to its form made it hard to tell where flesh ended and plating began. A familiar revulsion curled in her gut. Lily had shown her a piece like this once.

Sara crouched before the reiser, her fingers hovering uncertainly toward him.

"Sara!"

Chris's arm wrapped around her waist, pulling her away so fast she dropped the sack.

His grip was firm, grounding. His voice deep, too close to her ear.

"What are you thinking? That thing is poisoned—it could kill you."

Sara took a step back. Too aware of where his hands had been. Not for the first time—only before, he hadn't been upset. And everything around them had been still, warm, unbroken.

A memory surfaced unexpectedly, bypassing a mental barrier she hadn't realized was there. One she had built.

A river—sunlight filtering through the trees, the sound of water rushing over rocks. She'd slipped on the edge and gone under with a startled cry. Chris had jumped in without hesitation, his laughter echoing as he reached for her.

She remembered the way his arms wrapped around her, the strength in his chest as she clung to him, soaked and breathless. He'd brushed the hair from her face, the pads of his fingers lingering longer than they needed to. And then—his gaze had softened, all the weight he usually carried melting from his expression.

When he kissed her, it was hesitant, like he was afraid

he might break the moment. But it had been real. It had meant something. She'd felt it in every heartbeat.

Now, his hand hovered near her head again—but the warmth was gone. No softness in his touch, only concern threaded with frustration. No trace of the boy who'd kissed her like she was his whole world.

She blinked, and the memory vanished like mist. The space between them was colder than any river.

"I have been looking for—what happened to your head?" Chris asked, frowning. "Are you all—?"

Sara didn't answer. Her voice was lodged somewhere behind that memory, behind everything they used to be.

"I told you, I don't have poison," the reiser interrupted. "And I wouldn't hurt her."

Sara used the distraction to move away from Chris, and a past that didn't exist anymore.

"I thought you were dead," she said to the reiser.

"I wish I was," he rasped, then broke into a cough so deep it seemed to rattle his bones.

Sara turned to Chris. "We need to help him."

Chris crossed his arms. "He's dangerous."

"He's dying," she countered. "If we don't help, he will."

The reiser let out a weak laugh. "You want *him* to help me? I think he's enjoying this."

Sara looked at Chris. "Is that true? Do you want him to suffer?"

Chris crossed his arms. An answer that hurt more than she expected.

"Fine," Sara said, "I'll help him."

She walked towards the reiser, but Chris grabbed her arm. "I don't care how weak he looks. He is dangerous."

"Dangerous? He is suffering and dying,

Chris passed his hands through his hair and frowned.

She would never know what he had lived through, but after everything they had learned, she had hoped he would be a little more open.

"He saved my life not long ago," Sara said to the reiser, "and he has more reasons to hate me than you. The only thing he knows about you it your race."

"What are you talking about?" Chris said to her. "Hate you? What makes you think I—"

"Oh, he knows me." The reiser lifted his head. "He knows I'm Colonel Hayden Green. I killed plenty of his soldiers. Imprisoned the last of his guard."

Chris stepped closer, drawing his sword.

Sara stiffened, but she forced herself to stay calm. Her voice steady despite the images crowding her mind. "Well, I still beat you," she told Hayden, glancing at Chris. "I'm a *zhorta*, remember? I practically cursed all our races and helped destroy Hune. That's not all—"

"Sara," Chris said, his voice warning.

She didn't stop. "Magic runs through my veins. Hune's magic. Which he hates. *You* hate. And if that weren't enough—" she swallowed—"Murllen is my uncle."

Chris moved like lightning, shoving her back. Hayden groaned, claws raking the earth as he tried to rise, only to collapse again. He convulsed, coughing up blood.

Sara shrugged off Chris and dropped to Hayden's

side, her hands moving without thought. She searched the treetops for the owl—but there was nothing.

"I think we should get the armor off," she said, quietly.

This time, Chris crouched beside her. "It won't matter. He's too far gone."

Hayden's eyes opened, bloodshot and dull.

"What if it's like with Cielthos?" Sara asked, more to herself. "Like the curse, or a blindness? Something keeping us from seeing the truth? Lily could be right."

Chris rubbed his face with one hand. "The truth is—he's a monster who killed our people."

Sara didn't answer. She reached for Hayden's helmet.

"That won't change anything," Chris said. "I've seen them without their—"

She pulled harder, and when the helmet unlocked from the armor, its putrid scent choked her. Trying not to breathe, she slipped it off, ignoring how her hands became wet, and the layers of dead skin tore away from the metal.

Chris stared, unmoving.

"I told you," he whispered. "It changes nothing. I'll help you—but I'll do it for *you*, and—gods, I don't even know how."

Sara tossed the helmet away and wiped her hands on her skirt. Her attention was drawn to a small crack in Hayden's shoulder armor. Something his helmet had been concealing.

"Your major had a good idea," Hayden whispered, eyes fluttering. "Murllen betrayed us. I need your help—"

"My help?" Chris scoffed. "That's not likely."

"Believe me," Hayden said, "I'm sick and shocked, too, but—" He gasped for air, but something was blocking his throat.

Sara scanned the ground and spotted a sharp-edged rock. She didn't hesitate. Her hand trembled—not from fear of what she had to do, but from knowing *how* to do it.

She jammed the rock into the fissure and twisted. Dark liquid oozed out. Hayden screamed, writhing, his eyes locking with hers.

He clawed weakly at the armor but couldn't free himself.

Chris moved beside her, sword in hand.

"Don't," Sara said, grabbing his arm. "Don't kill him."

"I won't," Chris said. "But you can't touch him again. Look at your hands."

Sara stepped back, startled to see a dark liquid trailing down her fingers. She didn't dare wipe it on her clothes —not even when Hayden had told them he had no poison left. Even less after her hand had stained Chri's uniform.

Chris used his sword as a lever, prying the armor open until Hayden slumped forward. Beneath the layers, he looked... human. Pale. Bearded. Coated in blood and black ichor.

"Let me help—"

"Stay back, Sara," Chris said. "I've got him."

She watched as he dragged Hayden out of the armor and propped him outside the cave entrance.

"Now would be a good time for rain," Chris muttered.

"Donald!" he called. "I need—gods be damned. We have nothing there!"

"What can I—" Sara said, but when Chris looked at her, a shiver ran down her spine.

"I don't know, Sara." He looked away for a second, and though his tone changed, his severe gaze didn't. "A freaking blanket to clean him? I'm not dragging this mess inside."

She flinched but spotted the sack her dad gave her. Chris's sack. She was about to grab it, but her dark hands held her back.

Chris was right. Rain would be great so she could clean her fingers, and Chris won't have to yell at her again.

A second later, a raindrop fell across her cheek. The truth of who she was weighted on her as she cleaned her hands in the pouring rain.

She reached for the sack, but just before dropping it by Chris, something caught her eye—her zhorta's coat. She pulled it out slowly, then turned away without a word and stepped into the cave.

John sat with a woman in his lap, stroking her hair. He looked up at Sara.

"What happened?"

She didn't have to answer. Chris and Donald walked inside, holding Hayden between their arms. John swore again but didn't move while Chris threw things out of his sack and Donald rushed to clean the injury on Hayden's leg.

The distraction allowed Sara to move to the far end of the cave, tugging her coat around her and lowering her hood. She didn't want to speak. She didn't want to listen. She just wanted to disappear into sleep—and forget.

DONALD STRETCHED AS HE STIRRED AWAKE. THE light outside told him it was late—maybe even afternoon —and the absence of the others confirmed it. Before stepping out, he knelt beside Amanda once more. Most of the night had been spent fighting her infection, waiting for the fever to break.

The rest of the night, he'd tried to act as a buffer— diplomatic peacekeeper between Chris, John, and Hayden. He had hoped Sara wouldn't fall asleep, but he understood why she had. Her body was still healing from the fall, and her spirit was raw from everything she'd lost... and everything she was still becoming.

He exhaled quietly and stepped outside the cave. Just two days ago, he'd been walking alone through the Soto Forest, chasing legends about a magical saber. Now, Hayden claimed the valsings were hauling a massive block of enchanted ice through that same forest—with reiser help. Amanda and he had been attacked because of it.

He still hadn't processed it all. Murllen, the reiser leader, wasn't just human—he was family to Sara. And Hayden, who looked like any other man, was something else entirely.

Chris had mentioned Cielthos's cave—how it had

clouded his mind, kept him from thinking clearly and at the edge of rage. Sara had thought a similar curse may have obscured something that should have been obvious. The reisers weren't monsters.

Donald had no answer for it. It made sense. They were all from different races, sure, but the same species. The same naming traditions. The same shape of eyes and bone.

He couldn't help but wonder: would the valsings have noticed sooner? Probably. That must've been why Gemli left their kind alone. Too sharp to fool.

"John, how's the morning going?" he asked as he spotted him seated on the edge of the clearing.

John didn't look up. He was drawing aimless lines in the dirt with a stick.

"Let's just say it's going."

The bitterness in his tone was understandable. Amanda had stirred a few times through the night, but she hadn't truly woken. John was preparing for a hard conversation—whether he admitted it or not.

Donald sat beside him. "You feeling better?" he asked, nodding toward John's head. "You don't look very—"

"I don't look what?"

Donald glanced down. His own clothes were a mess—filthy and stiff with dried sweat. He ran a hand through his hair and grimaced at the grime.

"I need a bath," he muttered.

John barked out a tired laugh and pointed toward the trees. "There's a river over there. But fair warning—Chris made that bastard clean himself before they left."

"Bastard?" Donald blinked. "Oh, Hayden. Right. I'm not worried. Rivers move so—wait, they left? Where?"

He tried not to sound offended, but the twist of pride was undeniable. Chris and Hayden without a diplomat? Dangerous. Chris's idea of negotiation came sharp and fast, usually via blade.

"Chris said he trained around here. Thinks there's a refuge nearby. He didn't trust Hayden enough to leave him behind."

Donald frowned. "But, Amanda?"

"She can't move fast, and we need supplies. Chris thinks there's a way to save the prisoners. I still don't trust that reiser."

Donald lowered his voice. "And the saber?"

John shrugged. "According to the bastard, if what the valsings are moving is the sword, it's already near their lair—or worse, inside."

Donald sighed and scratched at his scalp. It made sense—Chris needed to move quickly. Still, Donald hated being the one left behind. He needed something to do. Judging by the tension radiating off John, so did he.

A soft sound behind them made him turn. Sara was stepping out of the cave, a worn book cradled in her hands. There was something different about her now. Her posture held a weight he hadn't seen before—shoulders squared like a soldier's, eyes too old for her youth.

For a heartbeat, he saw his queen in her.

"I'm not worried about the saber," she said quietly. "We'll find each other."

Donald felt a chill skitter down his spine. There was

no fear in her eyes—just certainty. That same unsettling stillness he'd seen in Gemli. Something ancient moved behind her gaze. The worst, her tone—distant and polite, not kind and comforting.

"Think the answer's in that book?" John asked.

"I doubt it," Sara said with a faint smile. "But I'm too slow to travel, so I'll do what we zhortas do best—read."

John shook his head, half-amused.

"I don't think Chris left you behind because you're slow. I think he's terrified something might happen to you."

"Or," Sara said with a small shrug, "he's mad I made him see the reisers differently."

Donald tried to soften the edge. "Maybe he's not upset at you, exactly... just what you made him face. Right, John?"

John stared at the trees. "No. Sort of. I don't know."

Sara took a few steps away, then paused and turned back.

"You know what, John? I can't explain how much I hate Rafael for what he did to my family. But I still appreciate that he moved us to the Soto Forest. You can despise Hayden all you want, but he saved Amanda. He spoke to you and Chris last night. Thanks to him, they know where the prisoners are, and where to find Murllen. And I'm sure he knows you've been killing his people for years."

She didn't wait for a response. She just turned and disappeared into the trees, the book pressed to her chest.

John looked helplessly at Donald, palms raised. "What? I can't just—"

"Just try to get it," Donald said, voice low.

John rubbed his face with both hands and groaned. "Chris is going to kill me if she doesn't come back."

Donald nodded, though he wasn't truly worried about Sara running off. She wouldn't leave them behind. Her heart was too big, her love too stubborn.

And that—he feared—was what might get her killed one day.

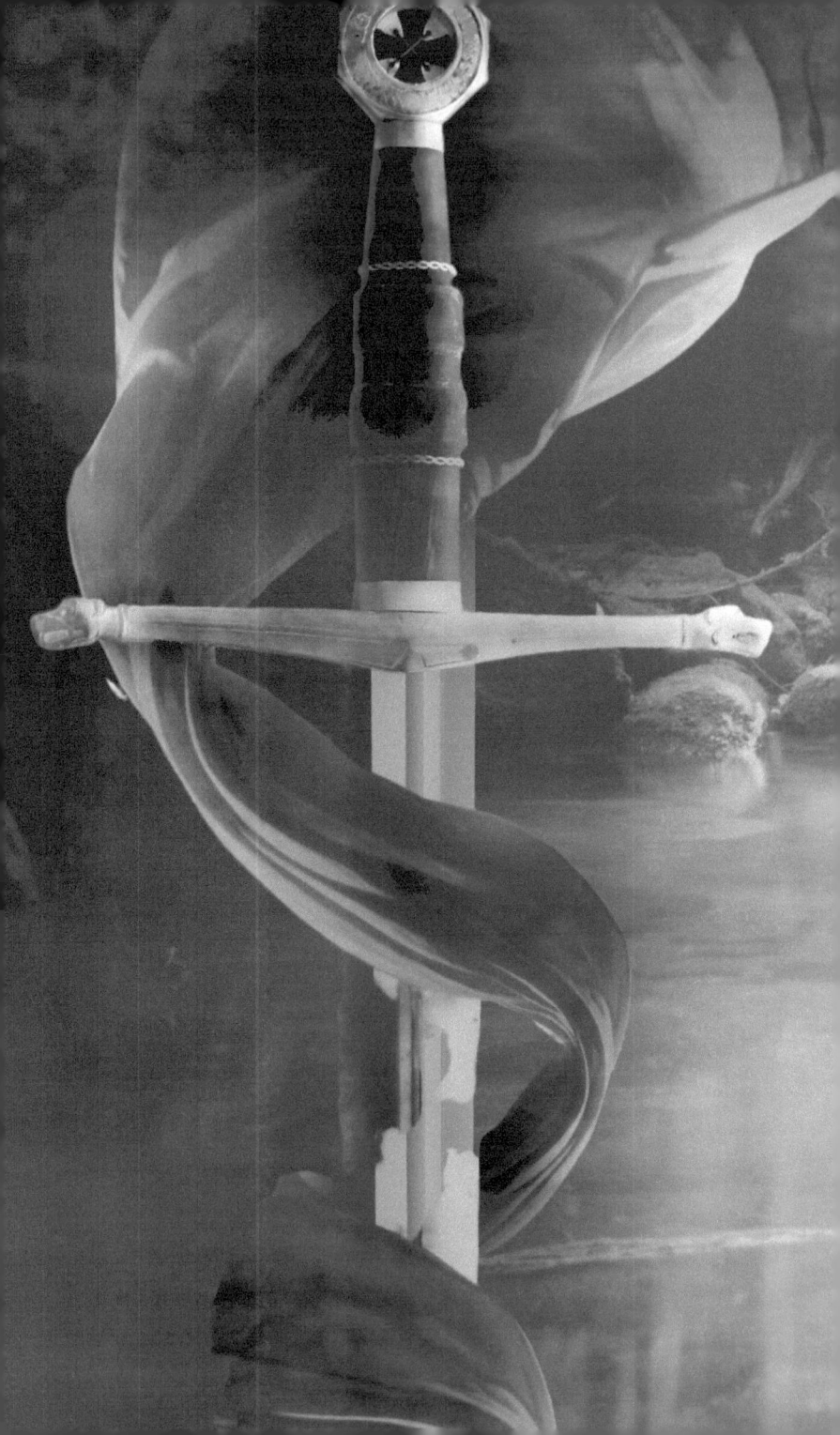

CHAPTER TWENTY-FIVE

The morning was cold and foggy, like most mornings in the swamps, but this one held a different kind of tension—Murllen's mood had shifted. In the last few days, sparring with Rafael and toying with Orson had kept the general in good spirits. Gemli had also kept to his chambers, occupied with rituals for the saber and preparations for Sara's arrival. That helped.

Murllen slowed his pace. Lately, every time Sara slipped into his thoughts, the pull deepened—sharp, persistent, and impossible to ignore. He hadn't expected to care. But she had escaped Gemli. *Outsmarted* him. And that, he had to admit, stirred something dangerously close to pride. She carried his brother's blood—thin, human, but still his—and he needed to see it for himself. See *her*.

She'd even changed Rafael. The zhorta had once been arrogant, narcissistic, and soft—a carbon copy of

Leonard. But now? Now, Rafael protected her with a loyalty that made Murllen curious. Watching him suffer for her had been...fun.

The first time Murllen had met Rafael, he hadn't been impressed. Just another entitled zhorta, convinced the world belonged to him. Torturing that kind of man was always easy. But Rafael had surprised him—had begged, resisted, endured. And all for a human girl.

"General," a reiser called out. "Someone just arrived and asked for you."

Murllen frowned. Unexpected visits were rarely good. The caravan should have been far beyond the swamps by now, slowed by the humans' weakness. His men should have intercepted the saber already—but it was too soon for their return.

"Who is it, Sergeant?" he asked.

"One of Colonel Green's majors. The colonel sent him ahead. With a prisoner."

Murllen's gut tightened. He despised Hayden, but the reiser wasn't careless. If he sent someone early, there was a reason.

"Where?" Murllen barked, shifting into his fast, predatory stride.

"By the dungeons, General."

At the massive stone archway of the fortress's lower level, Murllen saw a frail silhouette collapsed on the cold ground. She looked more ghost than human—tiny, sick, hardly alive.

"What the hell is this?" he growled.

The reiser major straightened as others stepped aside.

"General, Colonel Green sent this prisoner—for her safety."

Murllen let out a laugh that made the major flinch. "Safety? You brought her here for *safety*? To *me*?"

He stepped closer, inspecting the woman. Her gray hair clung to her scalp, her limbs paper-thin, barely holding her upright.

"Explain," he ordered.

The major cleared his throat. "Days ago, she attempted to assassinate the human king."

Murllen's eyebrows lifted. "And Colonel Green couldn't dispose of her himself?"

"He... He said the king tried to kill her first. Green placed him under watch and insisted it was up to you to decide her fate."

Amused now, Murllen crouched beside her. This one had history in her bones—though at the moment, she looked like death itself.

"And what exactly am I supposed to do with this—" he paused, "—human?"

"Her name is Alleta Riddley."

Murllen straightened at once. "Oh well, now this makes sense. Major, you should have started with that."

It was no wonder he hadn't recognized her. The powerful woman he'd met bore no relation with the dying being at his feet. Her skin was more gray than white, and her muscles only worked to fold her bones. Only if he tried hard could he find hints of the red that had once made her look stunning.

The battle he'd had with her husband came to mind. Colonel Alexander Riddley, had stood between

Murllen and his soldiers, foolishly sending the king away with his son's guard. As if that noble act could stop anything.

Murllen smiled at the memory. Alexander had fought well. Briefly. Even without Gemli's magic, the colonel hadn't stood a chance against him. Most days, Murllen wondered if anyone did. After training in that asylum, he doubted it.

And now, the man's widow lay crumpled before him.

Gemli had warned him about the colonel's son, but Murllen hadn't believed it. No child could live up to a father like that. Still, if this woman meant anything to the boy—*Christopher Riddley*—then perhaps her suffering could be useful.

He leaned down. "Hello!" he shouted into her ear.

Alleta startled awake. Her eyes fluttered open, focused, and widened at the sight of him. She recoiled, dragging herself back until her spine hit the stone wall.

Murllen turned to the major, grinning. "Splendid. You didn't break her on the way here."

Then he addressed her directly. "I'm *so* glad you're alive."

He spread his arms in mock welcome. "Welcome to my home—the fortress." His voice carried a sharp, threatening edge that made her shudder. He relished it.

"But where are my manners?" he said, grabbing her by the arm and hauling her upright. "I'm General Murllen. Leader of the reisers. The man who killed your stupid husband. And soon, your son."

Her eyes filled with tears—but she didn't let them fall. She met his eyes.

"You're lucky I'm not a soldier," she rasped. "You'd be dead already."

She yanked her arm free and braced herself against the wall. "And you'll never kill my son. He's already dead."

Murllen tilted his head, mock concern painting his face. "Is that what you *hope*? That your little boy is already gone?" He clutched his chest. "Such motherly devotion."

His voice darkened. "I hate to disappoint. But he's alive. On his way here. I'm sure he'll be so happy to see you."

Alleta's tears spilled this time, silent and slow. She lifted her bound hands.

"If it weren't for these," she whispered, "you'd be blind."

Murllen laughed again. "Poor woman. Sick *and* delusional."

Then his voice dropped to a cold murmur. "Tell me —was it the sight of your husband's remains that broke you? Or was it when they brought back his face, mouth hanging open, skin peeled, no eyes left?"

She slumped to the ground, shaking her head.

"Oh… you didn't *know*?" he whispered. "I suppose your son spared you that particular horror. How sweet."

He crouched in front of her again. "But don't worry. I'll make sure you see your son's face when I'm finished with it."

"You coward," she hissed, trembling. "My son is dead!"

With a sudden scream, Alleta tried to strike him.

Murllen grabbed the front of her dress and slammed her into the wall.

"I am not a coward," he snarled, nose inches from hers. "And I am not stupid. He's alive. And I *promise*—you'll see him again."

He released her, letting her crumple to the floor. For a moment, he considered kicking her. But no. She wouldn't survive.

"Major, you are free to go." He turned to another reiser. "Pick her up and follow me." Then, more to himself, he added, "We need help from the caring reisers on site."

LIKE EVERY TIME MURLLEN APPROACHED THE asylum, memories clawed their way to the surface. He remembered his own training here—brutal, endless. After killing his brother, Gemli had taken him to Reign Mountain. Murllen didn't know how long he'd been kept in that cave. Long enough. Long enough for the difference between pain and reality to blur, for his mind to fracture and rebuild itself around agony.

The reisers inside the asylum didn't wear armor. Their job was to raise and protect the young until they were strong enough to be suited up and sent off to war. Because of that, the most dangerous reisers were not out in the field—they lived behind these walls. And if Murllen wanted to lead them, he had to become one of them.

On Gemli's orders, the reiser in charge had trained

him personally. The sorcerer claimed to have incarnated Murllen into the armor—fusing it to his flesh, enhancing his power, elevating him above the rest. More importantly, he would be their new leader.

Aside from Murllen, none of the reisers needed to wear armor anymore. Gemli grew particularly angry every time Murllen asked how it was possible they didn't know it, since, according to the sorcerer, it had changed decades ago. He'd never gotten an answer beyond agonizing pain. Years back, he'd stopped asking, making that issue, one of the sorcerer's only weaknesses he knew.

Need it of not, the armor fascinated him.

Before they were deployed, each reiser was bound into a grotesque suit—a hide of dried skin soaked in poison and vital fluids. Then came the iron plating, fused and sealed with more of the same. Once bonded, the armor grew with them. They never took it off.

Here, in the asylum, the reisers learned more than battle. They learned obedience. Detachment. They were conditioned to protect the race, not individuals. Their training taught them to sever emotion, to erase personal desire.

Murllen had never believed it was the lessons that made them forget. It was the armor.

The asylum held secrets older than some chambers of the abbey. And it was better that way. That's why he hesitated to leave Alleta here. But if she was going to survive, he had no other choice.

"Knock," he ordered the reiser beside him.

The heavy metal door groaned open. Murllen stepped forward.

"That will be all," he said coldly, scooping Alleta into his arms.

The reiser hesitated, glancing from Murllen to the open threshold.

"If you don't want to find yourself in the dungeon," Murllen said, "go do something useful elsewhere."

Without waiting, he crossed into the shadows.

The door slammed shut behind him, plunging them into absolute darkness. Metal locks slid into place. Footsteps echoed, retreating. Alleta shivered against him.

A soft, humorless laugh escaped his lips.

"Don't worry," he muttered. "Looks like hell, but it's not. That's out there."

UNLIKE THE FORTRESS OUTSIDE, THE ROOM smelled clean. The heat inside softened the ache in Alleta's muscles, almost melting the pain from her bones. If it hadn't been for the monster beside her, she could have let herself drift to sleep—just for a moment—forgetting the world that still waited beyond these walls.

"You must drink that," a firm voice cut through the quiet, startling her. A dim light flickered on.

"I won't be needing that today," Murllen replied flatly. "Like every other time I'm here."

The lights brightened, and Alleta had to close her eyes against the glare. As she blinked, shapes came into focus—a modest wooden table, a pair of chairs, a neglected flowerpot, and a celosia that partially obscured a small patio ringed by open hallways.

It was... normal. Too normal. That was what unsettled her most.

"Of course you won't drink it," the voice said again, now clearly feminine. "You. Always breaking our laws."

Murllen dropped her into one of the chairs with little care and sat across from her.

Alleta scanned the room. A woman stood by the far wall, no older than Chris. Her deep red hair caught the light just as Alleta's once had, and her freckled face, green eyes, and glowing skin made her look youthful—almost innocent.

But the sharp line of her mouth and the undeniable curve of her pregnant belly gave her a different air altogether. Commanding. Dangerous.

"Well, well," Murllen drawled. "I thought your kind couldn't reproduce, Genevieve."

She descended the last few steps and stopped on the other side of the table.

"That is shocking. I had no idea you knew our rules," she said, mimicking his mocking tone. "Why the stupid question, though? This is the consequence of your last command."

Murllen's mocking grin faltered, and a cold churn twisted in Alleta's gut. The idea of him fathering anything turned her stomach.

"Interesting," he said, his tone darker now. "Maybe the dear colonel wasn't so useless after all." He moved closer, eyes fixed on her belly. "I can't wait to meet that bastard's offspring."

His hand reached out, but the woman was faster. She struck him across the face with the torch, gripped his arm, and shoved him against the wall with a strength far beyond what she should've possessed.

"Touch me again," she growled, "and we'll find out how well you live without your armor."

Murllen laughed. "You know it's permanent. I'm not like the other reisers."

"Exactly. More interesting to test," she said coldly. "And don't flatter yourself, Thornton. The only true reiser in this room is me."

Alleta blinked. Thornton? The name wasn't common, but the man she remembered bore no resemblance to the monster in front of her. And Genevieve... she looked like she could've been Alleta's daughter, not her enemy.

Murllen pushed past and dropped into a chair again, casual and unbothered.

"Well, Genevieve, as delightful as your company always is, I'm here on business. Where's your boss? Where's Estela?"

"Dead," Genevieve said, flat and indifferent.

Murllen stilled. The mocking edge vanished from his voice as he leaned forward. "When?"

Genevieve arched an eyebrow, folding her arms. The silence stretched just long enough to cut.

Murllen cleared his throat, leaned back, and forced a scoff that didn't quite land. "Well... I never cared for her anyway."

But his expression didn't follow his words. The mask slipped just for a second—just long enough to reveal something quieter, unreadable beneath.

He exhaled through his nose. "The relevance is that we have a new house ruler. New ruler, new rules?"

Genevieve rolled her eyes.

"You're already breaking them," he went on. "Look at you—glowing. What was it your mother used to say? He tapped his chin a few times. "Oh, yes, you should not have preferences until your leader establishes his own offspring, and well...we know I do not plan on doing that."

He chuckled while turning to Alleta. "Let me explain things to you, Mrs. Riddley. Reisers aren't like us. They have no affection or passion. If I cut off the head of the reiser responsible for that unborn thing, Genevieve wouldn't feel a thing. Think about it, knowing that the pieces of that reiser would rot in the mud like your beloved Alexander wouldn't even make her flinch."

Alleta's throat tightened. Her breath caught, caught on grief, caught on the weight of what she'd lost.

"Don't believe me?" Murllen gestured toward Genevieve. "She told you her mother's dead like she was announcing the weather. What's the point of fooling around with something like this?"

He touched his chest and looked at Genevieve. "I guess my human experience prevails here and I don't see the point of...umm... I don't know, go through the procedure? Or I guess with these new rules, touching you? Why waste time without the attachment?" he shook his head amused at himself. "That's my weakness, I suppose. I'm all about the emotional attachment."

A soft, unexpected laugh echoed across the room.

"That's your excuse?" Genevieve's expression lightened, though her eyes stayed sharp. "We all know why you can't sire children. After what Gemli did, you're broken. Mutilated."

Murllen's chair scraped back violently. He lunged, knocking the table aside and pinning her to the wall by the throat. To Alleta's surprised, she didn't fight.

"Go ahead," she gasped. "Kill me. They'll call you a defector. They'll destroy you."

He growled again, but his grip loosened.

"Keep dreaming, stupid reiser."

Genevieve stood firm, breathing hard. "I will—because I know who should be leading us."

As she walked toward him, the light revealed the marks from Murllen's claw on her neck. Her voice cracked with fury. "Colonel Hayden Green will replace you."

Murllen's grin returned. "That's your plan? If he fails, your bastard takes over?"

Genevieve's hand moved, almost protectively, toward her belly—then stopped.

"You're adorable, Genevieve. I might never put a bastard in you, but believe me, Hayden's spawn won't be part of what's coming."

"That's not for you to decide," she snapped.

"Not yet," he agreed. "But it will be. You said it yourself—I'm good at breaking your rules."

Then he turned to Alleta. His tone cooled.

"Anyway, back to business. This is Alleta Riddley. She's very important to me. Heal her. Keep her alive until I return."

Genevieve barely glanced at her. "She's old. She's sick. Not my concern."

"So rude," Murllen cooed, patting Alleta's knee. She jerked her leg away.

"Genevieve, play nice. This is no ordinary human. She's a mother and just like you, she believes her son can defeat me. Isn't that sweet?" He leaned toward Alleta. "I want to reunite them. Once Commander Riddley arrives, he deserves to see his mommy again."

Genevieve's lips pressed into a line. Murllen took a step closer.

"Need a reminder of your duty? Or has the safety of reiser offspring slipped your mind now that you're carrying dear Hayden's child?"

Genevieve flinched—barely—but it was enough.

"Oh, what's this?" Murllen beamed. "Feelings? For him?" His voice dropped to a hiss. "You're becoming one of *them*."

Her gaze sharpened like a blade. "You are an idiot. Of course I care. He's our rightful leader. Everyone outside these walls knows it. They trust him. They *follow* him—not out of fear, like they do you."

The room fell silent. The two stared at each other, motionless, but radiating threat. Alleta couldn't tell who would win in a fight. Genevieve might be half his size, but there was a feral, coiled power inside her—something that reminded Alleta of Chris when he came home from war, haunted and deadly.

Murllen reached out, gently curling a lock of her hair between his fingers.

"Well then," he said softly. "Looks like your dream of

seeing a rightful leader in charge will have to wait. That bastard in your belly will need time to grow."

He kissed the strand of hair, then turned to leave.

"Hayden Green won't return to this fortress," he added with a cruel smile. "Not breathing, anyway."

The moment his hand touched the door, the room plunged into darkness. Alleta gasped. The door creaked open, and the swamp's putrid stench seeped inside. Murllen stepped out. The door closed—and the lights flared back to life.

Alleta remained in the chair. She turned to Genevieve, who hadn't moved. Her eyes were closed, and her breathing came in steady, deliberate waves.

Alleta recognized that kind of breath. It was the weight of mourning. The invisible pressure that sat on your chest when someone you loved was gone, and you had to keep moving anyway.

"Do you miss him?" Alleta asked softly.

Genevieve's eyes opened, sharp and cold. She stepped forward. Alleta's hands trembled as the reiser reached out and pressed her forehead.

"No," Genevieve said firmly.

But her eyes betrayed her, drifting toward something that wasn't there.

"I miss the opportunity to watch someone *destroy* your race—along with the bastard we call our leader."

Alleta lowered her gaze, lips pressed tightly together. Up to that moment, that was exactly what she had hoped from her Xander and now Chris to do. To destroy the reisers. "Why didn't you kill him?" she whispered. "You could have."

Genevieve walked toward the celosia, her voice cold again. "You're right. I could have. But it's forbidden."

She paused, then looked over her shoulder.

"Can you walk?"

Alleta stood slowly, bracing herself against the wall. Her legs protested, but she nodded and followed.

Silently, they moved together, deeper into the asylum.

CHAPTER TWENTY-SIX

Dead branches clung to what had once been lush green walls, weaving brittle nets across the stone barriers surrounding the patio. A translucent dome enclosed the space, shielding it from the toxic atmosphere of the swamps. Long ago—when dances and garden parties had been common and war a distant rumor—Alleta had visited the castle in Tundra on her husband's arm. She remembered walking through similar breathtaking indoor gardens, trailing her fingers along vines and blossoms that no longer bloomed.

Unlike that castle, the rooms in there lay in darkness. The silence pressed in as they passed shadowy corridors, where figures—reisers—glided past without a word or glance. Their steps made no sound. The weight of still-ness had replaced the once-vibrant pulse of the place.

Genevieve led her toward a staircase, but then stopped abruptly, raising a hand to halt her. "Wait here," she whispered. "I don't want them to see you."

Alleta obeyed, pressing against the wall. From the far

landing, a tall reiser descended the stairs, followed by a line of children—none older than five. Their pale features mirrored humanity so closely it made Alleta's breath catch. But they didn't speak or fidget. Instead, they moved in eerie unison, hands clasped, gazes forward.

A small smile broke across Alleta's face as memories stirred—laughter, sticky fingers, and bedtime stories under a blanket of stars. She thought of her son as a boy, and of other children now hidden in refuges, or worse, marching in chains.

Once the children disappeared through a side door, she stepped close to Genevieve and whispered, "Are they all right? Why do they seem so... serious?"

Genevieve didn't answer at first. Alleta's heartbeat quickened—was her question a misstep?

But then Genevieve turned, and for the first time, a soft pride lit her face. She placed a hand over her abdomen without hesitation.

"They are perfect. Healthy and safe." Her tone darkened. "But we don't let them play when they cross the patio. They have no protection yet. The outside—it would hurt them. They need to fear it."

Alleta watched the closed door where the children had vanished. Beyond it, she heard faint laughter, and the tightness in her chest eased.

The staircase, though modest, proved a challenge. Alleta's body ached from exhaustion and captivity. Genevieve didn't rush her. At the top, the reiser extended an arm, steadying her. The gesture, simple as it was, tugged at something raw inside Alleta.

There was no way she could ever despise Genevieve

—or any of the little ones behind that door. Perhaps learning that it was Thornton, not a reiser, who had killed Alexander had softened something in her. And maybe it helped that Genevieve didn't look like the soldiers outside. But would any of that be enough to change Chris's mind about who the real enemy was?

The infirmary was small but clean. A bed stood against one wall, a tall cabinet against another, and in the center, a wide table with drawers beneath. Genevieve helped her to the bed and then stepped out to call someone. When she returned, she stood in the doorway, arms crossed.

"What makes you think your son can change Hune's future?"

Alleta looked down, lacing her fingers together. Her voice was barely audible.

"I'm the mother of Commander Christopher Riddley. Widow of Colonel Alexander Riddley." She drew in a shaky breath. Something in her, maybe exhaustion or defiance, pushed her to add: "My son now leads what's left of the human army. Just like his father did. I'm sure Murllen would enjoy torturing both of us. I just hope... Chris is still alive."

Genevieve stepped inside, retrieving vials and a cup from the cabinet. As she moved, her tone shifted, almost as if speaking to herself.

"Evil had no meaning to me until I met a human. Murllen—then called Thornton." Her voice trembled, just slightly. "Are all humans soldiers like him? Full of hate and sick desires?"

Alleta met her eyes. "No. Some are. But most aren't."

Genevieve nodded slowly, then handed her the cup of water with two small tablets.

"I started to figure... Recently, Murllen has been bringing humans into the fortress. I had hoped they were all evil. It would explain why we live in hiding, trying to survive this horrible place and your race... At least we were safe from you all here. But if your race isn't evil... then why are you allowed to live in Hune while we are stuck behind this disgusting armors."

Two reisers entered the room.

"She needs a bath," Genevieve instructed. "Clothes. Food. Preferably warm. And rest."

The reisers hesitated, staring at Alleta like she might shatter beneath their gaze.

"Isn't she human?" one of them asked.

"Yes. And these are your leader's orders."

A tense silence followed.

"Estela will die again if she sees us now," muttered the other reiser as they opened a drawer and began pulling out clothes.

"Murllen wants her alive," Genevieve added, her tone grim. "That alone is cruel enough for this poor being."

Alleta felt her blood pressure drop when both reisers turned to her. Her eyes were clouded with sorrow, and their hands grabbed her with pity.

And somehow, that hurt the most.

THE ASYLUM WASN'T JUST GENEVIEVE'S HOME— it was her life, her purpose, her burden. As the firstborn of Estela, the ruler of the asylum and their former leader, her path had never been her own. The ancient laws were unyielding: her life would be spent within these walls, raising and protecting the next generation of reisers. She could only join the impregnation protocol if her procreator died and a new, unrelated leader took control of the reisers.

With Murllen as their new leader, she hoped that day would never come.

Genevieve had grown up in a different asylum than the one praised in their sacred books. Years ago, weary of her daughter's relentless questions, Estela had shared truths not written in any script—truths that changed everything. Things were already bad, and they would get worse.

Genevieve sat in a infirmary's chair, her posture straight but her shoulders heavy, watching as the other reisers finished tending to Alleta. After, she would attempt to heal the human woman herself—a daunting task, given her state. Alleta's age wasn't the issue; it was the grief etched so deeply into her soul. You could see it in her eyes—grief that devoured her one heartbeat at a time.

She understood that kind of sorrow very well. You didn't recover from it. You either learned to carry it or let it pull you under. Contrary to how she'd acted, the death of her mother had left a weight on her heart. She missed Estela more than she admitted. They had shared more than blood—they had shared duty, ideals, and a connection only a ruler and her heir could know. Now, the very choices she'd once questioned fell on her shoulders, and silence had become her only counsel.

She let her hand rest gently over her abdomen, remembering what her mother had told her long ago.

Before the war truly began, Gemli had forced his way into the asylum—with Thornton at his side. He made his demands with the ease of someone who believed himself untouchable. Estela was to train the creature they brought with them—a twisted creation they called Murllen. She would anoint him as her challenger and ensure he took the reins of power. If she refused, Gemli would cast every infant and young reiser out into the wild to die.

Their race had always protected its young above all. Somehow, Gemli and Murllen knew this. They exploited that sacred bond, and Estela had no choice but to obey. Murllen would train within the asylum, sharpen his skills, and eventually use them against his own kind.

As heir to the asylum, Genevieve had spent her youth becoming the strongest warrior within its walls—not just out of tradition, but because of what Murllen represented. Her mother had trained her relentlessly, ensuring she could outmatch him if the time ever came.

She was grateful she had never needed to fulfill her other responsibility. Estela had explained long ago how the ruler of the asylum always formed an instant bond with a new leader—if they were unrelated.

Genevieve had vague memories of her mother, happy talking to a powerful reiser. Their former leader and her father. But she knew it would never happen to her. Murllen had no rightful claim to their race, since he was born a human, and she doubted his successor would be part of her reiser either.

She had never expected the chance to change her people's future would fall to her. But fate had other plans.

A few weeks earlier, Murllen had broken protocol again, bringing a reiser outside the scheduled cycle. Genevieve shouldn't have met him. Because of her position, impregnation wasn't part of her tasks. However, since the others were occupied, she had stepped in. She told herself it was routine—she only needed a sample of his blood. Nothing more. She would figure out the rest later.

Sometimes, she wished the secrets behind the impregnation process hadn't been lost with the curse. As legend told it, her ancestors and the valsings had once tried to conquer Hune, incurring the wrath of the gods. In return, the valsings were cursed to walk around Hune but never have a home and obsession over their image, while the reisers were confined to an infertile, hostile land, unable to leave the fortress.

In remorse, or perhaps guilt, the valsings had given the reisers certain technologies—armor to survive outside, and the designs for the impregnation method. But when Genevieve's predecessors sought their aid again, the valsings denied any role in the curse. Their newer generations claimed Hune as their birthright and moved freely, as if their ancestors had never sinned.

Genevieve didn't care for perfection—only resilience. She wanted to strengthen her kind, not reshape them. It shattered her heart to force her children into armor, to seal them in steel and fear and still expect them to thrive.

That visit had begun like any other. The reiser had waited in darkness until the door closed behind him. When the dim light flickered on, he drank the sedative left for him on the table. Clipboard in hand, Genevieve descended the stairs moments later.

She asked his name and rank again, even though he had already given it. A test. But something felt off—he moved too easily, his gaze too clear. The sedative wasn't working.

In the lab, she asked again. "What is your name?"

"I told you that already, human," he replied. "Are you a prisoner here? You seem upset, but not afraid."

She looked up, truly meeting his eyes. For a heartbeat, trust flickered in her chest—unexpected, but undeniable.

"I'm upset because you aren't supposed to be here, but I'm not a prisoner. I'm in charge of the asylum. Rest assured, I'm not human. Like you, I'm a reiser, but since I don't go out, I don't need to wear armor."

Genevieve offered him another cup with one of the valsings' solvents to get his blood ready.

He watched her carefully. "Can we take it off... and not die?"

His voice slurred as the sedative began to pull him under—too slowly. He tried to remove the armor himself, fumbling and bruising his arms. Genevieve couldn't help but laugh softly.

"What do you think you're doing?"

"I want to see."

She gently caught his hands. "We don't allow you to see."

Then he doubled over in pain, growling low. He collapsed hard, and for a terrifying moment, she thought he might be dead. But his eyes opened—glazed, pained, but awake.

On very rare occasions, the reisers needed to open their protection. Genevieve had learned what to do, and using a special key, she slid open a small fissure of the armor.

All became clear to Genevieve. Although hard to believe, he had been born with a natural resistance to their sedative, a clear sign he was strong enough to challenge their leader. A suitable challenger, aside from strength, needed to have a cannier mind. The regular sedatives and process of impregnation wouldn't work with them.

Even when her mother never thought Murllen would allow it, she'd taught her what to do. Since their minds would fight the sedative, their armor would poison them. Their race didn't need too many challengers, so it was a safety measure to prevent riots. As the ruler of the asylum, she could decide if he should die right there.

Genevieve removed his helmet, allowing him to breathe the clean air in the room, and opened the top of his armor. The reiser's heartbeat and breathing normalized, and he became able to focus again. She took a step back.

"How have you done this before?" she asked.

But she knew the answer—he hadn't. Others must

have never finished the process. His lucidity must have concerned the other reisers, and instead of preparing him, they'd drugged him to fall asleep, hoping he would forget everything. She couldn't blame them, though. Her mother wasn't very compassionate or forgiving.

"I don't... Sorry—I guess?" he said, hazy with confusion.

She cursed and poured him another mixture. He had to sleep. It was the only way to keep him safe. If Murllen found out—

"Are you trying to kill me?" he said, managing a crooked smile. "Because I'd rather die at your hands than—"

"I'm trying to save you."

The way his eyes softened at the corners and his smile barely lifted his lips reminded her of the way their former leader used to look at her mother. That's when Genevieve finally understood his true role—and the bond her mother had once spoken of filled a hollow space in her heart she hadn't realized was empty.

"I have to save you so you can go out and protect us."

She leaned closer and whispered in his ear, "You were supposed to lead us, Colonel Green. Murllen is a usurper and has threatened to destroy our future."

For a moment, she thought he hadn't heard. But then his nose brushed her cheek, and she froze. Somehow, he had freed his hand—and he was gently holding a strand of her hair.

"Hayden," he said. "Since you are not a soldier, I'm not your colonel."

Genevieve's skin tingled, heart pounding. Her entire

body responded to his nearness. Logic blurred, boundaries dissolved.

"This is wrong," she whispered, trembling. "You aren't even supposed to be here."

Hayden leaned close, his breath warm against her ear. "Then just pretend I'm not."

Something in his voice—deep, grounding, real—drew her in. Her fingers grazed his hand, and the spark that passed between them nearly brought her to her knees. When he stood, his armor fell away completely. He pushed her one step back, and the room turned warmer when she felt his hands on her waist.

"What is your name?" he asked, breathless.

She hesitated, the weight of destiny crushing her chest. Hayden picked her up and sat her on the bench. "Please, I need to know."

"Genevieve."

He cupped her cheek and looked straight into her eyes.

Genevieve felt the quick rhythm of his pulse beneath her fingertips and, breathless, she brushed her hand along his cheek.

"Genevieve..." he whispered, voice rough with longing.

She drew back, her hand lingering a second longer than it should. "No... it doesn't matter. You won't remember this—me."

He leaned in, his lips barely grazing her cheek. "Then you'll remember for both of us."

Her resolve cracked.

Before she could think of a reason to stop, her lips found his. His hands found her waist, steadying her, grounding her. The warmth of him melted through her doubts and swallowed the loneliness she'd carried for what felt like lifetimes. In that stolen moment, there was no war, no curses, no fate—only the echo of his name blooming quietly in her soul.

When the moment passed, she said nothing—just helped him back into his armor with trembling hands. The sedatives were taking hold. Her tears fell freely now, silent witnesses to the impossible thing they'd shared, and the cruel knowledge that he would forget it all.

"I'll... miss you," he whispered.

Genevieve steadied herself. She lifted the helmet, ready to seal him away again, but he stopped her.

"I heard you. About Murllen. I'll do something—I don't know how—but I'll try. And more than anything, I won't forget you."

He pressed his forehead to hers.

"I'll come back, Genevieve. I'll find a way."

Now, as she sat beside Alleta, hand protectively over her belly, Genevieve let herself smile—just for a moment. She would never forget Hayden. And she would never treat their child like any other reiser.

She finally understood her mother's distant smiles and the silence that followed her visits with the leader she once loved. The same sorrow now nested in her chest.

Murllen's voice echoed in her thoughts like a curse, and her throat tightened. By now, Hayden was likely already dead.

She hadn't expected to see him again, but knowing he was gone shattered something inside her. Her body moved through the motions, but her soul remained at the moment he whispered her name. He could've changed everything. He could have saved them.

But now, he was just a memory—a dream that died before it had a chance to become real.

ALLETA COULD HEAR THE WIND BATTERING THE stone walls of the asylum, and for once, she was grateful to be somewhere warm. Even if it was still her prison, she had found a strange kind of peace within its walls.

In her current state, there was nothing left to lose. She was tired—tired of walking, of fighting, of trying to keep hope alive for herself and the others. Even her prayers had dulled into silence.

The door creaked open. Alleta held her breath until she saw the reiser's face. Genevieve stepped inside.

"Thank you," Alleta murmured.

"You're still ill," Genevieve said gently. "And even I can tell you're depressed."

Alleta exhaled and rested her head against the thin pillow. "Wouldn't you be? If you lost the man you love—and your only hope is never seeing your son again?"

Genevieve glanced toward the door, then stepped closer and sat beside the bed. "I'm a reiser. I can't possibly understand what you feel—neither the emotions, nor the choices." Her fingers crept toward her abdomen as she absently played with the blanket's edge.

"The rules of human love and attachment... they don't apply to us."

Before Alleta could ask more, Genevieve's eyes went wide. Her skin blanched, and she gripped her belly, covering her mouth to stifle a cry.

Alleta bolted upright and knelt beside her. "What is it? Are you in pain?"

Genevieve shook her head, but the tears she tried to swallow escaped anyway. "Something's wrong. I think... I think the little one is dying."

Alleta gently moved Genevieve's hand aside and placed her palm over the reiser's belly. From the size, she guessed the child wasn't due for weeks. She waited... then felt the tiniest kick drum against her skin.

"You mean *that*?"

Genevieve could only nod, silent and shaken.

"You don't know what that is?" Alleta asked, surprised. "I thought you were trained to care for your offspring. You must have seen pregnancies before."

"Of course I have," Genevieve whispered. "But... this is different."

She tried to stand, but her limbs trembled. Alleta steadied her and urged her to sit again.

"At least rest. You don't want the others to see you like this."

Genevieve nodded, eyes darting to the door before she wiped her cheeks.

"We do care for our young," she said at last. "I've seen hundreds of impregnations—but never anything like *this*."

Alleta remembered Murllen's surprise when he'd first

seen Genevieve. At the time, she'd assumed it had to do with Genevieve's rank or role... but maybe it had been something else entirely.

"For us," Alleta said gently, "this is very normal." She pressed her palm to her belly again and smiled. "It means the little one is strong and healthy."

Genevieve placed her hand lightly on top of her stomach but didn't press down. Her fear still clouded her face, making her look younger—uncertain.

"How does it... normally work?" Alleta asked, easing onto the bed beside her.

Genevieve took a shaky breath. "We collect blood from the reisers outside and mix it with blood from those in here. The blend is cultivated... with other materials, some from the valsings. Then the mixture is placed in special vessels that allow it to grow." She looked away. "Don't ask me how. I don't know. Others carry the vessels—not inside their bodies. We nourish and protect them until it's time. It looks like this"—she gestured at her belly—"but the child... it's never really inside us."

A thousand questions burned in Alleta's mind, the kind Alexander or Chris might have leapt on. Perhaps it explained why the valsings had withheld their support in the war. But none of that mattered right now. The only one she could help in this moment was the frightened young woman beside her.

"No one has ever had a baby like this before?"

Genevieve shook her head. "Not that I've ever heard. I suppose... maybe my mother did. But she never told me, and with Murllen around, there was no need to talk about it." She looked down again. "I thought human babies just... rested until they were born."

Alleta chuckled softly at that, but when Genevieve didn't smile, her humor faded.

"So how did *this* one happen?"

Genevieve flushed and looked away, the silence more telling than anything she could say.

"In that case," Alleta said, her voice kind, "I'll assume this little one is just like ours. Growing peacefully, kicking to say hello."

Genevieve's eyes filled with tears again. "What am I going to do? I knew this was bad, but—I don't understand human pregnancies. I don't want to lose this baby. It's... all we—I have left."

Alleta reached out and gently lifted her chin. "I saw you speaking with Murllen." Her voice softened. "This child is not a mistake. You can do this. And this little one... they're lucky to have you."

"You're a prisoner," Genevieve said quietly. "How can you believe that?"

"I saw enough before. And I've seen how you've cared for me since. You may not think you have love in you, but your actions say otherwise."

Genevieve's hands trembled as she touched her abdomen again. "I wish things were different. I wish... he could know about this."

Alleta leaned in and wrapped her arms around her. She let Genevieve cry on her shoulder, brushing her hair as if she were comforting a daughter.

Murllen had been right.

They weren't so different—both trapped, both

mourning. He had taken the man Alleta loved and condemned the father of Genevieve's child.

And now, both of their children—one born, one still growing—were a threat to him.

Their future was as fragile as the life fluttering beneath Genevieve's hand.

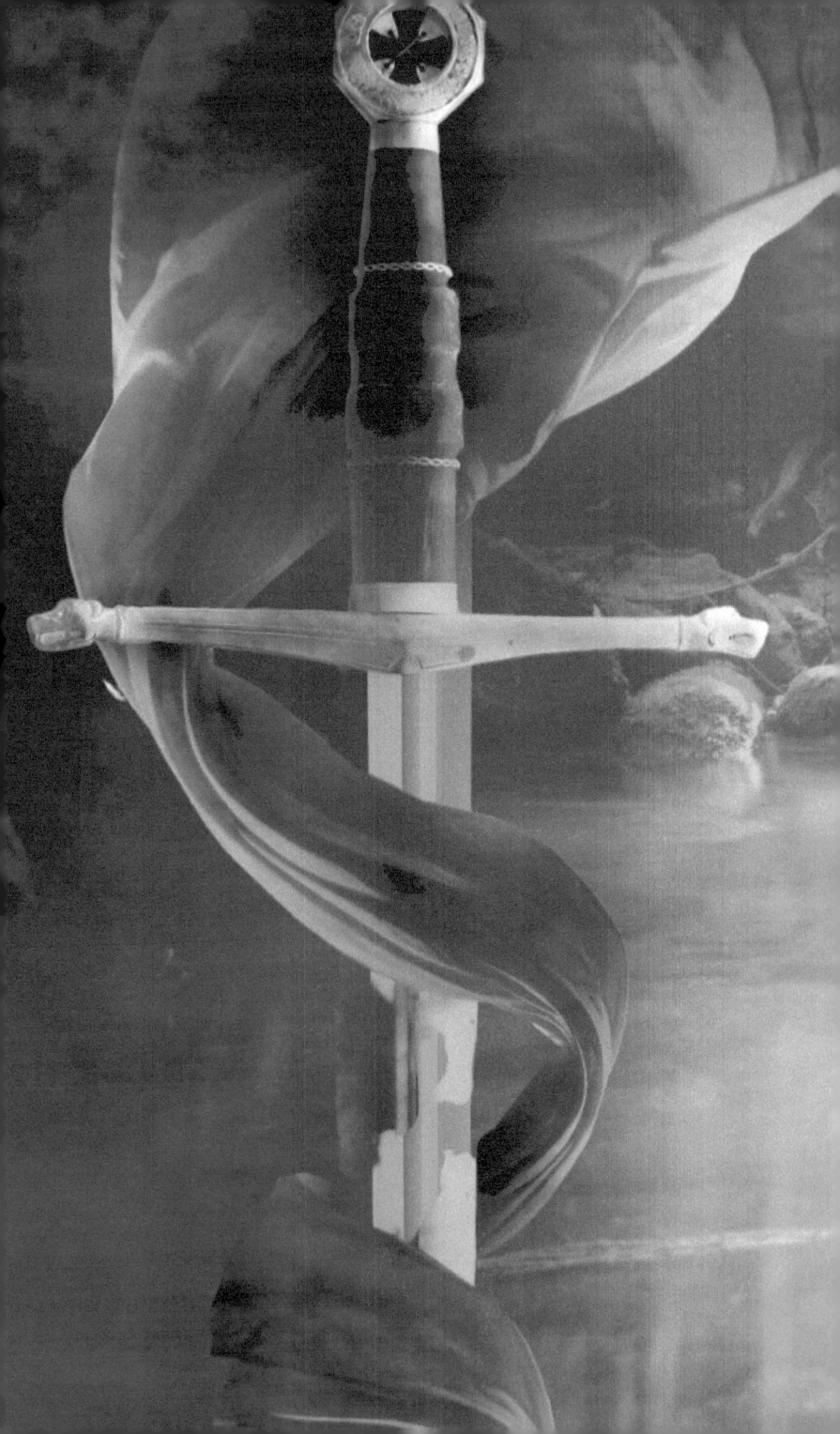

Epilogue

S ara sat against a tree and exhaled heavenward. For years, her life had been simple: take care of the gardens, sometimes help in the kitchen or the infirmary, and then study. There were so many things to learn about Hune, and the abbey kept so much lost information.

However, among those scrolls, parchments, and books, there were none that she had been afraid to open. The one in her hands was different, and she wondered how it had ended up in Cielthos's hands.

The book was a journal, and it had been written in the typical zhorta's style. She was familiar with it because she had used it to write her own studies before.

There was no rule that said all zhortas needed to be human, even when most were. Although it was before her time, she knew that in the past, there had been valsings who'd left their communities to join the zhortas. Still, finding the reisers' language in a well-known style surprised her and made her wonder if she had lived with them before.

It crossed her mind that the author had chosen the language to protect the book's secrets. However, once she read his name and part of the contents, all doubt left as her body turned cold and her heart slowed down.

The rough state of the book made sense. Cielthos hadn't taken care of the volume; he just wanted to gain its knowledge. Now he wanted her to learn from it, too. She feared this, but she understood how important it was.

The journal in her hands explained how the foundations of Hune worked and how to understand its power to manipulate it. Because Cielthos had given it to her, it wasn't strange that it spoke about magic. The fact that, in the first chapters, Gemli explained how he had mastered control of the trees around the abbey was, though.

According to the journal, Gemli became a zhorta because they rescued him by the forest of Laconia years before the war was even part of a conversation. He didn't know he had the ability to use magic until years after being sent to the Soto Forest. Saint Peter's Abbey had always belonged to the zhortas, but no one had lived there until they had to, and when Gemli visited it, the library became his second home.

During his trip there, he got lost in the forest. It took him several days and almost dying from poison before he figured out that he could affect the roots' movement and heal himself—something which, according to him, even wizards had trouble mastering. Just like her father had mentioned. Gemli believed that this was due to his reiser nature.

He stayed in the abbey for a long time, and within those walls, he read about magic, sorcerers, and wizards. The book contained detailed explanations of how to manipulate Hune's magic, with examples of what he had done and how he understood Hune's foundations.

His journal ended with a mention of the discovery of a legend, one he had grown up listening to with his former race and knew was real. He didn't explain his plan, but after reading about his past, Sara understood him.

Born a reiser, he had grown up in their fortress. In the journal, he talked about a place called the asylum. He wasn't supposed to remember what had happened to him the only time he visited it. And because he did, he was sentenced to death.

Sara had grown up around secrets and knew their importance, but she didn't support trying to kill someone to preserve them. She found herself in the same position she'd put Chris in. Her hate for Gemli had no comparison, but from the book, she learned that his own leader took him out of the fortress, broke his armor, and left him to die in the middle of the swamp.

It didn't take long for Gemli to figure out the reisers' armor did nothing but make them look like monsters. The atmosphere didn't kill him, and the scarce food he ate didn't, either. After he recovered with the zhortas, he talked to the Prime Zhorta at the time, but with no success. The Prime Zhorta told him to leave his former race in the past and forget what had happened to him. The reisers' destiny wasn't his anymore.

Sara's hands shook, and a few tears fell for the injustice that people in the past had done to the reisers. One act of kindness would have saved Gemli from becoming the monster he was now.

No one helped the reisers, and everyone blamed them for destroying Hune. The reisers learned to hate and blame the humans for their luck, all while the valsings denied their part in the history and the zhortas ignored the knowledge they gained.

She hoped the others would come to understand—not to forgive the reisers, but to break the cycle, to keep history from repeating its cruel rhythm.

Even Chris hadn't understood. Deep down, she believed that's why he left. He hated what she'd made him see—what he couldn't unsee. And just like before, he walked away, even when she just had asked him not to leave her.

She wiped her eyes, but the ache in her chest lingered —a quiet, constant pull she'd spent months trying to forget. And then, before she could stop it, her mind drifted back to the desert in Tundra. Back to the moment Chris looked at her—no, looked *through* her— and told her she wasn't real.

"You're not real," he said, his voice low and broken, just as her soul began to shatter.

"What are you—" she started, stepping toward him, clinging to the hope that he was joking, that any second now he'd grin and say something ridiculous. But he didn't let her finish.

"This is all crazy," he muttered, turning away, shaking his head. "You're a dream. Just a... I can't believe I'm even doing this."

"Doing what?" Sara asked, her voice trembling as she fought to hold back tears.

"This. *You*," he said with a sharp exhale, his expression closing off. "You're a hallucination. A scream from my mind trying to keep me sane while I was—"

"No." Sara shook her head and reached for his hand, but he pulled away. "You're wrong. I'm real. Just like you are. You know it." She crouched, grabbed a handful of sand, and let it fall through her fingers. "How do you explain this? The sand you feel, the flowers you smell, swimming in the river... holding me?"

"I can't do this anymore," he said, voice hollow.

"Please don't..." Her voice cracked as tears spilled freely. "Don't leave me. I need—"

"The war, Hune—everything is changing," he said, his voice rising as he stepped back. "I need to focus on what really matters."

She had no words for the way his rejection hollowed her out. Back then, she couldn't understand what he meant. He wasn't a soldier, just a boy she thought may be a zhorta and hadn't discovered it yet. Back then, all she knew was that something inside her had broken, and she didn't want to feel that pain again.

She straightened, breathing through the ache in her ribs. "Then this is the last time I'll think of you," she said, her voice distant and trembling. "You won't see me again... because I won't remember you. I *am* real. But you won't be a part of my life anymore."

And just like the zhortas had taught her to forget nightmares, she erased every moment they'd shared.

Because if she didn't, the ache would consume her. Because remembering him as someone who didn't believe in her was more painful than forgetting altogether.

She had loved him. And the heartbreak of being forgotten was a weight she couldn't bear—not then.

Now, she let herself remember. It still hurt—but the pain didn't break her. It shaped her. Strengthened her.

Chris had been right: the war had changed everything.

It had changed *her*.

And the girl she used to be... felt like someone else entirely now, someone she doubted still lived inside her.

The way Gemli talked about the magic of Hune, as if it were his last resource, sounded familiar. Too familiar. She didn't understand magic, but it was all she had left.

The empathy he managed to inspire in her soul after only a few pages made her fear she could end up turning into a monster like he had.

A dangerous thought—especially if she truly was the heir of the Great Wizard.

The only way to prevent that darkness from taking root was to learn how to wield her power... using the lessons of her enemy.

I HOPE YOU ENJOY THE book. If you want to learn how everything started, you can read the Free prequel here

BOOK 3 EXCERPT:

WISDOM & JUSTICE

Knowing a reiser had murdered the human commander—and their absurd king, Leonard —*should* have made Murllen's day.

But the circumstances were far from ideal.

He only believed the story because the reiser had marched in with Leonard's half-rotted head swinging from one clawed hand.

And now, instead of celebrating, Murllen was forced to summon a meeting of all high-ranking reisers—*an inconvenience*.

"With all due respect, General," a reiser colonel said, "we must consider the possibility that this is a deception by the sorcerer."

Murllen didn't bother to answer. Instead, he stared at the reiser holding the decapitated head.

"Do you know how long I waited to kill this human?" he said.

The reiser shifted uneasily, subtly inching the head away from his side.

"*Decades,*" Murllen said with a smirk. "This moment should have been memorable—one of the happiest of my life. *Our* lives. And now? You've *ruined* it."

He turned away and walked to the window, scowling at the silhouette of the asylum in the distance.

"If what you say is true, you also executed the other human I was looking forward to meeting. The commander." He turned back. "What would *you* do about it?"

Continued here:

ACKNOWLEDGMENTS

For your patience, support, belief in the cause, staying
with me and tolerating the time that I took away from all
of you to sit down and write. During these years, I
learned so much from all of you. For listening to my
stories, complaints, and successes. For your help and
critiques, for all of these and more.

To Each one of you, who loves to read mysteries and took
the time to read my take on them. My amazing coaches;
Scarlett and Bryan, my mystery group friends, Mom,
Gloria, Teddy, Josephine, and You up there...

Thank you.

ABOUT THE AUTHOR

Hi, I'm Monica Red, and I have a passion for forging worlds where magic collides with destiny, and adventure is never far from danger—or from the heart. From sweeping romantasy to daring steampunk adventures, my stories are filled with peril, secrets, and bonds strong enough to change the course of kingdoms.

My greatest inspiration is my daughter, whose courage and imagination remind me why stories of love and resilience matter. At home, I live with two loyal dogs, five outspoken birds, and a husband who insists that golf and sports are the only safe escapes from the battles, quests, and rebellions unfolding in my head.

When I'm not writing fantasy, I step into another realm of storytelling under the name Montie Red, where cozy mysteries bring twists, secrets, and the occasional murder to small-town life. Whether the journey is through enchanted forests, skies filled with airships, or quiet streets hiding dangerous secrets, I'm always chasing the spark of a good story.

Thank you for traveling these worlds with me—arm yourself with courage (and maybe a little tea), and let's embark on the next great adventure together.

facebook.com/AuthorMonicaRed

instagram.com/monicaredauthor

pinterest.com/MonicaRedAuthor